WELCOME TO THE
APARTMENTS

FEATURING
44 BALLOONS BY NICOLE WATTS
ARRANGED BY ROBIN
SCORNED BY LEONDRA LERAE
NO PLACE TO RUN BY SEVYN MCCRAY
FLOWERPOTS BY DRUSILLA MARS
GRANDMA'S GIRLS BY LE'VONNE

THE APARTMENTS

Published by KREATIONSK
KREATIONSK.COM

Cover by Nicole Watts - NWattsStudios.com
Typesetting / Illustrations by Nicole Watts - NWattsStudios.com

FEATURED AUTHORS

NICOLE WATTS

ROBIN

LE'VONNE

LEONDRA LERAE

DRUSILLA MARS

SEVYN McCRAY

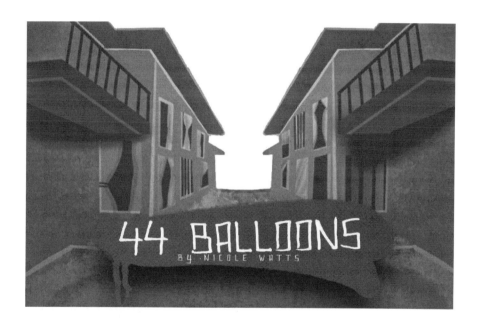

6 : 3 0

Parked at the rest stop Whisper Cooper sat quietly with her AirPods in her ears. The sound of Rod Wave's "Street Runner" had her in her zone. In her lap sat four ounces of THC oil, a syringe, a pack of party balloons, four packs of peanut M&M's, Krazy Glue and a single serving laxative pack. Beside her sat an elastic headband, and a small box that held two of the world's smallest cellphones and an ounce of Crystal.

She rapped along with the music as she ripped the vibrant plastic pack of 50 party balloons. After emptying them out onto her lap, she picked one up and blew into it. The balloon expanded, reading, "Happy Birthday." It was funny. Today was actually her birthday, and she was going to be spending it with her man getting to the check. Releasing air from the balloon, she reached over in the glove compartment and grabbed a pair of scissors. Then she cut the balloon and opened up the small eight ounce water bottle that contained the oil. When she

3

stuck the syringe inside, it made contact with the thick, golden syrup-like substance. Extracting 3ml, she sat the bottle down in the cup holder. With the balloon in hand, she spread it open and squirted the gooey liquid inside. She tied the balloon as tiny as she could get it and clipped the excess. After doing that forty-four more times, she was finally done with the easy part. Whisper always fucked up. That's why she thought ahead and bought multiple packs of M&M's.

Grabbing a bag, she gripped it like a bag of chips and gently pulled apart the end. She poured a handful into her mouth and laughed as a text was read through her AirPods.

Message from D'Marco: Cash App finna be jumpin bae. The block dry."

Pouring the rest of the candy out, she picked up her phone and smiled at the jailhouse photo of the two of them then unlocked it. With her long, acrylic nails, she tapped away at the screen.

Whisper: Cash out or crash out baby. We finna ball out. See you soon.

D'Marco: Facts! Love you babe.

Whisper sat the phone aside and counted out twenty balloons then shoved them inside the bag. Once the pack was full, she opened the super glue and dabbed a few drops on the inside of the wrapper then sealed both ends together. No one could tell they weren't M&M's, and that's just how she wanted it. After filling another two bags, she put all the supplies into a trash bag and pushed it under the seat.

Whisper stepped out the car. She grabbed the candy and stuffed it into her boy shorts. She tapped as she looked at the bulge in her underwear. She loved that song and would often rap it.

4

Whisper loved a good laugh, and even while doing something as serious as this she was going to laugh.

Adjusting her oversized sweats with big pockets, she smiled thinking about seeing her man. She missed last visit because she forgot her ID. This time she made sure to have it. Taking her seat and smiling, thinking about D, she grabbed a headband, bag of Crystal, and phones then went into the glove compartment again. Grabbing the needle and thread, she shut it. Sewing the bag and the phones to the headband, she put it on then looked in the mirror. Adjusting the headband, she sat back and started to pray. She did this all thirteen trips, and the fourteenth was no different.

Roddy Ricch's "War Baby" began playing as Whisper started the car. She drove the hour drive to the prison.

8:00

Whisper pulled up to a booth after driving over a small dirt road. Out stepped three officers. One approached the car while the other two stood guard.

"Windows down and identification out," the officer said as he handed her an inmate visitation form.

First, Whisper rolled all the windows down. Then she popped the trunk and waited for them to search it. Once they were done, she showed her ID then drove a mile down to the prison parking lot. After finding a spot, Whisper scribbled down "DF5734 D'Marco Porter" and her own information. Looking at herself in the pull-down mirror, she smiled then closed it.

5

Her slides hit the dirt as she stopped out of the car and closed the door behind her. Walking around to the trunk, she grabbed her hoodie and tossed her cellphone inside. Along with her purse, she grabbed a small ziplock bag that contained thirty dollars in ones and five dollars worth of quarters. Locking up, she headed down the dirt pathway until it changed into a concrete walkway.

Taking a look at the small beige building that read "Visitation," she followed the path to the door. Entering the building, Whisper kicked off her slides and walked with her socks to the visitor line. There were a few people ahead of her, so she asked the woman behind her to save her spot. Against the wall sat a vending machine and the machine for photo tokens. She inserted three dollars into the machine. Out came three golden tokens. Printed on them was the prison's logo. Stepping back in line, she thanked the woman behind her then stepped up. After fifteen minutes it was her turn.

Whisper placed the hoodie on a tray along with her slides and keys then handed over the Ziplock bag with her money. She was feeling nervous as hell as always. This part could make or break her. The correctional officer behind the desk instructed her to put her arms out and turn around. Once Whisper was facing the line she had been in, she raised one foot then the other. They wanted to make sure nothing was in her socks.

"Hair up," the CO instructed.

Whisper lifted her hair to show the head band then let her hair down. Once clear, she was instructed to walk through a metal detector as her hoodie and shoes went through an x-ray machine. Taking a deep breath, she stepped through waiting to hear a beep. She always blamed it on her jewelry. Once given the, "All clear," she waited at a large metal door until the CO handed her a printout of D'Marco's mugshot and housing information.

BEEEEEEEP! The large door began to open. Whisper stepped out along with a few other people and entered a cage. The Cage held three separate cages to ensure that you will not be going anywhere.

The first cage opened and Whisper knew the hardest part was coming soon after. After another beep, the second cage opened for the group to enter. As that gate closed behind them, they waited for minutes until another beep signaled for the opening of the third and final gate.

"Niggas ain't going nowhere," she joked to the woman next to her as they exited into the last cage and out to the Catwalk as she liked to call it. The Catwalk held two different paths. The one on the left led to the visitation building for Building C where D'Marco was housed. On each side of the path sat two guard towers, each watching as everyone headed down their given path. Whisper shoved the money in her pocket then began putting on the hoodie. First her head then her right arm. Pulling the hoodie down over her left shoulder, she sneakily reached in her panties and grabbed the bags of candy. With them now in her left hand, she shoved them in her left pocket then continued putting on the hoodie.

Inside the visitation room, she was greeted by a familiar face. Cesar the CO. As usual, he flirted with Whisper as he collected her ID and printout with D'Marco's information. It always gave her the creeps. When she told D about it, he told her not to worry unless she wanted do something about it. His "do something" included things Whisper wanted no parts in. So she dealt with the flirting and bullshit.

"Table two." He opened a large bar door.

Inside sat twenty round tables with four chairs each. They sat inside a red square that the inmates were not allowed to step out of. Outside those lines sat vending machines that carried drinks, snacks, ice cream and hot food. At the head of the room sat a large counter that the COs sat behind to watch the inmates.

Whisper pulled out the money and headed for the drinks. She pretended to scan the selection, but she was really peeping her surroundings. There were cameras everywhere and she felt like everyone was watching her.

So far everything was going good. She selected a Mucho Mango Arizona from the drink machine. Then she moved on to the start of the show, the candy.

With pockets and arms full of each item from the machine, she made it to table two and dumped everything out. Then she emptied out her pockets. As the candy hit the table she looked around nervously at the guards standing a few feet away before she tossed the second pack of M&M's in with them. She then took her hair down and removed the headband. Finally, she placed the band on the table and sat down to watch the door the inmates were brought through.

"HAPPY BIRTHDAY, BABY!" was all she heard as the door opened. Out came D'Marco with a huge smile. Placing his ID card on the counter, he grabbed a clipboard and signed them up for pictures. With his long, moisturized head full of curls he strolled over like the man in town. D'Marco smiled at the love of his life, but it wasn't Whisper. With dollar signs in his eyes, he approached the table where Whisper sat watching him. Standing to her feet, she opened her arms to embrace him.

"Happy Birthday, Whisp." He hugged her tightly while looking over his shoulder at the table and the packs of candy and headband.

"Thanks, babe."

They took a seat. Instantly he reached for the band and tied his hair up. Looking over to Whisper, he asked if she could see the phones or drugs? She let him know he was cool. Then he popped the Arizona open and took a sip.

"So what you finna get into tonight?" He reached his tattooed hand out and grabbed the first bag of chocolate. Ripping a hole in the bag, he poured a few in his hand and admired them. Whisper was getting better at this shit. Her packaging was on point this time around.

Whisper began telling him the plans for the night while he counted each balloon he swallowed. In between balloons he took a sip until the balloons and drink was gone. Whatever Whisper was talking about went in one ear and out the other as he swallowed balloon forty-four, the last and final balloon.

"Let's take our pictures." D stood to his feet.

Doing the same, she followed behind him to the photo wall where there was a cheaply decorated wall. Handing the inmate photographer the three tokens, Whisper and D waited their turn then stood in front of the wall. Whisper felt she looked bummy but as long as her makeup and nails were done she'd be good. To D she looked just fine. He enjoyed their pictures. Whisper always had them in different poses, and today was no different.

"Wrap your arms around my waist," she ordered.

D did as he was told. Bending over, Whisper poked her ass out and flipped off the camera. She had the photographer take two shots of that pose then one regular pose.

"That's how I want you to fuck me tonight." She smiled as D took his photo.

9

D'Marco smiled at the photo, thinking about jacking off to the picture. With a smile and a hug he let her know he had to go. Whisper kissed him and slipped him the laxative. Then she headed to the table where all the snacks were still laid out. She gathered them all and tossed them in the trash. The inmates weren't allowed to take anything back to their cells so the candy was just to distract them from the drugs. Again Whisper flirted with the guard and went on her way feeling uncomfortable again.

Once Whisper was out of the prison gates and in her car, she made her way to the booth where they searched her trunk again then let her go.

Twenty minutes into the ride home, Whisper revived a text from D'Marco that had her a little upset.

D'Marco: Aye bitch who is HK?

Whisper pulled to the side of the road and took another look at the phone, wondering how he found out.

Whisper: Who?

D'Marco: Bitch don't play stupid I'll fucking kill you. You had this nigga in my grandma house? You lucky.

Taken back by how D came at her she decided she was going to come clean with him and tell him what the fuck was up.

Whisper: A nigga I been fucking. And what you going to do about it? I sure did fuck him there. What the fuck do you expect I'm always taking care of your helpless ass grandma nigga.

Thirty seconds late,r her phone rang. Answering it on the first ring, she put the phone on speaker and listened as D began to curse her to Hell and back. He was so tight in his chest. Whisper couldn't believe it.

"...bitch you so fucking lucky!"

1 0

"You gonna let me talk?" She reached under the seat to find the rest of the M&M's.

Locating a fresh bag of them, she shoved a few in her mouth then began speaking. "Check this, you're the one who said we ain't together. You made that clear a million and one times. When I come visit sure we act all lovey and shit, but it's show. When you say you love me, it's cus them packs are in your face. You love the shit we do. When I say I love you, it's cus I love you, Nigga. You make me suffer through long nights on the phone, talking about this life we're gonna have, all these kids and this house and shit... then tell a bitch, 'I can't be in a relationship cus I'm in jail.' You think a bitch supposed to just wait twenty years? No, I'm doing the same thing you doing, talking to people. I know you got bitches. I know for a fucking fact you got bitches. So don't sit up here and act surprised I'm fucking a nigga." Whisper let it all out.

At this point she wasn't even sure if D had understood her. After rustling on the other end of the line, he finally spoke.

"Do you love this nigga?" The hurt in his voice was apparent as he sighed, waiting on her answer. "Whisp, imma take that as a yes."

"Yeah, I do, and what you gonna do about it?"

"I'ma kill that nigga." That was all that was said before the line went dead.

* * *

12:00

Pulling into an alley, Whisper cut the stereo down as she watched her neighbor being a weirdo out back by the trash can. She wondered what the fuck he was doing. His weird ass was always lurking around like a creep. He was an older dude with no family or friends. He never spoke or made eye contact with anyone. Whisper thought he was a cop, but Mrs. Porter called the man slow.

Getting out of the car, she clicked her key twice then headed toward the mailbox where she gave him a fake smile and collected the mail. With a stack of catalogs and two letters from D'Marco, Whisper headed up to the second floor where she stayed with Mrs Porter, D'Marco's grandmother. While she fumbled with the key, Whisper heard her name being called from downstairs. Pausing what she was doing, she walked over the railing and smiled knowing damn well she shouldn't have been.

"What's up?" she yelled down at the slim, six-two, brown-skinned thug. He stood there dressed in an all-blue sweat suit with a fresh fade and his jewelry shining in the Cali sun.

'God this man is fine!' she thought, even though she was supposed to be done with him.

"What you doing over here?" Confusion was written on her face.

"Check it out." He waved her down.

"Nah." She stopped looking over the railing and went back to unlocking the door.

Whisper found it funny that HK was here out of all places. At this time, in broad daylight, without a care in the world. No phone call to announce he was coming or even a simple text.

"Whisp! On Crip, come down here. Quit playing, cuz!" His strong and authoritative voice turned her on, and she honestly loved him despite all his betrayal.

With a weird feeling in her stomach, she let him know she'd be right down after she put her things away. Even though she said she was done with him for good. Entering the two bedroom apartment, Whisper sat the mail down and called out for Ms. Porter.

1 2

She headed to the back room to see why she wasn't answering. The neighbor, Patricia, was supposed to check on her every hour to see if she needed anything while Whisp was away. To her surprise, Ms. Porter was sitting in her bed fully dressed and on the phone with someone. She sucked her teeth.

"Let me call you back. She's here." The old woman rolled her eyes then hung up. "Where you been?" Her tone was off in every way.

"You know where I been." Whisper's response was full of irritation. "Why you dressed? Somebody coming over?"

Ms. Porter had this funky attitude and twisted look on her face. All Whisper kept thinking was, *'Try it, old lady.'*

The relationship between the pair had been off for some time now, and they were honestly just putting up with each other for De'Marco. If it wasn't for that nigga, they would have been throwing blows.

Ms. Porter shook her head and looked Whisper up and down. She said nothing as Whisper stood there asking if she needed anything. She couldn't believe the young girl had been so reckless and not given a fuck about anyone but herself. Whisper took her not responding as an answer.

"Look, I gotta run downstairs real quick." Whisper headed for the bedroom door.

"In my house, Whisper?" Ms. Porter finally spoke up.

Turning around and tilting her head slightly to the left, she caught an attitude. "What?"

"You fucked him in my house," Ms. Porter called her out.

Whisper was stuck in her tracks.

"What are you talking about?" She played dumb, but Ms. Porter already knew.

She had known for some time this was going on but chose to say nothing. Whisper and D'Marco were all she had at the moment, or so Whisper thought. Unknown to her, Ms. Porter was getting her affairs in order and had already found another person to come work for her. She was over Whisper and all the sneaky activity she had been up to in her apartment. Sneaking a random man in wasn't even the start of it. Ms. Porter had been suspecting other things but had no one in her family to take care of her, so she said nothing. With that over, she would be letting the young girl know exactly how she felt and what she knew.

"I told D'Marco." Ms. Porter spoke with a smug look on her face.

Still frozen in the same place, Whisper didn't know what to say. Her mind started going in a million and two different directions. Slowly taking in a deep breath, she decided she wasn't even going to trip on it.

"Look Mrs. Porter, I love your grandson and alladat, but um… you think I'm his only bitch? It's twenty four hours in a day. We talk for about ten of them. All damn day long I hear him typing in my ear to other bitches. I'm not dumb, and so what I got a nigga? I'm grown." Whisper gave her the nice version. "Shit, you still keep in contact with his exes."

"You fucked a stranger in my house when you thought I was sleep. You've been bringing drugs in here since we've met. You don't think I see people dropping packages off to you when they're taking me to chemotherapy? You're wrong, Whisper."

Whisper was taken back because all of this shit was D'Marco's fault. Whisper was a normal ass girl from South Central. She smoked her weed, listened to her music, and didn't fuck with nobody. She called herself hood-adjacent. She grew up there, knew about it, and was raised in it, but that was never her thing. She liked movies, gaming, and as corny as it sounded to her loved musicals and was a big fan of nature documentaries. The only thing hood about her was the way she looked. It didn't mean she didn't have that side, though.

Shit, back when she was a young girl, she was in the streets heavy. She was a fighter, a shit talker, and finesser. Her innocent looks could fool anybody. That's what D most liked about her. Her innocent look and the fact that she was down to line it up with anybody. After being close friends since childhood, in their teen years they made it official. Well, sort of. See, D'Marco told Whisper behind closed doors that she was his girlfriend. That was until a few months into their relationship when the girls started coming, and the verbal and physical abuse too.

Whisper, so young and so in love with D, did what she had to do and lined it up with every bitch she caught him with. It got to the point where D told her *'I been trying to get you pregnant, but it looks like you'll kill the baby before it even gets a chance with all the fighting you be doing.'* That was at seventeen, and it stuck with Whisper. Cutting her to the core. She wanted nothing more than to grow old and start a family with D.

Whisper fell back and stayed to herself, becoming withdrawn from society and only coming out when she absolutely needed to. For a year she was unseen and unheard from all of her peers. It had gotten so bad that everyone thought she had moved. Then suddenly one bright summer day, at the age of eighteen, Whisper got dressed, feeling like a million bucks. With her hair down to her back, her tight cut off shorts, and spaghetti strap shirt, she stepped into the summer sun. For the first time in a whole year, she felt different like a new person.

The first thing she did when she stepped foot off the porch was head to the local gym where the summer program was going on. All of the neighborhood teens would be there.

As Whisper approached, she got looks from every which direction. She spoke to people and even played a few games with some of her old homegirls. All the while feeling this high like never before. She was on Cloud Ten because Nine was definitely too low for her. That's when she stopped what she was doing, and her eyes landed on Mecca. Mecca was a kid who had a crush on her and had no shame in telling her. He was a few grades under her so she always kept him at a distance but tonight he was looking right.

Taking a long drink of Bacardi, Whisper handed the bottle back to her girls then dipped off to the basketball court sideline where Mecca stood rolling up a blunt. They exchanged words, and next thing they both knew whisper was bent over his aunt's kitchen tablet getting some of the worst dick she had ever gotten in her life. Which was crazy because she had only ever slept with D. They began arguing. Whisper laughed it off, and they exited the house.

When they made their exit, Mecca was met by two of his friends and Whisper's good friend Vani who she hadn't seen in a long time. Vani and Whisper began catching up while the boys headed across the street and into one of their yards. After catching up both girls headed across the street where Mecca wanted to show his ass.

Whisper was still on Cloud Nine and very much horny as Mecca claimed his dick was burning. Whisper hadn't had sex in over a year, so she knew it was all talk. She aired him out as having a weak dick and In response Mecca said her pussy was trash. Whisper, still high off life, told him she could prove it wasn't. Grabbing one of his friends, they headed inside. Whisper was sadly disappointed by the type of dick his friend was giving out. She didn't even bother to learn his name. Sucking it up and realizing she was just going to have to get herself off, she decided to get dressed and head out. On her way out she caught the third

1 6

friend looking at her. He was the sexiest of them all, but Whisper – no matter how crazy she was feeeling – knew she couldn't fuck three guys in the same night. Batting her lashes, she brushed past him and headed out with Vani.

Heading back to the summer program, she partied the night away still high off life. The next morning she received a text. It read "Meet me on the block." It was from Andre, the third friend and he wanted to talk. Whisp had no idea how he had gotten her number but didn't care. Still feeling on top of the world, Whisper got dressed and went to see Andre. He met her on the block they had met on the night before. They exchanged greetings then went to hang out in his garage. They talked and laughed then he leaned over and kissed her. Still not satisfied with the events that took place the previous night, she went with it. One thing led to another, and Whisper's mind was blown. He had done things D had never done before. She was honestly pleasantly surprised. When things were done, she got dressed. He walked her to the corner, and that was where they both ran into Mecca and the other friend who she still didn't know by name.

Mecca seemed heartbroken in fact he was heartbroken. He would later go on to bash Whisper on social media about giving him an STD and how she was a whore. It was all so entertaining for Whisper.

Later that night, Whisper stood on the porch scrolling social media, laughing about Mecca and his post when she saw a post that crushed her high on life attitude.D had gotten her enemy pregnant.

Whisper broke down into a trillion pieces. The voice in her head came to a halt, her speeding thoughts were gone. The sexual hunger and desire that had been looming over her was gone. All that was left was a hollowed out shell of a person. In that instance, she went back to being withdrawn. With her feet moving and her brain on autopilot, she found herself standing blindly in an intersection. She didn't know how she got there or even why she was there. All she knew was she felt high again as she held her arms out and felt the breeze of air swooshing past with every car.

She didn't understand it. She felt so alive and so dead at the same time. With every passing car she got more excited as they were mere inches away from a tragic outcome. Laughing uncontrollably, Whisper smiled with tears streaming down her eyes. Twirling in a circle and feeling free and liberated, she took in the crisp night air.

Until suddenly she felt hands pulling her down and red and blue lights surrounding her. It was an officer who had been passing by and felt she was trying to harm herself. The officer got in contact with her parents and Whispered ended up in the hospital being diagnosed with severe Bipolar Disorder, something that goes untreated in kids until they're around eighteen. Her highs and extreme lows plus her hyper sexuality said it all.

Finally understanding what was going on, Whisper slowly withdrew from the world again for eight more years for fear of having an episode like that again.

PRESENT DAY

"How is this D's fault?" Ms. Porter asked, bring Whisper back to the present day. "He's not the one bringing drugs and strange men…"

"If anybody is strange, it's your weird ass grandson! You think that nigga is God's gift to earth when he's nothing but a fucking inmate. He ain't shit, the drugs are his. Who you think sending them here?"

"Get…"

"Whisper held her finger up and silenced Ms. Porter. "Nah, you know what? Fuck you and your grandson. You can call your grandson and tell him call his dirty ass baby mama or one of them bitches to come watch you, bitch. Cus honestly I'm sick of your shit. All you do is sit up here and complain about how bad your life is. If your ass followed the doctors' orders then maybe you'd fucking feel okay for a change."

Whisper's phone vibrated in her pocket. She pulled it out and looked at the screen. Then she shoved it back in then focused back on Ms. Porter.

"I'm calling him now," she threatened.

Whisper snatched the phone from Ms. Porter and walked out the room, leaving her to herself as she exited the apartment and looked over the railing at HK.

"What?" she yelled down.

"On Crip, just come down. We gotta talk, cuz." He looked upset.

"HK, I can't right now. Shit crazy, come back tonight." HK shook his head "No," and demanded she come down now or he'd come up.

"Five minutes, that's it." Whisper sighed then gave in as she took the stairs two at a time ready for him to leave her alone.

When she got down there, the first words that he spoke gave her chills.

"Your boyfriend is dead" There was no trace of any emotion, no jokey-jokey manner, or none of that. He was cold and searching Whisper's face for any trace of emotion.

"What?" She felt like she was punched in her gut.

HK began to tell Whisper the reason he had come to see her during the day. A few hours ago, HK had gotten a call from one of his old prison cell mates saying his name was ringing hard in the prison. Whisper didn't care; she just wanted to know about the dead part.

"Ten minutes ago, I got a call saying they just brought ya boy out of his cell in a body bag. I got a video, Whisper. This shit ain't no joke. We both know you took that shit up there. Ya boy likes to– you know." He made a smoking gesture.

"D doesn't smoke meth." She got defensive.

"That's your problem, Whisper, you don't listen. I'm telling you the nigga dead. I was behind them walls for twelve years, I know what these niggas do. Now I'm telling you, the nigga dead."

HK pulled his phone out and cut the screen on, "Look…"

Whisper stopped him from talking and answered the unknown call from Ms. Porter's phone. Like HK had said, D was dead and it was information that the man on the phone who believed he was speaking with Ms. Porter that confirmed it. He couldn't answer questions or give out details yet. All he was doing was notifying the family.

"I gotta go." Whisper tried to walk away from HK, but he grabbed her by the arm and pulled her close.

"Why was my name brought up?" he asked in a menacing way.

"After the drop, he called me and was like, 'You been fucking that nigga HK.' I don't know who told him. I promise I'm as surprised as you. Now let me go." She snatched away then headed upstairs as he talked shit and threatened her.

She had enough problems on her hands.

When she entered the apartment, all 300 pounds of Ms. Porter was standing in the hallway with her walker. Whisper was in shock. Since she'd been there Ms. Porter had been confined to her bed and her wheelchair.

"Ohhhh, bitch, you walking now?" Whisper was done with her. "What other tricks you got for me today?" She laughed to keep from crying about D.

Ms. Porter went off, calling her all types of names as she struggled to make it to the couch. Whisper didn't give a fuck, though. She had other things on her mind. Like the fact that D was dead after she just took the nigga 44 Balloons and some Meth. Formulating a plan in her head, she walked herself through a list of things she needed to do then got on it.

4:52

After hours of arguing and talking shit to Ms. Porter, Whisper was finally done packing up her shit and putting it at the door.

"I hope you and yo bitch ass grandson rot in hell. You old bitch," Whisper said, opening the door to start moving her shit downstairs.

Ms. Porter had said some of the most vile things ever to Whisper as she was packing her things up and the one thing Whisper wanted to tell her she had been saving for this very moment.

"Yeah, you'll be there with us in Hell, Whisper." Ms. Porter laughed. "You were such a sweet girl, Whisper. I don't know what happened to you."

"Your grandson happened to me. That's why his bitch ass dead down!" Whisper shouted, lugging a suitcase out the door. As she sat it down by the railing, she could see several LAPD squad cars coming through the alleyway deep as hell. It was like a scene out of the movies as the deep orange sky placed a glow over everything. As she admired the beauty, in this time of chaos came the sound of helicopters as they hopped out with black boots and bulletproof vest then swarmed the building with guns drawn.

Heading back inside, Whisper locked the door and told Ms. Porter to shut the fuck up or else. Whisper needed to think, but the only thing on her mind was how she got into all of this in the first place.

EIGHT MONTH EARLIER...

Whisper sat at home with her siblings, enjoying the night. They had just gotten back from the movies and were all in the kitchen bugging their mother to cook for their grown asses. Sitting on top of the deep freezer while scrolling on Instagram, Whisper stopped on a photo.

The account it came from had been inactive for years. To be honest, she should have been unfollowed it.

Staring at D'Marco's photo, she couldn't help but get butterflies in her stomach. He was no longer the teen she had fallen in love with. He was now a man. With his thick and healthy beard and curls that hung way past his shoulders, she smiled. He had some weight on him and overall looked good. Double tapping to give it a like, she continued scrolling for a moment. Then a notification popped up on the top of her screen that read "Whisper Cooper?'

She replied with a, "Yeah," then instantly got another message telling her he wouldn't be able to keep messaging because he was using someone else's phone. He gave her a phone number and asked her to text him.

After giving it some thought, she didn't see the harm in it and shot him a quick text. That text turned into an eight-hour phone call, which turned into old feelings surfacing on both parts. Whisper felt like her best friend was back and D'Marco felt like the girl he he fucked up with could potentially be back. The days went on, and they both spent countless hours talking and reconnecting until D finally asked where Whisper had been for the past eight years.

D'Marco felt like Whisper just vanished off the face of the earth one day. He explained she was there then one day gone. He saw her one summer night then got locked up the week after. He always wondered what had happened to her.

Whisper, now grown and over it, explained to him what happened. He apologized for everything. For the beatings, the mental abuse, and cheating. When he was done, he gave his side of the story. D'Marco felt bad. Deep down inside he knew he did those things but couldn't remember them. He admitted to being off pills most of his teen years. Then he went on to tell her he didn't think she loved him.

Whisper smacked her lips and rolled her eyes. "You were my first boyfriend, D. You took my virginity."

Whisper held on to her virginity for a long time. She turned down lots of guys. Shit, her first real kiss was at sixteen. Up until that point she was queen of the pop-kiss. To her it was special, he was special.

"I was the first for a lot of girls. It doesn't mean anything."

"It means everything to a woman. What do you mean?"

"My baby mama..."

Whisper stopped believing what he had to say at that point.

To him his baby mother was just like a nigga. That was something he said out of his own mouth. She didn't care about him and only wanted him for sex. Whisper knew that part to be true based on the shit she had seen first hand.

"I apologize, Cooper." He chuckled, using her last name. "I didn't think you were that serious about me. One day you were at my house with my sisters then the next you were gone. We grown now. Let's start over."

Against everything in her, she agreed to start over which would prove to be one of the worst decisions she's ever made. As the weeks went on, the talks grew. Before she knew it, she was head over heels again.

* * *

Laying in bed surrounded by her pillows, listening to the latest Youngboy, she rolled over with a sigh. She was so used to D hitting her line that she had a bad feeling in her gut. Something was wrong and she could feel it. She had already sent him three texts for that day without response and didn't want to seem like she was pressed. Shaking those thoughts off, she opened up her Messenger to a message request. It was from Juan, a nigga she had talked to in her teen years. She laughed at the thuggish type of content he was posting. She knew this nigga was nothing but a teddy bear.

In their teen years Juan was obsessed with Whisper, but whisper wasn't really into boys at the time. She still thought boys were nasty and her friends often teased her about it. The farthest they got was a two second kiss pop kiss then Whisper moved away. A few years later, the two ran into each other, but Whisper was instantly turned off by him. It was nothing against him. It was the choice of people he hung around, specifically D's baby mother. She wasn't his baby mama at the time, but Whisp had a strong dislike Whisp for the girl. Their beef was from the sandbox and would most likely be for life.

Juan: Whisper, what's up? I ain't seen you in a long time.
Whisper: What's up. I know, how you been?

Juan began telling her about what he had been up to. The two exchanged several messages, then Juan began fishing for answers about Whisper. All the while Whisper had one question for him. Was he still friends with D's baby mother? He assured her they hadn't spoken in years then asked Whisper about D'Marco. Whisper had never even mentioned D at all. Whisper lied like she hadn't been in contact with him.

After a few more messages, Juan asked her on a date. Whisper agreed, thinking, *'Why not?'* as she continued to scroll through Facebook.

A few days had passed since Whisper had spoken to D'Marco at this point, and she was worried. She hit his line one more time then went back to doing her. Tonight she was going to chill with Juan and catch up.

As she stood in the mirror flat ironing her hair, she got a text from an unknown number.

Unknown: Whisp, it's me. My phone been tripping. A lot of shit going on right now. I'll hit you up in a few days.

Whisper: Okay, hope you're okay.

A call came after she responded. Whisper answered to hear his deep voice. The girl melted at the sound of it. D had twenty minutes left to use the rented cellphone before he had to send it back to another inmate.

Although Whisper was turned on, she could hear sadness in the way he spoke. When she asked what was wrong, D asked had she ever met his grandmother. She hadn't, but had always heard about her.

Stressed, D began to tell her how his grandmother had been in and out of the nursing home for the past year and had recently been admitted to the hospital. He was afraid she was on her way out the door soon. After confiding in Whisper, he felt somewhat better then began to ask her about her week. He missed her and wanted to ask her something. She had become a part of his day to day. "You sound busy. What you got going tonight?"

"Going out," she responded, looking in the mirror, trying to get her lashes to stick.

"Where?" He was a little curious, knowing she was a homebody.

"With a friend," was all she said.

Whisper knew D didn't want to be in a relationship. He made that clear from the start. So when he hit her with the, "With a nigga, huh?" she was surprised. His voice was deeper than normal.

"Yeah, is that a problem?"

"Nah,"

"What's his name?"

"Juan," she said, not feeling like she had to hide it, but asked was it okay with him out of curiosity.

"Do I know him?" He disregarded her question.

"Actually you do." Whisper explained that Juan had mentioned him.

"Have fun. But look I gotta give the phone back." He got off in a hurry not even wanting to ask her the question anymore.

Whisper felt some type of way but continued getting dressed.

Later that night she and Juan chilled for a few hours then she headed home. Over the next few days, they continued to hang out. Whisper had even spent the night. All the while still maintaining her talks with D. One night as she was chilling with him, D hit her up from his own number.

He wanted to ask Whisper something serious. She stopped what she was doing as he began telling her about his grandmother, Ms. Porter, again. She was being released from the hospital, and there was no one to help her out at night. She was in the process of finding a nurse but needed someone for a few nights. The thing was Ms. Porter didn't trust anyone. A few hundred dollars for a few nights was fine with Whisper. She agreed, and D gave Ms. Porter Whisper's phone number. After speaking, Whisper and Ms. Porter came to an agreement.

The next day at fivethirty, Whisper stepped out of her sister's car into the sunset. The olive green building that stood in front of her read Green Vista. There were bums standing around talking, and the smell of something delicious was in the air. The sound of kids fussing and mothers yelling made Whisper laugh as she remembered her mother once doing the same.

"Here we go," Whisper said as she entered the gates leading into the U-shaped courtyard. Inside she spotted a Hispanic couple on the grill with a Black couple next to them playing oldies.

Whisper nodded at them then made it to the elevator where she hit the up button. After waiting a minute, the kids who were playing let her know it wasn't working. Heading up the stairs she finally made it to the apartment and knocked on the door. After a minute, the door opened and a woman named Hellen introduced herself and let Whisper in.

Whisper was expecting the apartment to be run down like the rest of the building but it wasn't. There were photos everywhere, and little keepsakes lined the shelves and entertainment area. The smell of baked chicken hit her. She instantly became hungry.

Ms. Porter sat on the couch, looking at Whisper as she entered. Her first thought was Whisper looked sweet and innocent. Her grandson had been talking her ear off about her for a week now, and everything he said about her look wise was true.

The two exchanged greetings then got to business. Ms. Porter let Whisper know what she'd need her for the next few days. She offered Whisper a plate. As Whisper ate, Ms. Porter told Whisper she had heard about her and hoped there would be no problem if no D's baby mother stopped by.

The first thing Whisper thought was, '*It's Always On Sight,*' then, "*I'm too grown.*" Instead, she asked what made her ask that. D's aunt had mentioned their many brawls. Whisper assured her she'd keep it cool unless Shorty wanted to line it up. She was always down for the fade and would stay ready.

After their chat, Hellen left and the pair began to get to know each other. The first few nights went well. Whisper would spend the night then head home and chill. About a week later, Whisper was scheduled to see D for the first time. Her visitation was finally approved by the State of California and Correctional Department. She was excited as hell. She had got a fresh silk press and even swooped the hell out of her edges. With her scarf tied and bag packed, she kissed her mother goodbye then headed out with her sister.

Whisper made it to the Vista, and Ms. Porter wasn't feeling well. She was rushed to the hospital where Whisper stayed with her. About nine o'clock at night, Whisper finally got in contact with D. He was far from concerned about his grandmother at the moment. Right now, he needed Whisper.

D: I can't wait to see you tomorrow. You got shorty address you riding with?

Whisper: Yeah, I'm excited.

Whisper grew butterflies. This was the man she had envisioned her life with. Putting the pain in the past, she was looking forward to seeing him.

"Do you need any water?" Whisper offered Mrs. Porter as she sat watching CNN.

Mrs. Porter declined the offer, so Whisp went back into her phone as Aaron May's "In Love" played in her AirPods.

D: Can you bring me some M&M's?

Whisper: Yeah.

Whisper had no problem with his request. What was a simple pack of candy? Right? She asked herself.

D: I'm not talking about candy. Call me and make sure you're alone.

Whisper excused herself from Ms. Porter's room and made it down the long empty hallway. Entering the restroom, she called D. He answered with a, "Hey Babe, "which was new for Whisper. She acted like she didn't hear him and asked what was up.

D wanted Whisper to bring him a pack of M&M's full of balloons that contained THC oil. At first Whisper thought about it and declined. After going back and forth for a bit, Whisper agreed only once. D told her to give him five minutes then he'd call her back. Two minutes later, she received a text from an unknown number.

Unknown: Pack ready. Where we meeting?

D called back immediately and let her know someone would be texting her.

Whisper responded to the unknown number with the address to the emergency room. They responded with a set time they'd arrive and that was it. Whisper spoke to D for a few more minutes, then he disconnected the call. When she made it back to the room where, Ms. Porter was on the phone with D.

Exactly an hour and fifteen minutes later, Whisper got a text saying come out. Whisper excused herself then headed outside to the parking lot where a group of police officers sat guarding the ER as she walked out.

Whisper got another text describing her outfit then began looking around confused she had never done anything like this and found it crazy. There were a few cars, so it could have been anyone texting her. Feeling uncomfortable, she began to turn around, as a car window rolled down and a light skinned, tatted thug with long braids stuck his head out.

Whisper's phone buzzed again. It was him telling her come to the car. When she approached, he smiled and licked his lips. The bag of M&Ms sat in his lap along with a gun. In the driver's side was a woman. He looked Whisper up and down one more time then passed her the M&Ms. She tucked them in her hoodie then headed back upstairs.

Later that night, Ms. Porter gave Whisper her key to spend the night and get ready for her visit with her grandson.

As Whisper made it to the Vista, she took a long look around before stepping out of her Uber. There were a few men standing outside the complex. and the clouds of some and bottle places around had her nervous. Sucking it up, she placed the keys between her fingers making sure they were secure. With the tips pointing out between her fingers, she got out and grabbed her bag with her free hand. Bumping the door closed with her hip, she started walking with her head held high. Never show weakness was what she thought as one of the men started to speak to her. She ignored the man and tightened her grip on the keys, ready to do damage if needed.

Whisper already didn't like the building; this was just another reason she thought as she headed to the elevator. After a few minutes she decided to take the stairs. Making it up to the apartment, she began to look around before releasing the keys and opening the door. When she opened it, the heater hit her. Cutting on the light, she cut the heater off and took a seat. It was late.

She was worn out as she cut on the television, thinking about the candy. Pulling it out, she inspected the bag. It had a loud smell to it. Other than that, it looked just like a normal bag of chocolate. The seal was intact and everything. Realizing she didn't know how the hell she was going to get this in, she got up and headed to the room Mrs. Porter said she could use. There were two rooms just a few feet away from the living room the first was Mrs. Porter's room. Opening it she looked around at all of the trinkets and photos from her life. Stepping in Whisper began looking at all of the photos. The old woman had changed so much in her life and Whisper began to wonder how she made it to the Vista. Going into the woman's closet Whisper grabbed a pillow and blanket then made it to the second room. Opening the door she turned on the light of the small room and shrugged her shoulders. There was a full size bed a small radio and medical supplies stacked by the wall. Covering the bed then tossing the pillow on the bed she sat her things down and opened the window. The cool California air washed over her and she began getting to buisness.

First, she tried in her bra, then her pocket, and eventually she settled on in her underwear. Walking back and forth in the mirror. she kept checking herself until she had it down pat. When it hit four, Whisper got a text from her ride. She let them know she'd be at their place in an hour.

Putting on gloss and checking her outfit, she smiled. She looked cute even with all of the restrictions. No blues, greens or oranges. No wire bras or even long unnatural hair. Whisper couldn't even be a bad bitch for the day like she wanted to. Taking another look at herself in the mirror she headed out. Locking up Ms. Porter's place she headed out and met up with Trina, her ride.

When she got to the large brownstone apartment in Downtown Los Angeles she looked around and got New York vibes. Entering the building there we large wooden spiral staircase that had seen time pass. Taking the worn stairs to the fifth floor she knocked on the door to apartment 504 and a girl about her age answered. Letting her in the woman asked for

Whisper to excuse her mess. It was a tiny studio with hardly anything in it. Whisper didn't judge. She took a seat on the woman bed as requested then waited. While waiting she began to text D. After ten minutes Trina was ready and they headed down stairs to see another woman waiting in a red Van. She called Trina then got out and locked her car. She introduced herself and Poppy and they headed to a black Kia. Poppy stood out side as they got in and took their seat.

"I thought you was bringing that weird bitch from last time. This one is pretty." She got in with a blunt on her lips.

"Thank you," Whisper smiled from the back and they both laughed.

The three-hour ride to the prison went by smoothly. Whisper didn't talk much, but she did listen to the women talk about all their prison bae stories.

When they arrived, the car was searched, and the women walked Whisper through the process of getting in. After a lengthy wait, all three women were let into these cages. That's where Whisper transferred the drugs from her panties to her pocket. Then they all headed to building C.

Whisper's nerves were bad as she looked at the guard towers that had officers with guns pointing down at their path. Her heart was beating out of her chest. She kept telling herself to put one foot in front of the other. The sweltering desert heat d made sweat pour down her forehead. When the group finally made it to the visiting room, Whisper followed the women's lead and got her table number. It was right at the front of the room where the correctional officers stood watching everyone.

Whisper bought hella snacks like D told her then took her seat and put the M&Ms with the rest of the candy in the center of the table. Chest still thumping, she waited until she heard her name being called.

Standing to her feet, she smiled as D brought her into a big hug. He squeezed her and kissed her deeply. Breathless, she stood there giggling then was scolded by the CO.

"Fuck you, Cesar!" D shouted then gave her his full attention. "Fuck them. So what's up?" He looked at the table behind him.

Turning around, Whisper smiled at a familiar face. It was a cat she knew from the neighborhood named Sir. He was with Trina. D got permission to double tables, so they all sat together.

D and Whisper talked and exchanged sexual looks as he began popping the balloons like pills and taking sips of Powerade. Twenty-two balloons Whisper counted. He did it with ease. When he was done, he smiled at her then crinkled the bag in his hands.

Whisper's body was finally at ease and D could tell by the way she became talkative and loosened up. She had a smile that wouldn't go away and D liked that. Their conversation was even better in person. Time flew by. Before they knew it the visit was over. A bell rang, and all the inmates stood up. They were given two minutes to say their goodbyes. That includes hugs and kisses.

D grabbed Whisper's hand and she stood up. He brought her into a hug and held her tightly.

"I love you, Whisper." She could feel him poking her in the stomach and giggled.

"I love you too," she began rubbing on his package as he lifted her chin and French kissed her.

She never wanted the kiss to end. As another bell went off, D stepped back and told Whisper he had to go. Falling in line, he kept looking back at her as she headed out with the women she came with.

On her exit she waited for her ID and was greeted by the CO who had introduced himself as Cesar. He flirted for a bit then gave her back her ID.

Once out the prison walls and back on the road, Trina and her friend began telling Whisper how they didn't know she was with the shits. They thought she was a nerd, but Trina's man told her about Whisper back in the day. They also brought up the drugs. They didn't peg her for that type. Whisper asked how they knew. Obviously, the vending machines didn't carry chocolate. That was also something she had noticed. About thirty minutes into the ride, Whisper's phone began blowing up.

Her Cash App was jumping. Every memo read "Gift for D." Then she got a text saying "Expect more. By the time she reached The Vista she had well over two bands in her account. D hit her line. He let her know half of the money belonged to her and to hold on to the rest of it. More was to come before the night was over.

As Whisper lay on the couch looking at her Cash App go crazy she felt she could get used to this. It wasn't as bad as she thought it would be. That's where she fucked up at.

As the money was coming in, a text popped up. It was Juan wanting to hang out. Whisper agreed then caught an Uber to see him. When she got there, Juan was all over her. Whisper was still high off seeing D. She gave into temptation with Juan with D on her mind the whole time. Falling asleep in bed with Juan she woke up in the middle of the night to see her phone on her charger. She thought that was odd because she didn't take it out of her bag.

"Do you love him?" Juan asked.

"What?"

"D'Marco. Do you love him? You're taking care of his grandmother and shit."

"What are you even talking about?" Whisper asked, confused as to why he was bringing D'Marco up again and how he knew she was taking care of Ms. Porter.

"You texting him and shit. Going to see him."

That's when Whisper put two and two together. This nigga had been in her phone and read the texts between her and D. She snatched her shit up and left. When she made it home, Juan began calling and texting like crazy. Eventually he popped up and met her on the porch where he confessed he didn't want to lose her. He was in full blown tears telling her how D was in jail and couldn't treat her like he could. Whisper being an asshole began with the water works too and gave a hell of a show as she told him she didn't want to lose him too. Whisper didn't want to lose the dick and add to her body count, so she figured she might as well play the role. That calmed the nigga down and told him she wasn't going anywhere. *'Bitch ass nigga,' she* thought as he spoke. She really wasn't that interested in what he was saying, but for the sake of the dick she spoon fed him exactly what he wanted to hear. When he finally left she headed, in to get some rest.

As the went by, Whisper and D had got deeper into their friendship and started to explore the future and what could be. Their visit had both of them in their chest about each other. Whisper had fallen back in love with the man she vowed never to love again.

A few weeks later, Juan called and said he had some weed. Never one to turn down a good smoke session, Whisper ordered her Uber to go see him.

When she arrived Juan had the biggest smile on his face. He hadn't seen Whisper in a while and was glad she was there. Whisper, on the other hand, just wanted to get high.

Hugging him he let her know he had to run next door then would be right back. Heading in and taking a seat on the couch, she pulled out her phone to see it had died. After plugging it up, she took a seat then seen Juan's phone sitting next to the television. Picking it up to see the the time, she couldn't do anything but sit there and laugh. Juan had an Android phone and when you get a message from Facebook the person who inboxed you, profile photo pops up in a bubble. Whisper couldn't believe whose photo she was seeing.

Clicking on D'Marco's baby mother's picture, Whisper read the conversation then read the last message over and over until she heard Juan coming.

"Had fun last night bestie."

Sitting the phone down, Whisper acted as if nothing happened. Juan came in with a Wood and took a seat. As he rolled up, he kept looking at Whisper like he wanted some. When he finished rolling up, he passed it to Whisper. She took a few hits.

The conversation was basic, and Whisper was waiting until the Wood was gone to show this nigga the bitch she had always been. She hated to bring "Cooper" out, but he went there.

"So what's this?" She picked up his phone and showed him the conversation. "I thought you don't fuck with that bitch. Why was she over here?"

"That's my best friend, what you mean?" He got defensive and took his cheap ass phone with a little force.

"Why tho?" was all she said.

"Don't be like that. She thinks we should be together," he confessed.

Whisper cocked her head to the side then swung on him, landing a blow to the jaw.

3 6

The nigga didn't know Whisper was real deal crazy and was two seconds away from doping his ass again.

"Y'all was taking about me!"

They were both now on their feet.

"You said you ain't see the bitch in years. Now she yo best friend? Nigga, you's a weirdo, on my mama." Whisper stole off on him again, landing a blow in his chest.

With her fist landing dead in the middle of his chest he stumbled back. Then he tried to block the next blow.

"You's a bitch, my nigga! What type of nigga goes and befriends a bitch that the girl he wants don't like? Nigga, she don't like yo ass. Fucking weirdo."

Whisper unplugged her charger and grabbed her bag while Juan tried to explain himself. Whisper ain't care. She walked out with him following as she ordered an Uber to The Vista. As she stood outside, Juan kept trying to talk to her until she dropped her shit and started swinging on him. She was pissed and cracked him in the jaw like a nigga. Squaring up, she was ready for the fade.

"You a pussy, nigga, and I hope you and that bitch get y'alls." She kept swinging and eventually began trying to choke the life out of him until a car pulled up and started beeping.

Whisper punched him one more time then grabbed her shit and got in. The whole way to The Vista, all she could do was think about how pussy that nigga had been to link up with a bitch she had beef with.

When she made it home, she headed upstairs and straight to Ms. Porter's apartment. She let herself in, kicked off her slides, and went straight for the fridge. While grabbing a soda and making a sandwich, she laughed about how she doped the nigga. He definitely deserved it.

Later that afternoon, D shot her a text telling her something funny happened today. When she asked what, he told her his baby mother brought their son to visit and mentioned her. Whisper, already on one, responded by telling him to tell that bitch keep her name out her mouth. D explained that all she asked was did he remember Whisper.

She didn't care. She ain't want her name in the bitch mouth at all. The conversation ended there, and Whisper ate then took a nap. Later that evening, an ambulance dropped Ms. Porter off, and the two went on with their normal routine.

What was supposed to be a few days turned into Whisper eventually moving into The Vista with Ms. Porter. She'd take care of her and go to chemotherapy with her every week. Their relationship was cool. Ms. Porter liked Whisper for her grandson and would often let D know that.

Whisper sat at the dinner table, braiding her hair while texting D and listening to Family Feud in the background. Ms. Porter was nodding off as Whisper received a text from an unknown number.

Unknown: I'm outside but the place is surrounded.

Whisper got up and looked out the window to see police down the block at a neighboring apartment. Letting the person on the other end of the call know it was the next building over she slipped on her slides and wrapped her hair. She stepped out with a joint. Heading downstairs, she lit up her paper and waited.

Minutes later a nigga dressed in a plain white tee came waking into the courtyard from the back. He had a pack of Polo boxers in his hand and a smile on his face. He looked to be in his early twenties and was tatted up from his hands to his neck.

"My bad. I ain't been out here in years. This should be it."

He handed her the boxers then asked to hit the weed. Whisper laughed then handed it over. After taking a few hits, he passed it back then disappeared into the night. Whisper finished off the joint. She flicked the roach then headed upstairs. Before entering, she tucked the boxer pack on her right side under her shirt. Once inside, she headed straight for the restroom where she emptied the box to see a Ziplock bag full of balloons.

This was the first time she was given balloons by themselves. She sent a text to D letting him know that. He gave her instructions on how to fill them then asked how many there were. There were twenty four balloons. They disconnected the call. Whisper hid the balloons in a box of tampons before going back to doing her hair.

The next night, as Whisper got ready for bed, she got a text from the last unknown number that hit her. It was the guy from last night. He said he needed to drop off a few extra and rewrap the first package. His next text stated he was ten minutes away.

Getting the box of tampons, Whisper headed out to meet him. When he walked up, Whisper was impressed. He was dressed in an expensive button up shirt with slacks and dress shoes. He smelled amazing. Under the light, she finally got a good look at him. He was slim, about six-two, and his brown skin was flawless.

Handing the box over, Whisper waited on him to do what he needed to do. He laughed and told her they needed to go somewhere private. Not wanting to go anywhere with this random man, she did something even stupider. She invited him upstairs under one condition he had to be quiet. Ms. Porter was sleeping and she didn't want to wake her. He agreed, and they headed upstairs.

Inside of the apartment, he made himself comfortable on the sofa and poured the Ziplock bag out the box of tampons. He reached in his pocket then sat four more balloons down and asked if they had Saran Wrap. Playing some light music, Whisper got the wrap and took a seat on the other end of the sofa. Watching him carefully as he ripped a small piece of plastic, he placed a balloon inside then twisted it and sealed it with a lighter.

Finally he looked over at Whisper and introduced himself as HK, something that Whisper was never supposed to know.

"Whisper," she introduced herself with a handshake.

His cologne hit her in a pleasant way as he sat back and stared intensely at her. Reaching in his other pocket, he pulled out a blunt.

"You got weed?" He invited himself to say.

Whisper excused herself to her room and grabbed the small ziplock bag she had got from Choppa and Easy, her downstairs neighbors. When she got back to the living room, HK was still laid back like he lived there. She took a seat at the far end of the sofa with the bag in hand. HK handed over the blunt. Examining the Swisher Diamond, she passed it back.

"What's wrong, cuz?" He moved closer, looking deep into her eyes.

Whisper loved a good gangsta and all the lingo that came with it.

"Don't laugh." She blushed as he began unbuttoning his shirt.

Whisper could see just how tatted he was as sat there in a beater. Stuck looking at all the gang related ink she confessed something to him. "Um, I only know how to roll papers." She laughed.

HK thought that was cute and let her know he'd teach her. Scooting closer, he grabbed the bag and poured a few nuggets out. As he began breaking down the weed, Whisper got a text.

D: *What you doing Coop?*

W: Doing my hair.

D: I'm excited to see u. Two more days.

W: I know. You got everything set up?

D: Yeah, but look it's another drop tomorrow. I'll give you the details then. Gotta go. Love you.

W: Love you too.

After HK broke down the last of the weed, he walked Whisper through breaking the blunt down and dumping the guts he made this eye contact never once looking away. He was sexy as hell, and all she wanted to do was kiss him. Stuffing the tree into the blunt he carfully rolled it up while licking the edges of the blunt. Whisper desperately wished it was her as produced a lighter and lit it up. Inhaling deeply, he passed it to Whisper. She hit it then laid back. HK placed his arm around Whisper's shoulder, and she melted into him.

As the blunt traveled back and forth, the pair began getting to know each other. Whisper learned HK's birthday was the night before, and he only came because his boy had nobody else. It was last minute for him, and he rushed while bagging up. That was his reason for coming back. After explaining himself, the conversation took a turn to everyday shit as they bonded over music, movies, and growing up in South Central.

HK got the impression that Whisper wasn't the type of girl for this lifestyle. He could see it in the way she talked and the things she liked. It was clear as day to him that she grew up around the life but was never in it and he liked that.

"Damn, I was supposed to be somewhere." HK checked his watch and saw that he had been there for more than three hours vibing with Whisper.

"Let me get my coat and shoes. I'll walk you out." Whisper got up and headed into the room where she put on a hoodie then headed back into the living room for her slides.

"You ready?" she asked, pink in the face as he licked his lips while looking her in the eyes.

"Yeah." He began putting on his shoes then buttoning up his shirt.

Whisper walked HK downstairs and to the parking area. They both confessed how much of a good time they had then hugged each other. HK looked down at Whisper and lifted her chin with his right hand. Looking deep into her eyes, he went in for a kiss. After their lips parted, he told her to head upstairs. He'd watch her from there.

As Whisper headed upstairs she couldn't help but think about the kiss. He had been so smooth with it. Sighing, Whisper entered the house and began cleaning up before heading to bed.

Laying there silently, the realization that she probably would never see him again set in. His vibe was everything, and she enjoyed the night. She dozed off and woke up to her alarm going off. With sleep in her eyes and cotton mouth she got up and headed to shower. When she was done, she cooked breakfast then sat it in the oven to stay warm while she got Ms. Porter ready for her doctor's appointment. The cancer had come back, and she was going to figure out her treatment plan.

After breakfast, Whisper called transportation and took a seat on the couch as Ms. Porter sat in her chair. Still pink in the face from last night, she couldn't help but smile. Ms. Porter noticed but said nothing about it.

D: GM, *twenty minutes.*

Unknown: *Fifteen minutes away.*

Whisper responded to both texts with an "Okay" then got a call from Transportation saying they were on the way up. It took them ten minutes to get her downstairs without the elevator, which saved Whisper some time.

"I forgot my wallet," she lied as they loaded her into the back of the ambulance.

Heading back upstairs, Whisper took a seat and waited for the next text. Five minutes later, she got it and headed down to the lot. There was a car with a woman parked behind the ambulance.

"Cooper?" the woman said as she approached.

Whisper nodded then approached the driver's side window. The woman handed her a grocery bag, and Whisper quickly stuffed it in her backpack.

"Bye, Cousin!" Whisper waved as the woman backed out.

All the while, Ms. Porter grew suspicious.

* * *

Whisper had been sitting in the waiting room for hours when her phone displayed a random number. She let it go to voicemail. They called back.

"Hello?" she answered.

"What's up, cuz?" HK's voice came through her AirPods.

"Who is this?" She played stupid.

He reminded her who he was, and she asked what was up. He asked her about her day. That led to an hour-long conversation. Whisper was giggling as Ms. Porter came out with a nurse. Cutting the call, she asked about the visit but got the runaround. Ms. Porter didn't want to let anyone know how bad it was really getting for her.

Not wanting to push, Whisper left it at that. They headed home. She cooked dinner, got everything settled with Ms. Porter, then began getting ready for tomorrow's visit. She still had yet to check what was in the bag from this morning. When she opened it, it was another pack of M&Ms. She was confused but went with it. When she was done packing up her candy, she got in bed.

HK: *I'm on yo side. Finna pull up.*

W: *For?*

HK: *I wanna see you.*

Whisper, wanting to see him too, let him pull up. She received a text from him saying he was at the door. When she opened it, she was surprised to see a young boy no more than sixteen with him.

"My bad. My brother ain't wanna wait in the car." HK held up a bag of weed and a bottle of Remy.

Whisper reluctantly let them in and let them know they had to be quiet. They took a seat and began rolling up. Whisper locked the door then took a seat by HK.

Leaning over as he broke down the weed, he waited for a kiss. Closing the distance between them, Whisper gave him a kiss then sat back. She had butterflies as he began telling her about his day. They smoked and drank, then HK said he had to drop off his brother. Walking them to the door she shook his brother's hand then gave HK a hug. As HK held her tightly, he kissed her on the forehead then told her he'd be right back.

Whisper doubted that, and headed off to bed. As she drifted off to sleep, she got a text from HK letting her know he was at the door. Surprised he kept his word, she headed for the door. She opened it to see him dressed in Nipsey blue from head to toe. When she let him in, he grabbed her and began kissing her. Between kisses he asked where the bedroom was at. Never completely breaking the kiss, they maneuvered through the house to her room.

Once inside, HK cut the lights off and began undressing Whisper. He had been thinking about doing this since the moment they met. Kissing on her neck and rubbing on her ass, he pushed her down on the bed. He pulled off his hoodie and undershirt in one motion. Under the dim lighting from the television, Whisper could see the full extent of how tatted he really was.

Gliding her finger along the nice size 62 that was placed in the middle of a skyline, she smiled. His body was perfectly sculpted and all she wanted to do was feel him inside of her. HK slid down his pants then boxers. Leaning in for another kiss, he spread her legs.

"Ona set, I been thinking about you all day." He kissed on her neck while guiding her to lay on her back.

Whisper got butterflies as he slowly began to leave a trail of kisses from her neck to her breast. Gently sliding in, he kissed her then placed a hand firmly behind her head and held her tightly as he gave her slow deep strokes. With every stroke he went deeper. In heaven, Whisp began to moan in his ear.

"You like this Crip dick?" He asked picking up the pace.

Whisper was, in fact, loving *the crip dick*. She had never been with the other side before. All her family were Bloods, so naturally she stayed away.

"Mmh, yes," she moaned lightly.

"Tell me you love it." He began kissing on her neck as she breathed out how much she loved the dick.

Pulling out and rolling Whisper over, he forcefully spread her legs and gripped her by the hip with his right hand and entered her from the back. First slowly in and out as he watched her bite the pillow while moaning out in pleasure. Then he sped it up and drove her crazy.

"This is mine." He went as deep as he could get and stayed there while breathing heavily in her ear. "You understand me?" He pushed himself deeper while asking again. After a few more strokes, he pulled out and came on her back. About to roll over, Whisp was stopped. He pinned her back down with one hand and began stroking himself for a few seconds then went back at it.

"This pussy so fucking tight," he moaned in her ear as he legs began to shake uncontrollably. "On Crip, you gone make a nigga crazy." He pulled out.

Flipping her over, he placed one of her legs over his shoulder and pulled her in as close as she could get. With his hands pressed against her waist, he drilled her while not breaking eye contact.

"Fuck, fuck, ahhh!" He pulled out and let his nut drip down her pussy.

With a smile an a *cuz,* he collapsed on her chest.

What felt like love to Whisper was twelve years worth of pent up sexual tension. Unknown to Whisper, HK had just got out of prison a month earlier after doing twelve years for armed robbery.

Laying there in his arms, she could do nothing but run back the scene over and over. At 3 A.M., they ate a bowl of cereal, got high, then he got dressed and left. Whisper got up and got ready to go see D'Marco.

After setting Ms. Porter up for the day, she went to meet her ride. It was the dude who had dropped the first pack off at the hospital. Halfway there, they pulled over at a Rinky-dink gas station and swapped cars.

Dude's wife joined them. She would be driving because he didn't have a license. When they made it to the prison, Whisper checked herself then headed in.

***

When D came out, he was so excited to see Whisper that he kissed her without warning. She felt so bad, seeing as what she had just used her mouth for. With the candy already on the table, they began to talk as he popped balloon after balloon into his mouth with no problem. As they laughed and talked, D finally got to the third pack. Whisper knew it wasn't hers because it looked sloppy.

Popping a balloon in his mouth, he began to chew, and Whisper scrunched her nose up. D said exactly what she was thinking, why was there candy inside?

D had to be very careful as he ate the candy and swallowed the balloons. As he popped what he thought was an M&M in his mouth and bit down, he knew he fucked up. Not wanting to get caught and charged, he swallowed the broken balloon and told Whisper he had to go. Kissing her, he got up then walked away without saying anything further.

Upset and not understanding what was going on, she tossed her trash and got left with tears in her eyes.

Once outside the prison, she met dude's wife. They headed to back to their house. Whisper took a seat on the couch as they argued about the wife going out. That was the least of her worries. She was in her chest about D and his hasty exit.

"No! I'm going out! That's it!" There was a silence for a moment.

The wife was a little upset about the way her husband was looking at Whisper earlier when they pulled up, so she claimed she had to do something and use the car. They argued while Whisper smoked the weed they offered her, not knowing she could hear everything.

D: whi

D: lov u

Her phone began ringing, and she excused herself outside to answer the call. When she did, D was babbling about how he loved her but could never love her the way she would want him to. Then he began going on about how she fucked up by fucking Juan. He went on to say how he could never be in a relationship with her while he was locked up. All of those things hurt Whisper, and she didn't know why he was saying what he was saying. What hurt the most was his laughs. They cut deep.

Whisper asked was he okay. All he would say was he was too high for this shit. Whisper tried to get his cellmate on the phone, but it didn't work. The phone went dead. Whisper tried to call back a million and one times until she finally gave up. Hurt, worried, and an all over mess, she decided to head in.

Heading inside, Whisper took a seat and dried her eyes. Finally, dude talked his wife into riding all the way back to South Central with him so there would be no problem. She agreed then they got into the car and headed on their way. Before they hit the highway, the couple stopped at the liquor store and bought beer and tequila.

Dude drank and smoked as his wife drove. Half way back to South Central, they pulled over and switched spots. Whisper objected, but dude assured her he could drive. He took another shot before putting the car in drive and doing ninety. Things were moving so fast. All Whisper could do was close her eyes and pray they didn't crash. Swerving in and out of traffic, Whisper looked up to see dude's wife on her knees, leaned over the console, blowing smoke into his mouth, and laughing. Dude swerved again avoiding the center devider. His wife fell back on her ass. Whisper let out a few drops of piss as she clutched the door, hoping they didn't crash.

Whisper was full of fear and sadness when they pulled up to The Vista. When she got settled in, she checked on D but got no response.

A few days later, D hit her up and asked why she wasn't texting him. She asked the same. All he said was he could have died. She told him she didn't know what he was talking about and told him about the crazy ride home. He didn't want to hear it. He wanted Whisper to feel sorry for him because he almost died. He still had yet to tell her how. Frustrated, they hung up on each other.

They never really spoke on the situation like that, but D did confess he popped a balloon filled with Meth. That was the first time he had Whisper bringing it in. She was pissed and decided to quit. All they agreed on was the weed.

D and her fell out for a few weeks. The money slowed up. Meanwhile, her relationship with HK grew. He seemed to be the perfect man, but sometimes perfect isn't always what it appears.

A month later D and Whisper finally made up and Whisper agreed to make the trips alone from now on. She had gotten a car and had gone on plenty of trips. This week was no different. She got the product, bagged it up, then hid it in the bathroom. When she was done, she put Ms. Porter to bed then got ready for HK to come over.

When he showed up, he was dressed in all black from head to toe. His usual vibe was now replaced by a cold energy. Something had changed. She couldn't put her finger on it. Asking if he was okay, she kissed him. He pulled back.

Seeing what type of mood he was in, she backed off. He asked to use the restroom then walked past Whisper without waiting for her response. He was in there for a minute then flushed and cut the water on. When he came out, he was on the phone.

"I gotta go. I'll be back, something came up." He left in a hurry.

Feeling played, Whisper headed to bed. She had another trip to D in the morning.

When she woke up, she got dressed then when to get the candy out the restroom. It was gone. She called HK and got no response. Having a mini heart attack, she started plotting and planning. She had enough money to reup and be good by next visit. D was going to be the problem, though. Sitting there thinking for a few minutes, she got her plan straight.

She got Ms. Porter dressed for the day then headed out. She headed to the beach where she sat and ate grilled shrimp and fish. She needed to clear her head from all the bullshit. She still really wasn't over the meth incident. And HK, that was a whole different can of worms. Calling D with her AirPods in, she bit another shrimp while waiting for him to pick up.

"What's up Whisper?" he asked.

"Hey, you ain't gonna believe this. I got a fucking flat. I'm not even going to make it."

"Damn, try to set a visit for tomorrow."

"Okay, I gotta go." She hung up and went back to her meal.

Later she planned to lie about not being able to get a visit. When she made it home, she told Ms. Porter the same thing then went to bed. She was heartbroken about HK. As she laid in bed, she sent him an email. She had all of his information from the time they had spent together. She helped him with job interviews, and other things he was having trouble doing as he adjusted to the free world. That's why she didn't see his betrayal coming.

Chalking it up as an L, Whisper copped her pack then continued on with life. She would continue with seeing D weekly and dropping off the packs all the while missing HK.

***

Present Day

Whisper received a text from an unknown number. It was HK, letting her know he was pulling up. Whisper felt a way and didn't want him to come over. It didn't take much for him to sweet talk her. He showed up dressed in a pair of Forces, a white tee, and a backpack. Whisper let him in and shook her head

Whisper took a seat, and he took one next to her. Reaching in his bag, he dropped two rolls of cash on the table. That was half his apology as he gently pushed her down onto the sofa and began kissing on her neck. Giving her dick like the very first time, he let her know he missed her then dipped. Whisper was left confused and didn't know what to do as she showered and thought back to what happened.

When she was done, she sat on her bed, wrapped in a towel. Someone was blowing up her phone like crazy.

"Hello?"

"Yes, do you know Henri King?" The woman on the phone had a professional tone.

"Uh, yes."

"How do you know him?" She raised her voice.

Whisper rolled her eyes, "Does it matter?"

"Well, that's my husband, and I'm pregnant. Just leave him alone." The woman hung up.

If Whisper wasn't sitting down, her knees would have buckled under her. Blocking her number and Henri's too, Whisper decided she was going to be done with him for good. He stole from her and was married with one on the way. Nah, he had to go.

Whisper stayed up all night thinking about HK and how he ruined what they had and her birthday. She was supposed to be having the time of her life and getting to the money. Crying herself to sleep, she woke up the next morning and prepared for her last trip. She was done with these niggas, and they didn't even know it. She was going to play the roll with D then never speak to him again after the last pack touched down.

All Whisper really wanted was love and money. In the pursuit of both,\ she felt like she lost herself and life as the police got closer. D was dead, HK had a wife, and her, she nothing but a wet ass and broken heart.

THE NEXT DAY 4:52

After hours of arguing and talking shit to Ms. Porter, Whisper was finally done packing up her shit and putting it at the door.

"I hope you and yo bitch ass grandson rot in hell. You old bitch," Whisper said, opening the door to start moving her shit downstairs.

Ms. Porter had said some of the most vile things ever to Whisper as she was packing her things up and the one thing Whisper wanted to tell her she had been saving for this very moment.

"Yeah, you'll be there with us in Hell, Whisper." Ms. Porter laughed. "You were such a sweet girl, Whisper. I don't know what happened to you."

"Your grandson happened to me. That's why his bitch ass dead now!" Whisper shouted, lugging a suitcase out the door. As she sat it down by the railing, she could see several LAPD squad cars coming through the alleyway deep as hell. It was like a scene out of the movies as the deep orange sky placed a glow over everything. As she admired the beauty, in this time of chaos came the sound of helicopters grew closer as the police hopped out with black boots and bulletproof vest then swarmed the building with guns drawn.

Heading back inside, Whisper locked the door and told Ms. Porter to shut the fuck up or else.

"Shut the fuck up!" She yelled.

Mr. Porter heard all the commotion and continued with the yelling. Not knowing what to do Whisper grabbed one of the trinkets Mr. Porter had collected over the years. It was a heavy stone elephant that had been painted with beautiful roses and the closes thing to Wisper.

Wisper replayed everything over once more as rage filled her. The pain of love was too much and the emotions she was feeling were overwhelming. Sadness from loving D, Anger for the way HK lied. Then there were the difficulties of her own psychological issues. All mixed together it was a deadly combination, one that she had been avoiding all along.

"Shut the fuck up! I'm not going to tell you again!" Whisper started to approach her on the couch.

"Help! HEEEEEELLLLLLP!"

Whisper brought the heavy stone down on Mr. Porter's head. First once and when she didn't stop moving she tried for a second time. That blow made the elderly woman's eyes roll back and her legs began to twitch. With rage still blinding her Whisper brought the stone down repeatedly until she stopped jerking and went limp. Dropping the stone Whisper walked to the window and looked out as the police continued to pull up in swarms.

3 YEARS LATER

"Yes officer?" Whisper said as Jaden two-year-old son cried in the back seat.

Beside her was her husband Jordan who was drunk. The couple had just come from an outdoor festival and little Jaden was ready for bed.

"Do you know why I am stopping you?" The officer pointed his flashlight in her eyes.

Whisper knew she had done nothing wrong. She was one hundred percent sure of it. She had made it her life goal to never do another crime for fear of losing her new life and true love. The officer pointed his light at a passed-out Jordan.

"You ran the stop sign and didn't use your turn signal back there," he began looking at Jaden. "Is something wrong?" he raised a brow.

"No, we were at the festival and he's a little worn out." Whisper reached back to soothe Jaden.

Instantly she knew she had fucked up as the officer pulled his gun then ordered her to put her hands up. Jordan jumped out of his sleep and the officer squeezed the trigger three times hitting Jordan in the side with all three rounds. Without so much as a blink the officer opened the driver's side door and pulled Whisper out and slammed her on the ground as she cried out watching Jordan's life fade away.

Everything became a blur and the days turned to years as Whisper sat in prison for the murder of D'Marco, Ms. Porter, and smuggling drugs. She was never the same after losing the one true love of her life, but she understood karma. As for her son he was placed in the care of Jordan's family and has not had contact with her since.

SHONDRA AKA SHON
SOUTH CENTRAL, CALIFORNIA 4:56 PM

"You alright?" Ro asked, snapping me out my thoughts. I was looking out the window at my daughter playing with the other kids in the building. I was glad she was getting along with them, but I had gone off into a daze, leaving me standing in the window way too long.

"Yeah, I'm alright. Just glad baby girl is finding some peace after what we have been through." I got out of the blinds and walked over to Ro. He was my best friend, and I was thankful for him. He had taken in me and my daughter in our dark times and promised to make sure we were straight. The third floor two-bedroom apartment was small, and a roach problem had started, but it was better than the situation I was in when I lived in Texas. I knew living here was not forever, so I had patience with my living situation.

"Choppa and Easy said they got some of that wedding cake OG and some new edibles. Go down there and get us something. That should get your mind right." Ro handed me two hundred dollars.

"Thanks, Ro. I'll be back in a second." I walked out the door.

When I stepped out the cool apartment, the sun and humidity hit me instantly as I made my way to the stairs. It was fourth of July weekend, and I was wearing cutoff jeans shorts and a crop top with sandals. My hair was pulled into a tight bun away from my face so I wouldn't sweat. The sun was shining my way, so I slid on my shades that were sitting on top of my head.

As I was making my way down the stairs a man dressed in slacks, a dress shirt, and reading glasses was walking up the stairs holding a pizza box and a newspaper. I'd seen him a couple times since I had been living in the building, and he lived on the floor above me. He was handsome, and a bit quirky, but I wasn't into conservative guys. It wasn't because I liked gangsta dudes, but my so-called husband was conservative, and behind his innocent looks, he was the devil. The way he walked around I could tell he was no good. Something about his stare told me he was hiding something just like I was. It was as though everyone in the building was suspect of something. Even Choppa and Easy.

"How are you, ma'am?" he asked as he walked past me.

"Fine and you," I replied as I kept it moving.

I made it to the first floor and went to Choppa and Easy's, door which was 1A. I rang the bell twice and knocked like they always requested when you wanted to buy product from them. Choppa and Easy were a couple from New Orleans. Choppa was thick as a Snicker and had a cute face, while her man was chocolate, rugged, and wore locks in his hair. They were cool, and Choppa made bomb Cajun food. Ro and Easy were close friends, so Choppa would give him food to bring to me and my daughter.

Easy opened the door, shirtless with a blunt dangling from his lips. Easy was sexy and his body was tatted from his neck to his waist. He always had his shirt off and his dreads hanging down his shoulders.

"What's up, lil momma? What you need?" he asked as he sized me with his eyes.

"Can I get a quarter and two brownies?" I smiled.

"You can get whatever you want, baby. I'll be right back, tho.'" He closed the door.

Minutes later, he came back.

"You saw that maintenance man-nigga? It's hot as fuck in here and my AC went out," he huffed as he handed me my product.

"Nah, I ain't seen him. He fixed mine a couple of days ago tho. It's so hot, it's going to keep going out." I handed him the money.

He shook his head and closed the door.

I yelled for my daughter and had her come upstairs with me because it was getting late. The grownups were coming outside, and people were setting up their barbeque pits to start their holiday weekend.

When I got to my floor, Ro was sitting outside with the radio and a bottle of Hennessey in his hand. He was talking to the neighbor. Her name was Whisper. She was a cute girl, but she had a look about her that told me she wasn't innocent. I saw her have drama with her man that looked like a drug dealer. Ro knew everyone in the building because it was owned by his family. He didn't live with me, but he lived in the next city. I had to be lowkey so South Central was home after not living there since I was sixteen.

I gave him the weed to roll and sat in the chair next to him. I sent my daughter into the house, then Ro and I got our party going. I looked at my Apple Watch and it was four fifty-six. I looked over the banister when I heard police sirens. I couldn't even put the blunt in between my lips when I saw three cop cars drive into the courtyard, almost hitting the kids that were playing. I stood up as my heart began to race.

"Go in the house and wait in the room. I don't know why they are here, but I won't let them see you," Ro assured me as he shoved me into the house.

"I'm scared. You think they are here for me? I don't want to go to jail for murder," I wept as I sat in the living room looking like I had saw a ghost.

"You not going to jail on my dime. I promise you," he assured me.

"You have been so nice to me, Ro, and I love you for that. If I don't go to jail tonight, I'm going to give you some pussy," I babbled.

He chuckled and then kissed my cheek. "You definitely need to do that."

I had never fucked Ro before because I didn't want to cross any boundaries with him. I was still traumatized from the sex I had with Villain for two years. I also didn't know how life would be with him after leaving my husband. I knew sex was an emotional thing, and I didn't want anything that delt with emotions until I was over what my husband did to me.

I got my daughter from her room and went into mine. I was so scared, so I hid in the closet with my daughter.

"Mommy, why are we in here? Are those police for us about daddy?" she asked in a soft tone. She knew bits and pieces about what happened by being in the room.

"No, baby, we're going to be fine." I tried to assure her, even though I wasn't sure.

As I sat waiting for the worst, I thought back to the life I used to live. The night I took my life back I will never forget. Things got ugly but it happened for the better.

SHON
HOSTAGE

I was sitting in Villain's office while he yelled at his workers. I tried my best to tune him out because I was buzzed on vodka and cranberry. I was wearing a sequin red ballroom dress that cost six grand from Valentino. My face was beat to the gods, and my hair was tightly curled and highlighted blonde. It was my father's birthday, and he was having a ballroom party. Business came before pleasure, so everything was at a halt.

I came from a rich mafia family that put money, drugs, and connects over their loved ones. I was my father's money maker when it came to his wealth. I had been married four times in the name of money. Every time my dad wanted to make a drug deal with a connect, they wanted me as a pawn. I was to marry them and do as they say. I would get paid and the husband's I had would shower me with everything a woman desired, but my latest husband was nothing like my last, and it was nothing I could do about it. If I said no to any of their proposals, I would be killed.

My husband, Villain was a born into a Russian crime family. When his father died, he took over the family's business and changed all the rules for everyone that bought drugs from them. When he laid his eyes on me in one of their meetings with my father, he had to have me, or the deal was off. I was fresh out of my third marriage because he died in a car accident, so I was free to move on. Now I had been with Villain for a few years and things got worse by the day, especially after this night.

"Find that motherfucker now with my money and drugs. If I don't get my money, I'm murdering somebody in the West family!" he roared, startling me a bit. I looked up from my acrylic nails I'd been picking at for the last thirty minutes.

"Villain, please calm down. I'm sure Rabby will show up. No need to seek violence," I pleaded. Rabby was my younger brother and one of my dad's runners. Rabby had a drug habit that the whole family knew about, but my father still trusted him to make moves. My father paid him well, but his habit had finally caught up to him. Now he was on the run with one hundred grand in cash and ten grand worth of kilos.

"Shut the fuck up, Shon. You are just trying to save your coke head little brother. You get a fucking allowance. You have no say in this, and this is man business," he boldly spoke.

"I think I do have a say so since I've been the pawn for the last seven years." I rolled my eyes.

Before I could get my eyes back to the front of my head, he slapped me so hard, I bit my tongue. After all these years of arguing, this was the first time be put his hands on me. I was stunned with my hand on my cheek. His goons gawked me, waiting on my next move.

"You talk a lot, bitch, and I am sick of it. But I got something for you. Your family robbed me after I helped them levitate in my empire. Therefore, I am going to rob them too. I know you are daddy's little princess, but I am about to show you and Mr. West who the real King is."

I stood up and stormed out of the office. I went into my daughter's room, and she was still awake. I laid with her until she fell asleep. I kissed her forehead and then gazed at her. Had I known that would have been my last time seeing her for two years, I would have run away with her in that moment.

I left out of her room and went to mine. I walked into our closet and started taking off my dress. Once it hit the floor, my eyes widened when I felt Villain put me in the chokehold. He dragged me out of the closet while I tried to get his arm from around my neck.

"Bitch, your family is costing me a lot of money and lost."

"Let me go!" I shouted, using my last breath. I felt myself blackout.

I woke up by a punch to the face, Villain was on top of me looking like a maniac. The pain was unbearable, and I tasted blood in my mouth causing me to choke. I tried fighting him back, but he punched me again.

"Don't try to fight me back, bitch, it's only going to make things worse." He gritted in my face.

"Why are you doing this to me?" I whimpered in pain.

"You are staying down here, and you will be my sex slave I've always wanted, until your brother is found, and I get all my money back. The basement is soundproof now and I put in a metal door. You won't be heard of until I say so."

I thought back on the last couple of weeks when he had construction workers working in our basement. He told me that he was building a man cave, and adding a shower room, but the whole time he was building a dungeon to keep me in for his sick fantasy. It had only been a couple of days my brother was missing, so he already had it planned to lock me up.

6 5

Villain raped and abused me for the rest of the night and left me in my own bodily fluids. Weeks and months went by, and it was the same treatment for me. Things had gotten so bad for me I gave in to the treatment and became submissive.

I had been down in the basement for almost two years, and I was losing my mind. I cried all day and night, and I was suffering from constant infections from being raped. Villain wasn't getting any help for me, but he sent his nanny he had gotten for Ava down to give me food. Food and water were the only thing keeping me alive. But he only wanted me healthy because he didn't want to fuck on skin and bones. His obsession of me being his sex slave had gone overboard. He wouldn't tell me if my brother was found of if the debt was paid.

I hadn't seen Villain in two days, and I was happy. I sat in the quiet, so I made up scenarios in my bed. I was laughing with myself when the nanny came downstairs with a plate of food.

"What's so funny, Mrs. Moore?" the nanny asked with a smirk.

"Oh, nothing.... I've gotten so used to entertaining myself, that's all."

"You poor girl. I wish I could get you from down here, but he is watching my every move with those cameras. But you haven't been looking so good, so I snuck you these." She pulled a bottle of pills from her apron pocket.

"What is this?"

"Antibiotics and Tylenol. They should clear up whatever is going on."

"Thank you so much, Darla. Were you able to get the phone for me?"

"Yes, but please make sure you don't get caught with it. I don't want anything to happen to me and my child."

"Trust me, I won't get caught. Thank you so much."

"You eat and take your meds." She rushed out of the room.

I ate my food and took the pills. I was thankful for the small shower room he had built in the basement. That was the only thing he didn't lie about. I took a long hot shower and then laid in bed. I cried myself to sleep, thinking about my daughter.

Days went by and I still didn't see Villain. That gave me time to make fake pages on social media. I didn't talk to anyone, because I couldn't trust a soul. I only called my mother and looked at everyone's pages. My mother was a prisoner too caught in my father's world. She was once a pawn like me. It was a never-ending thing for the women in my family seemed like.

As I was going through Facebook, I ran across a face I had not saw in a while that a friend tagged in a picture. I was hesitant to message him, but I did. When he knew it was me, we talked for days at a time. After two weeks, he was begging to see me, and I had to tell him the truth about me.

Ro: *Why can't I video chat you, or have your number?*

Me: *I'm going to be truthful with you. I am married, but I am not happy. I want to get away.*

Ro: *Why do you want to leave your man?*

Me: *He beats me...*

Ro: *I am about to video chat you now, so answer!*

I decided to pick up his video chat. I knew Villain wasn't coming and it was early in the morning. When I got on camera, I looked a mess.

"What's up, beautiful." He smiled.

"You know I am not beautiful. I am not the same seventeen-year-old Shon you knew." My tone was bitter, and my head was slightly down.

"You're good. Now tell me what's going on."

"I am living in a soundproof basement, and he has me hostage as a sex slave until my brother pays a debt."

"What the fuck. You are joking." I could see the anger in his facial expression.

I walked around the room showing him my space, and then I showed him the scars on my body.

"I am coming to get you." He frowned.

"Don't come here. He is crazy, and he is one of the deadliest drug dealers in Texas. My own father fears this man and can't save me. When the time is right, I will let you know."

"I don't like this shit, now a nigga ain't gon' be able to sleep at night. You better call me every fucking day. I'm going to come up with a plan."

"I will, and okay."

I hung up just in time. I stuffed the phone under my mattress and played sleep. I enjoyed the time he left me down in the basement alone. Now he was back, and he was crazier than he was before.

"Stop tightening up your legs so I can cum, damn." Villain forcefully pushed my legs open and then punched me clean in my nose. I felt myself daze out and my ears started ringing.

"Now open the fuck up." He smirked. The look in his eyes was demonic, and I felt sick to my stomach. The way he was acting he had to be on more than liquor.

"You are sick, Villain. I know my father has paid the debt by now. You have to let me out of here," I cried out, knowing it would get me in trouble. But I was desperate. I knew he would beat me rather I asked questions or not.

"Shut the fuck up." He gripped my throat and started pounding me until he got his rocks off.

He rolled off me and stood from the bed. He left the basement without saying a word to me. I raced out of bed and grabbed my phone. I locked myself in the bathroom as tears fell from my eyes. I looked at myself in the mirror and I had blood all over my face and my nose was aching. I was sure he fractured it with the pain I was feelings. I started shouting at the top of my longs as I cried. I was trying to get my emotions together. I hated when I cried because it made my pain worse. I looked inside the medicine cabinet and grabbed a bottle of regular Advil. I took a handful of them because I knew two just wouldn't do it for me. In that moment, I was hoping the pills killed me.

I was ready to text Ro, but he video called me before I could send the text. I didn't want to answer, but I did. He wasn't settling for regular phone conversation, he wanted to see my face.

"I want to kill him, Ro. I think he fractured my nose this time. Do you see this shit? I need a plan to get away from him and I need to take my daughter with me," I cried out.

"I can come tonight, and I'll murder that nigga. Your nose looks more than fractured it looks broken," he gritted through the phone.

"No, don't come tonight. I need to meet with my mother first. Give me a week or two and I will give you the address."

"I can't wait that fuckin' long. I'm flying to Houston tonight and I'll be on standby for however long I have to."

"Okay, I will keep you updated."

"Find you a weapon or something. You are going to need it."

Every day I talked to Ro about our plan. I was nervous but I was ready to get it over with. However, I had to see my mother before I did anything. I needed her help, and I needed her approval. I sent her a text to ask her a favor. I needed money and I knew she would give it to me.

I walked up the street as fast as I could, at ten at night, after I got a nine one-one call from my girlfriend Shon. She was crying and whispering on the phone, so I rushed straight to her house even though she told me not to. Her dad had forbidden me from seeing her because I was a gang member at seventeen years old. But I didn't give a fuck. He was no different than me. He wasn't a gang member, but he was the biggest coke dealer in the city. If it wasn't for his daughter, I would have robbed his bitch ass.

I made it to the side of her house and tossed a rock at her window.

"Shon!" I shouted toward her window.

I turned around when I heard footsteps in the grass. It was Shon.

"I told you not to come, Romel," Shon expressed in a low tone.

"You know I don't give a fuck about your dad being home. Did he hit you again? I'll fuck that nigga up!"

"Yes, he did, but please calm down. I don't want anything to happen to you."

"Ain't shit gon happen to me. You want to run away, we can." I glared at her with a serious look on my face.

"Really?" she asked in a bashful tone.

"Yeah, you know I got money, and we both will be eighteen soon. I promise I'll take care of you." I grabbed her hand and cuffed it in mine.

"I'm going to pack my things now."

At that moment, I felt a gun to my head, and then I heard it cock.

"Get the fuck off my property, motherfucker. Didn't I tell you to stay the fuck away from my daughter?"

"I don't give a fuck what you said. Your daughter is my friend, and I am going to be there for her," I said boldly.

"Please, Romel, just leave. I will call you tomorrow, okay?" Shon pleaded.

"You won't be calling shit on any phone I paid for. I'm glad we are leaving for Texas tomorrow. You won't ever see this low life nigga again," her father stated as he shoved his gun harder into my back. I turned to face him like a man.

"You can move your daughter out the hood, but the universe will bring her back to me. Mark my words," I spoke with pride.

"Whatever, nigga. Now get off my property. My daughter will be with whoever I chose, and it ain't you." He started walking me down the driveway with the gun to my chest while Shon looked on and cried.

When I made it home, I tried to call her phone, but it went straight to voice mail. The following morning, the number was disconnected. I felt like shit losing my best friend that day, but it wasn't shit I could do about it as a youngin'. After that night, I never saw Shon again.

"Yo, nigga, you alive?" my cousin Chink said, snapping me out my daze of a flashback of me and Shon's last encounter when we were teens. I was reading me and Shon's recent text as I thought of her. I had been talking to her for the last three months and things were only getting worse with her situation. I knew it was time to get her the fuck out the basement. After not hearing from her for years, she found me on social media and poured her heart to me. She was held captive by her husband, and she needed help getting away. My brain was moving a mile a minute as I thought of a plan.

"I'm going to go save Shon like I was telling you the other night," I truthfully told Chink.

He laughed. "Nigga, what? How the fuck you gon' get her out?"

"I'ma murk her husband, and then fly her and her daughter back to Cali. I'ma move her in the Vista's for a while. You know that's the lowkey spot, and your mom is the landlord now." I shrugged.

"Nigga, you about to fly across to Texas, murk her nigga, and bring her to the Vistas? Did you fuck her before her daddy put that shotgun to yo' back ready to blow out your lungs years back? You doing all this like she got some good pussy." He shook his head.

"She was my best friend, and she was a virgin, so no I ain't fuck. I knew I shouldn't have told your childish ass. You better keep your mouth shut or I'ma come back and murder you." I glared at him with a devious look on my face.

He laughed nervously. "You gon' kill yo' first cousin?"

"Yup." I pulled my blunt from my ear and lit it.

"Look, man, I was joking. I know how you felt about her back then, so I see why you want to help her. I got your back, and I won't tell a soul. If you need me to travel with you, I will. I want you to be safe, so I got your back," he told me in a serious tone.

"Yeah, I'ma need you to go with me. I am going to call Uncle Jo and see if I can use his private plane and pilot. I gotta take my shotgun with me. It's no doubt in my mind that I'm not gon' kill this nigga."

After I told Chink my plan, I called my uncle, and he wasted no time setting up my flight.

I left my house where I lived alone in West Los Angeles and drove to The Vista's. I wanted to see if my aunt was there and to get some weed from my homie. I parked in front of the building and stepped out my SRT Challenger.

I walked in the building. Kids were outside playing, and the sun had gone down. It was summertime so being outside was cheaper than running the air conditioner. I stopped at Choppa and Easy's door for my weed. I could hear Lil Wayne's song *Hell Yeah* blaring through the door. I knocked harder than usual just in case they couldn't hear me. Seconds later, the door came open. Choppa had a tough name for a woman, but she was a baddie. All I could do was lust over her from a distance because her man Easy was my homie.

"What's up, Ro? What you need tonight?" she asked with a sly smile. Her New Orleans accent was strong.

"Let me get an ounce of that fire shit Easy gave me the other day if you still have it."

"You were stuck, huh?" She laughed.

"Hell yeah, I was." I chuckled.

She closed the door, and minutes later, she came back with my pack.

I jogged over to the renter's office. Thankfully, the light was on, letting me know my aunt was still working. I opened the door, and she was packing to leave.

"I was on my way out. What's up, nephew?" she asked in a slightly rushed tone.

"Please tell me you have a vacant spot in here I can rent."

"Now, you know the only thing I let people sell in here is weed. If you tryna turn it into a trap, I can't let you rent." She raised her eyebrow.

"Nah, its nothing like that. I have a friend that I need to move in here with her daughter. It won't be for long though, just until she gets some things straight."

"I have a two-bedroom apartment on the third floor that's vacant. The rent is two thousand a month if she doesn't have section eight."

"Okay, I'll be back tomorrow with the money. I only got a thousand on me. I am going to pay it for six months."

She went into her drawer. She gave me a key and told me the apartment number.

It took me one day to get the apartment furnished for Shon and turn on the utilities. After the movers brought in the beds, I flopped on the memory foam and pulled my phone from my pocket. I sent Shon a text.

Me*: My flight leaves in the morning, I'll text you when I touch down.*

Shon*: Okay. I'm going to a charity event in a few of days and I will get to see my mother. Once I see her, I am going to put my part of the plan in motion. I'll text you the address, but please don't come until I tell you.*

Me*: Alright...*

ARRANGED

The following day I was on a flight to Houston. I stayed in a hotel under a fake name for five days. I was anxious and ready to get to Shon. I'd text her when I touched down, but she didn't text me back. I took those days to stalk the house she was in. I watched her husband go in and out every day with a little girl every morning. He came home with her at night. I assumed it was the child he shared with Shon. He was lucky she told me not to make a move before she called me, because I could have killed him at his doorstep.

Me*: I'm going to be ready tonight. I couldn't text you because this nigga has been down here for days. He hasn't put his hands on me though because of the event tonight. I have to look flawless. But as soon as I get to my phone, I'll tell you to come in.*

Ro*: I'm still at the hotel. I've been ready.*

Me*: Okay, I'm going to keep the front door unlocked when we come back. The basement is near the kitchen. If you don't find me in time, I have something to protect myself.*

Ro*: Okay...*

I quickly slid my phone under the mattress. I heard the door unlock and Villain appeared. He was dressed down in his best and looked like he wouldn't hurt a fly.

"You have an hour to get yourself together. Wear what I laid on the bed for you."

"Where is Ava?" I asked as I stood off the bed. Every time I saw Villain I asked about my daughter or when was he going to let me go. It had been two years since I saw her, and we lived in the same house.

"Get your ass upstairs, Shon, and don't start with the questions."

Not wanting to cause trouble, I headed upstairs to the room I thought we would share forever.

I took a shower, and when I got out, he had a hair stylist waiting to do my hair. She put in a thirty-inch weave and curled it flawless. I went back to the bedroom and put on the pearl-colored dress that was laying on the bed. I looked at the price tag. It was a thousand-dollar dress from Chanel. It wasn't my style, but I knew I couldn't fuss about it. I slid on the dress and walked to the mirror. I slid on my heels and gazed at my reflection.

"I'm too fine to be some asshole's prisoner," I uttered as I ran my hands down my hips.

I felt Villain's hand on my waist. "You look good. When we come home tonight, you are sleeping in the room with me. Oh yeah, me and your dad is cool. The debt has been paid." He started kissing my neck, causing me to cringe. I hated when he touched me. I knew it wasn't sincere. However, hearing him say he and my father was cool and the debt was paid made me angry. My father wasn't even worried about me, and he never tried to come get me. I was hoping he rotted in hell since he didn't care about me.

We walked toward the door. All I could do was look around to see if I spotted any of my daughter's belongings. I saw her coat hanging by the door and her backpack. I was hoping she was home when it was time for me to make my way out.

We made it to the venue and went inside. Villain was holding my hand, making sure I didn't leave his side. I drank as much champagne as I could, getting sloppy drunk. An hour into the event, Villain let me go talk to my mother. I would talk to her on my secret cellphone, and I told her what I wanted to do. She was standing at the bar with a wine glass in her hand filled with red wine.

"Beautiful Shon. How are you holding up?" she asked dryly. I could tell she was over her limit with wine.

"I'm on my last string. I'm leaving tonight. Can you still help me?" I glared at her with a serious look on my face.

She sipped her wine and then looked over her shoulder. She sat her glass down and dug into her purse. She handed me a credit card and a stack of money.

"That's five thousand, and the card is in my name and unlimited. I'll always keep money on it for you and Ava. She is at the house, so make sure you get her out of here too. Get a burner phone and call me in a few days."

I quickly slid the cash and card into my handbag. "Thank you so much, mom."

"Be careful, you know that motherfucker is crazy." She warned.

"I got it all under control," I assured her. "But why hasn't daddy tried to send someone for me and Ava? Does he not care about me now that he is all in with my perverted husband?"

"Your daddy is a pussy, but he will be taken care of. Don't worry about that. He didn't come tonight because he is *sick*." She shot me a side eye. I didn't know what she had up her sleeve when it came to my father, but I was hoping it was death.

"Okay, mommy. I'll be in contact."

At that moment, Villain came to get me from my mother. After Villain wrote the charity a big check, we were headed back home. My heart was racing as he sped the highway, drunk. I was playing out my plan in my head as Villain had his hand up my skirt rubbing my clit.

"I can't wait to get you home. I've been thinking about a lot of things too. I want to make things right with us. I want to free you from the basement, and you can live upstairs with me and Ava."

I turned my head quickly to face him. "Are you serious?"

"Yes, I love you, and I want to start over." He smiled.

As good of a game he was talking, I still didn't want to be with him. He put me through hell, and I could never forgive him. He degraded me and took away the confidence I used to wear naturally. He stripped me of my freedom and took me away from my daughter. I wasn't trusting anything he was saying, but I pretended as though I was happy. All I knew was I was going to need to see a doctor once I got away from him.

"I love you too, and I can't wait to see Ava."

We made it home in minutes. Villain walked behind me and kissed on my neck. When we got inside, he picked me up and walked down the foyer as we tongue kissed.

"I thought you said you were letting me come upstairs?" I asked when he made it to the basement door.

"I need one last fantasy of fucking you down here before I turn it into a mancave."

He put me down and gazed at me with seductive eyes. I was glad he decided to fuck me in the basement one last time. I had everything set down there for my get away.

"Your body is so beautiful, even with the marks I left. I'm so sorry I hurt you," he uttered as he took off my dress.

I didn't respond. I felt tears welding in my eyes. I was angry he wanted to make things right now that I was done. I was forced to give him my all and he ruined me. I felt anger rush through my body, causing me to cry more.

"What's wrong, baby?" he asked before laying me on the bed.

"I'm just overwhelmed that I am going to see Ava after two years." I wept.

"She is going to be happy to see you to."

He slid my thong off and dived into my kitty. The feeling of his tongue felt good, but I couldn't let pleasure distract me and cause me to stay. I looked down and Villain had his eyes closed as he feasted. I sat up slightly and reached for my phone under the mattress. I had a text message from Ro.

Ro: *Are you ready?*

Me: *Yeah, are you in the area? I'm about to make my move.*

Ro: *Yeah… Go in for the kill. I'm closer than you think.*

I sat the phone down and then went under my pillow. I pulled out a kitchen knife that I found in a packaged box that was in the basement. It was big and sharp like the knife Chucky the doll liked to keep.

Villain was still eating me out when I took the knife and shoved it in his back. He sat up in surprise and tried to attack me. I jumped out of the bed and headed for the basement door. I was going to lock him down there to bleed to death. Before I could open the door, it flew open. A man in a ski mask held up a shotgun and pointed it at Villain. I knew it was Ro, and I was happy he came in when he did. I moved out of the way so I wouldn't get shot. He let off three shots into Villain, causing him to fall down the stairs.

Ro snatched off his mask and gazed at me while I stood in front of him in the nude.

8 3

"Damn, you are still sexy after all of these years." He smirked.

"Boy, we don't have time for that. We gotta find my daughter and get the fuck out of here!" I franticly expressed.

"Get your daughter and whatever you need. Our private flight to California leaves in two hours." He instructed, getting back to the plan.

He walked down the stairs and let off three more shots into Villain making sure he was dead. I couldn't stomach death, but I was glad to see Villain taking his last breath. I slid on a sweatsuit and a pair of Nikes. I went straight upstairs to my daughter's room. She was asleep with the nanny in the twin bed next to her. I quietly started packing some of her things while they stayed asleep. Thankfully her nanny did not wake up, but Ava woke up when I picked her up from the bed.

"Mommy?" she asked as she yawned. She was now six years old. She had grown a lot and she looked just like me.

"Yes, baby, it's me. But go back to sleep. We are about to get on an airplane."

I tossed a comforter over her, silencing her. I didn't want to explain anything to her yet. I just wanted her safe with me.

Ro escorted us out the house and we jumped in his rental car. He went back inside to make it look like a robbery and kidnapping. After he raided my place, he found seventy thousand in cash and all of Villain's jewelry. Two hours later, I was on a private flight with my first love.

We got settled on our flight. My daughter had a snack that the flight attendant offered, and then she went back to sleep under her cover.

"Thank you for coming to get me. Where are we going exactly?" I asked as I gazed at Ro. He said I was sexy after all these years, and he was too.

"To South Central where it's not high profile. I would put you in a mansion, but you need to lay low in the ghetto for a while."

I turned up my nose. "Back to the city?"

"Yeah, you are going to be living in the neighborhood we grew up in. You will be safe, and I will be there with you every day."

"I didn't want to go back to South Central but fuck it. I am just glad to be away from my husband and family. I want to change me and my daughter's identity and never look back."

"I know you probably haven't let it sink in that you are running away with me, but I want you to know I am nothing like your ex. I'm not asking you to be with me or to have sex with me. Your situation had me mad when you told me about it. I knew I couldn't just not do anything to help you since you trusted me enough to pour out what was going on with you to me."

I sighed. "I hate the way things ended between us when we were teens, and I am sorry for only contacting you in my time of need. I should have run away from Texas years ago, but my family had a hold on me. I want to learn my worth again, and the only way I can do that is get away from my family, not leaving a trace of me."

"I got everything covered with that. You won't be staying in South Central forever. Just until I get your paperwork situated," he assured me.

After we talked for a while, I had fallen asleep. I woke up three hours later at Van Nuys airport. We stepped off the plane and got into a brand new black 5.0 Mustang. My daughter was still asleep, so I laid her in the backseat and put on the middle seatbelt across her. Ro drove to South Central. As he cruised the streets, my childhood came back to me. The good times when I was a free spirit running the streets as a teen.

"This is where you will be staying," he said as he slowly rolled past a green building. There was a sign in front of it that said *Green Vista Apartments*. He pulled in the alley behind the building and parked in a parking stall.

"Where are we, mommy?" my daughter asked when I took her out the car.

"We're at our new home, baby," I assured her.

When we walked into the building, it was quiet, and the sun was barely coming up. Ro escorted us to the elevator. He excessively pushed the button until he realized the elevator was out of order.

"This muthafucka work sometimes. We can take the stairs." He shook his head.

"That's fine. I can use the walk."

I picked up my daughter and we took the stairs. We stepped inside the stuffy apartment and Ro showed me around. He had furnished it for me, and I had to admit, he did a good job.

"I wanted y'all to be comfortable, so I decked it out. You won't have to leave, I'll run your errands for you."

"It's nicer inside, and you did a good job. I'll just need some cleaning products to sanitize for my baby."

He nodded. "Y'all get settled. I'll be in the living room if you need me."

Before he walked off, I grabbed his arm gently. He gazed at me with his big brown eyes. Ro was sexy and the man of my dreams. I was happy to have him back in my presence. But I wanted to get settled mentally before I made any intimate moves with him.

"Thank you for being there for me at the worst time of my life."

"You're welcome. I would have not been a real man if I wasn't there for you." He wrapped his arms around me.

"When the smoke clears, can we talk about us?" I shot him a bashful look.

"Whenever you are ready. I know what you've been through so I'm not even trying to take it there with you anyway," he assured me. He hugged me tighter, and then kissed me on the forehead.

I took my daughter to the second bedroom that was furnished for her. There were simple pink sheets on the bed, a Disney dresser, a few unopened dolls, and a television mounted on the wall. I sat her on the bed.

"I know this isn't what you are used to, but do you like your room?" I asked her.

"Yes, I like it, mommy. Is this where you have been for so long?" she asked in her small voice.

"Yes, baby, I've been here all this time, trying to get you away from the evil people that were raising you." I lied. Even though Villain was evil, I couldn't stomach telling her at such a young age that her father held me as a sex slave in our basement.

"Well, I like it, and I am happy to be back with you. Daddy was mean. I was only happy with Nanny." She dropped her head.

"Did he do anything to hurt you?" I asked with sympathy in my tone.

"No, he just yells at me when I asked for you and told me I would never see you again." Tears fell from her eyes.

I took her into my arms. My heart was breaking for her, but I was glad I was able to give her a better life.

"You don't have to worry about daddy anymore. We are here for good, and we are not going back."

I tucked her in bed and kept the door open. I went back into the living room and Ro was laying on the couch with his arm over his face. I didn't want to lay in the room alone, so I laid on the love seat. I woke up a few hours later and Ro was still there. He was on his phone and flipping through the television channels.

"Is there food in here I can cook?" I asked him.

He put his phone on mute. "Yeah, I got the frig filled while you were sleep."

I went to check on my daughter and she was lying in bed watching television. I went to the kitchen and started cooking. I was comfortable in the Vista's, but something kept telling me that we were going to get caught.

As the days went by, I started to become paranoid, but I kept my cool for the sake of my daughter. Ro was with me hours at a time, and only left me at night when I was sleep. But the day I saw the police pull in the courtyard deep, I thought for sure they were coming to get me for murder.

RO

BACK TO 4:56 PM JULY 2ND...

I knew the cops weren't for me and Shon, so I went outside once I made sure she and baby girl was straight in the room. I wanted to watch the commotion and wait on my cousin Chink. I called his phone to let him know the police had the building surrounded so to park away and leave his weed in the car.

I knew I traced every one of my tracks for me and Shon. After I secured her in my rental when I saved her from her nightmare, I took all the surveillance cameras in the house and burnt them when we got back to California. I had done my research on the kingpins in Houston, and Shon's husband was an enemy of the state. Nobody would be looking for his killer, and Shon and her daughter would be in the system as unfound. I had everything in the works for her, so nobody would ever be able to trace Shon or her daughter. I knew she was in contact with her mother though, but that was my least worry.

I looked around the once crowded courtyard. It was empty and the neighbor Whisper, the girl me and Shon was smoking with, had gone ghost. She was a quiet girl that always stopped and matched a blunt with me and Shon when we were outside chilling. Something about her quietness made me wonder what secret she was hiding from the world. It was like everyone was a suspect around this bitch, *even me*.

I watched them start going door to door. I tucked the rest of the weed I had in my sock and sat back down. I watched two cops walk toward me with their guns drawn to their side. The tall, black officer with a bald head walked to me. I stood up to face him.

"You live here?" he asked with his eyebrow raised. I watched his eyes gaze at my gold chain and then at my hands. I knew he had already profiled me, so he was looking at my hands to make sure I didn't reach for a weapon.

"Yeah, I live here. What's going on?" I asked in a confused tone.

"We're looking for someone. Have you seen this person, or do they live here?" he asked me as he passed me a picture. I gazed at the person in the photo. I had seen them before, but I wasn't going to tell the police that.

"Nah, I ain't see them." I shrugged as I passed him the picture.

"We need to look inside briefly just to make sure. Is anyone in there?"

"My wife and my daughter. You can look around if you don't start going through our shit." I frowned.

Before he could respond, the officer with him started listening to his walkie talkie.

"They found the person, we can head down," he told his partner.

The black officer glared at me once again and walked off. I let out a sigh of relief and then looked at my phone. Chink had texted me, telling me he was walking toward the building. I walked to the alley and met him.

"Damn, what the fuck happened over here?" Chink asked in a shocked tone as he looked at all the police.

"I don't even know. I hope they are leaving soon though." I shook my head.

"It's a lot of weird niggas in this building now. Ain't no telling," he replied and shook his head as well.

We walked into Shon's apartment, and I locked the door. I closed the blinds and we walked to the kitchen table. When we sat down, he slid me an envelope with my name on it.

"Sorry it took a little longer. The nigga was in Africa, so I had to wait for him to come down, but all that shit is official."

I took the paperwork out the envelope and read over them. It was a new social security card, and driver's license for Shon. There was a social security card for her daughter and a fake birth certificate.

"Damn, this shit looks official as hell. Good looking out." I nodded with a smile on my face.

"I told you I had your back. I know I clown a lot, but I got you. Now you and your girl can get out the Vista's and live how you been living before this."

"Yeah, it's only been two months and I'm ready to get the fuck out of here. Especially after the police running through here like they did."

"Well, I'ma get out of here. It's too hot over here, and I got a bunch of shit in my whip. Call me later, and I might come back." Chink stood up.

"Alright, man. We're having a barbeque this weekend, so come thru."

When I let him out, I went into the room with Shon. I knew she was going to be happy when she saw the documents, I had for her. She had been stressing and crying about what the future would bring, now that could be the least of her worries. I also had another surprise for her too that involved our future. I had done a lot of thinking and I knew for a fact what I wanted for our relationship.

"It's me. Open the door," I heard Ro call through the door.

I opened the door and let him in. I knew still had a frightened look on my face, and I'm sure he noticed I had been crying my eyes out.

"You're good. They were here for somebody else," he assured me.

I let out a sigh of relief. "Thank God. I was in the closet about to shit myself."

He laughed. "Well, you don't have to worry about it no more. Look what I got for you." He handed me an envelope. I wasted no time going through it.

"Oh, my goodness! I can't believe this is happening." I blushed as happy tears fell from my eyes. "Baby girl, go to your room for a little while. I'll come get you when I start cooking dinner," I informed Ava.

Ava hugged me, and then left out my room. I closed the door and locked it.

"You have been so good to me, Ro. I want to start where we left off as kids. I love you, and I always have. I owe you my life, but right now, I'm going to give my body to you." I pressed my breasts against his chest and then kissed his sexy lips.

"I love you too. When your pops tore us apart, I never loved another girl the way I loved you. But now that you are back in my life, I can love again and with the woman I wanted to love. Not only do I want to be there for you, I want to be there for Ava too. Let me adopt her," he confessed.

I smiled. "Are you serious?"

"Yes, I want to start a family with you and have y'all in my life forever."

"So you talking marriage?" I giggled.

"Yup, I'm talking marriage." He raised his eyebrow and smirked.

I tossed the envelope on the dresser and started to passionately kiss him. Everything worked out in my favor and I wasn't taking my second chance at life for granted. I knew Ro would never hurt me and I could now be myself. Knowing I was with a good man, had my pussy wet.

We stripped each other out our clothes and he laid me on the bed. He slipped my panties off and spread my legs. I moaned softly when I felt his tongue hit my clit.

"I promise I'll never take advantage of your body like your ex did," he uttered as he kissed my lips below. My body was tense, but I loosened up when he said he would never take advantage of me.

9 4

We made love to each other for the next hour and then I made us a nice dinner.

We spent the fourth of July weekend in the Vista's and Ro surprised me with keys to our new home. We moved out that week and the rest was history...

Shon and Ro move out of the Vista apartments to a mini mansion in the hills. Ro did everything for Shon while she was a stay-at-home mom. A year later they had a baby boy they named Ro, Jr. Shon was never found out by her family, and she went on to live a normal life. What a lucky lady...

THE END

PROLOGUE

The blaring sirens and screeching tires pulled me from my mid-afternoon nap. I had no idea what was going on outside. However, from my bedroom window, I saw nothing but flashing lights. I looked over at the bassinet, and my baby was still sleeping, thankfully. I tiptoed toward the window and peeked out. The sight before me scared the shit out of me. Police officers were climbing out of their cars with their guns drawn, and some were putting on bulletproof vests. I heard the sound of the SWAT trucks pulling up, and my heart fell completely into my ass. For the first time in a long time, I was scared. I couldn't help the tears that welled in my eyes.

I moved across the country to South Central, LA, into the Green Vista Apartments. It wasn't the ideal place, but it was what I could afford for me and my daughter. I had been staying under the radar for the last six months. I never left unless it was absolutely necessary. I spoke to my neighbors when I saw them, but I never said much to them either. I didn't know my neighbors too well, but one thing about the tenants of the Vista, we were a small family. We may not have talked to ea ch other often or chilled with each other, but we looked out for one another.

I swallowed hard as I watched more cops pull up. I felt like I had made eye contact with one of the officers, so I quickly pulled back and slid down against the wall. Looking at the time, I saw it was 4:52 PM. I knew that after today, my life would likely never be the same.

CHAPTER ONE

TWO YEARS EARLIER...

PROVIDENCE, RHODE ISLAND

"Have a seat, babe," I told my boyfriend, Danny, as I finished making him a plate. Danny was an up-and-coming dealer who pulled long hours in the streets. I was going to school to get my degree in nursing, so Danny hustled hard to make sure he could afford our bills and my tuition. I offered to get a part-time job to help him, but he told me that he would rather me just focus solely on school and he would handle the rest.

Tonight, he looked like he had the weight of the world on his shoulders. When he had called me earlier, he sounded stressed, so I decided to make his favorite meal tonight and give him some of the sloppiest head I could muster up to try and relax him. On the menu was something simple, Mongolian beef over white rice.

"Here you go," I said, sliding his bowl in front of him. I went into the fridge and grabbed a can of ginger ale, popped the top, and handed it to him. I went back and made my bowl before sitting across from him directly. "Are you sure you're okay?" I asked him as I scooped food into my mouth.

He sighed heavily. "Yeah, just some street shit. I'll be good, though. It's nothing your man can't handle." He gave me a small smile, but I wasn't buying that bullshit. Something was bothering Danny, and eventually, I would get it out of him. I sat across from him, said a prayer over our meal, and dug in. Usually, Danny and I would talk about how our day was and about what our goals were once we were done with this school and hustling shit, but today, our apartment was silent. It was awkwardly silent, and honestly, I didn't like it.

"Are you sure you're okay?" I asked again as I placed my fork down.

"Yeah, Mariah. I just said that." I crinkled my face because I didn't like his tone. I decided to drop the discussion and revisit it later. I lost my appetite, so I placed my food in the microwave and headed toward the bedroom I shared with Danny to grab something to wear. I was heading out tonight for drinks with my best friend, Kayla. Kay and I had been best friends since the ninth grade. She was a CNA by day and a bartender by night. We were heading to her job tonight for free drinks. I didn't drink often, but with me just finishing my midterms, I needed a damn break, even if it was only for one night.

I walked down the small hall toward the bathroom. I peeked into the kitchen and saw Danny was still sitting there playing with the fresh bowl of Mongolian beef I had made. I shook my head and walked into the bathroom. I cut the shower on, tested the water, and proceeded to wrap my hair as I waited for the bathroom to fog up. I stepped into the shower and allowed the hot water to run down my body. I closed my eyes to enjoy the moment before I washed up three times and climbed out fifteen minutes later. I wrapped my towel around my body and grabbed my makeup kit from the vanity above the toilet. I proceeded to do a light beat with perfectly arched eyebrows.

When I was satisfied with my look, I emerged from the bathroom and peeked back into the kitchen. I saw Danny was gone, but his plate remained at the table. I walked into the living room and didn't see him there either. I looked out the window and saw that his Nissan Altima was gone. I hurriedly went to my bedroom to grab my phone and quickly scrolled to his name to call him.

I placed the phone on speaker and listened as the phone line trilled as I proceeded to put my underclothes on. The call rolled over to voicemail, but I quickly called him again.

"What?" he answered on the fourth ring.

"Where did you go?" I questioned.

"Out. Why what's up?"

"What is wrong with you? You've never snapped at me like this before, yet everything I ask you seemed to be a problem." I could feel my eyes starting to well with tears, but I quickly patted them away with my towel. I wasn't trying to have to redo my makeup.

"I told you that I'm good, but you keep asking me the same dumb-ass question, which is only irritating the fuck out of me. Just take my word that I'm good."

"Fine. I'm heading out with Kayla for a few hours," I let him know.

"Hm, a'ight."

"Why you say that?"

"Nothin'. As long as you're staying focused on your classes, I have no complaints." I rolled my eyes because he rode me about school like he was my father and I was a grade school student. I knew he was only doing it to make sure he wasn't wasting his money, and I was fuckin' off in school.

"Of course. We'll be down at her job if you want to come by and have a drink with us," I offered.

"Probably not, but I'll keep it in mind. Enjoy yourself. Love you."

"I love you too." We ended the call, and I proceeded to get dressed. I kept it simple with some tight, distressed jeans and a turtleneck sleeveless shirt. I put on a pair of black suede, chunky heeled booties. I removed the scarf from my head and combed my hair down. I spun around in the mirror and blew myself a kiss before snapping a few pictures. I uploaded one to Facebook, one to Instagram and sent a few to Danny. Just as I was done, Kayla shot me a text letting me know she was at her job.

I wasn't actually going out for drinks with Kayla; I was more going to keep her company at work. It worked for me because it was free drinks and good vibes. I grabbed my wristlet, phone, and keys before heading out the door. I couldn't wait to get my first drink in my system and unwind a little bit.

CHAPTER TWO

DANIEL 'DANNY' MITCHELL

I dropped my phone in the cupholder after I hung up with Mariah. I was glad that she was staying on top of school and going out to enjoy herself. I had to admit, Mariah was a hardworking woman. When I met her two years ago, she was working part-time at Walmart. When I got to know her, she let me know she was in school to pursue a nursing degree, and I respected her grind. We kicked it for a few weeks before making it official. She had a good head on her shoulders. Four months into our relationship, her mother died unexpectedly of a severe heart attack, which stressed her clean the fuck out. She started slacking up in school and ended up losing her job. I understood it, but I made sure I was the one in her corner, reminding her that she would be okay. She withdrew from school that semester and was placed on academic probation for the following semester. She wanted to give up completely, but I refused to allow that to happen.

At the start of the following semester, I paid her tuition upfront and told her don't worry about finding a job. I convinced her to move into my apartment and told her to strictly focus on school. She was halfway through her degree, and I kept reminding her that her mother would want her to finish. As far as I knew, she was on the straight and narrow with school, and I couldn't be prouder. She was in the middle of the first semester of her senior year, and I was grinding twice as hard because I wanted to not only propose to her at graduation, but I also wanted to buy her dream house as a gift. All was well until last week, when my main spot was hit. That shit was a major blow to our operation because it housed all of our work. The good part was it was paid for, so I didn't owe the connect. The fucked up part was I was going to damn near have to wipe my savings clean to re-up again, and that shit pissed me off and stressed me out. I already had the word out for the niggas who thought it would be cool to rob me.

I pulled up to the spot and saw my right-hand man, Brandon, smoking a cigarette on the porch. I knew he was just as heated as I was, but this city was so small. It was only a matter of time before we found out who it was. I pulled my Altima to the curb and killed the engine. I grabbed the pre-rolled blunt I had in the second cupholder and climbed out, activating the alarm.

"What's good?" I greeted him as I walked up and dapped him up.

"Can't call it."

"How bad does it look?" Brandon had called me when I was out of town scoping out new spots. I wanted to come straight here but made a detour home and regretted it. Usually, if I said I was good with something, Mariah didn't press me, but her constant nagging today only made my mood worse.

"Wiped clean. Part of me feels like it's an inside job, but I'm struggling to believe that one of the niggas we take care of would do this shit."

I shook my head at the thought as I sparked the blunt.

"What you got stashed?" I asked.

"About two-hundred and fifty," he responded as he took the blunt from my hands. I nodded. Combined, we had just over half of a million dollars, which would definitely allow us to recoup all that we had lost.

"How much are you willing to put up to re-up?" I asked.

"At this point, all of it. It'll hurt a nigga for a little bit, but fuck it. We got spots that rely on that shit, and I don't want niggas to think that we're dry. Luckily, the spots are stocked at least for the next few days, but we gotta re-up ASAP," he explained. I nodded in agreement. I pulled out my burner and shot off a text to my connect. I didn't know if he was going to be able to get as much work as I needed in such a short amount of time, but I needed a miracle at this point. "What do you got?" he asked me.

"About three."

"We should be good then with some shit left over. We're going to have to find a new main spot because this shit will be hot." Again, I nodded in agreement. I had been trapping out of this spot on Mystic for over five years, and it truly pissed me off that someone hit it. I had always kept this spot low. My workers didn't even come here. If it wasn't Brandon or myself, nobody stepped foot in this place, which let me know muthafuckas were scoping out shit. I was kicking myself in the ass because I had clearly become too lax.

My burner went off, and I noticed it was from my connect, letting me know he would be coming into town and meeting with us tomorrow. I sighed heavily as I thought about the amount of fuckin' money I was about to have to put up again. I pulled out my regular phone and started looking up properties. I hated having to start over, but it was what it was at this point.

"You hear anything yet?" I asked.

"Nah, everyone right now is tight-lipped, which I expected. I know it's only a matter of time before someone gets greedy and starts flapping their lips. It doesn't matter how long it takes. Whoever it was that hit us is getting popped on sight."

"Fa'sho."

I pushed myself off the porch and headed inside. The moment I walked inside, I shook my head. The door was damn near off the hinges. All the furniture that was inside was either cut open or flipped over. The muthafuckas even smashed pictures that I had hanging on the wall. From the outside looking in, this looked like a regular-ass apartment, but whoever came knew it was a trap house. When I made it to the bedroom in the back where the work was stashed, the fools had damn near ripped the closet door off the hinges. The mattress was pushed off the bed, and all the bedding was thrown on the floor. I shook my head as I turned and walked away.

"I already have one of my niggas on the way with a new door. I know we're not staying here, but we at least have to return it in somewhat decent condition," Brandon spoke. I nodded my head in agreement before chopping it up with him for about another hour. Once his people arrived with a new door, I dapped him up and headed out.

I would have to let Mariah know that for the next few months, my time home was likely going to be scarce because it was grind fuckin' season. I needed to double the money I spent within the next six months in order to get back on track with my plans, and with a lot of fuckin' hustle, the shit would happen.

1 0 8

CHAPTER THREE

MARIAH GREEN

SIX MONTHS LATER...

These few months have been stressful as hell, but today was the day that the shit was all going to pay off! Graduation day was finally here, and I couldn't be happier. Over the last four and a half years, I had cried more than I wanted to, but this very moment made it all very worth it. I couldn't help the tears that started falling when reality set in that my mother wouldn't be in the stands cheering me on. She wholeheartedly supported my career choice and my time in school. It killed me that she was gone, and although it's been a few years, I missed her more and more each day.

I took a deep breath before patting my eyes and walking out of the bathroom at the auditorium where graduation was being held. I walked into the main area where all of the grads stood, and just as they lined up, I quickly found my place in line. I felt my watch vibrate, so I checked it and saw it was a message from Danny letting me know that he was here.

Things between Danny and I had been weird for the last couple of months. He let me know about his spot being robbed and how much money he had to give up in order to re-up along with Brandon. I couldn't lie. I was nervous as fuck when he told me because he was basically wiping us clean. We had bills to pay, and I had my final semester of school to pay for. He told me not to worry about it, but it was easier said than done not to worry. True to his word, I never saw a termination notice for a bill or an eviction notice on our door. I never got a notice from school that my tuition wasn't paid, so I continued to put my faith in him as I have for the duration of our relationship. I couldn't wait to begin working so that I could help him around the house, although I knew he wouldn't ask.

I thanked God and my mom for Danny because he was the true definition of a real man. Never in our relationship had I been approached by a female about him, and it was a great feeling, especially with Danny being in the streets. It's always said that a street nigga has a saddle full of bitches, but that wasn't the case with Danny, and I took pride in that.

Two hours later, I was sliding out of the auditorium just as the rest of the line was filing back into their seats. Walking into the main area, Danny was standing there with balloons, flowers, and a small graduation bear. I ran and damn near jumped into his arms. He spun me around in a circle as he hugged me tightly and planted a kiss on my cheek.

"Congratulations, beautiful! I'm so fuckin' proud of you." He planted a soft kiss on my lips as well.

"Thank you so much. I appreciate you so much! I truly couldn't have done this without you."

"Nah, you could've. You're smart enough to where you could have tackled this shit solo." I blushed as he planted another kiss on my forehead before handing me the things he was holding. "Come on. I have something to show you." He grabbed my hand and led the way out to his car. I placed everything on the backseat and climbed into the passenger's seat.

"Where are we going?"

"Don't worry about it. Just sit back and relax," he told me. I reclined the seat slightly and closed my eyes, enjoying the warm May breeze. I didn't realize I had dozed off until he was tapping me and waking me up. Looking at the time, I saw that I had been out for about an hour. Looking out the window, I saw we were outside of what looked like a three-level house. I snapped my head in Danny's direction.

"Where are we?"

"Home," he smiled. My hands shot over my mouth as I looked at the house before us. I fell in love with the outside, so I knew the inside was going to be something else. I climbed out and made a dash to the front door. I ran up the stairs and straight through the front door. I stopped in my tracks and looked around. The hardwood floors were glistening, and the open blinds allowed the sun to come through the windows and bounce off the floors, giving the open space beautiful lighting. I took off running room to room, up and down the stairs. I was in awe that not only did this house belong to me, but that Danny had found it himself.

"Babe," I yelled as I came down the stairs toward the main entrance. "This is absolutely gor-…" I almost flipped face-first down the stairs when I got to the middle of the stairs and spotted Danny kneeling with a black velvet box in his hand. This time, the tears reached my eyes and fell before I could even stop them. I couldn't believe what was happening. "What are you doing?" I cried out. I sniffled and wiped my face, but the tears weren't stopping.

"You've been my rock through a lot these last few years. When your mom passed, you could have given up, but you grieved and pushed through. You remained dedicated and determined, and it has paid off. You've never judged me for anything I've done, and you rarely nag," he chuckled. I couldn't help the smile that adorned my face. "You're everything I've wanted in a woman. Mariah Green, will you do the honors of becoming my wife?" he asked. I couldn't help but chuckle and nod my head. Everything I felt like I wanted to talk about, my voice got stuck. I made my way down the rest of the steps and directly in front of him. He grabbed my hand and slid the gorgeous rock on my left ring finger. He held me tightly and nuzzled his face directly into my neck. I couldn't stop crying and staring at the ring. This had been a dream of mine since I was a little girl. I cried a little harder, again realizing I was experiencing all of this without my mother.

Danny continued planting kisses all over my face until we locked eyes. Nothing needed to be said. He planted his hands on my hips and moved in for another kiss; only this one was deeper. I wrapped my arms around his neck as he ran his hands up and down my body. Once his hands went under my short dress, I began fishing for the waistline of his pants. I wasted no time unbuttoning his buckle and his True Religion jeans before allowing them to drop down to his ankles. He ripped my thong off as if it were a piece of paper and flung them to the side. His fingers found my center with ease and began thumbing my clit. My knees began giving out as he brought me to a quick orgasm. He tightened his hold on me as I released my juices all over his hand and these newly shined floors.

"Damn, Ma," he said, not removing his lips from mine. I rode the wave as I felt a second orgasm building up since Danny wasn't stopping. I was stroking his dick, and it was hard as Chinese arithmetic. I could feel his veins bulging. Once my second orgasm hit, I wasted no time literally jumping in his arms. Caught off guard, he held me tight, but I landed right where I wanted to, sliding down his rod. I broke the kiss and threw my head back in pleasure. Danny immediately started bouncing me up and down his member while he bit his bottom lip. The slight curve he had found my spot right away, and he hammered away at it. I tried to stifle my moans, but he was making it hard. Giving up, I formed my mouth in an O shape and shuttered as I felt yet another orgasm ripping through me.

By now, I was sure there was a mess beneath us, but I had not a fuck to give. Turning around, Danny placed my back up against the door and continued slamming into me. I tightened my hold around his neck as nut number four hit me. I was done. I could hardly move, but Danny's energizer ass still hadn't come up off of his own nut. I lazily released my arms from around his neck as he kept slow stroking. He chuckled as he turned me around again, but this time, he pulled out and placed me on my feet. Just as I was about to walk off, he grabbed me and turned me around, pushing me down so that I was leaning on the steps in front of me. He wasted no time returning his member to its rightful home.

"Gah damn," he said. Looking over my shoulder, I witnessed him focused on his shaft slamming in and out of me. With the little bit of strength that I had left, I began throwing my ass back and tightening my walls. "Fuck, Ry, chill out with that shit," I smirked but continued. Danny could go all damn day, but I was tapping the fuck out. When he pulled back for another stroke, I squeezed my muscles, pulling him back in, and that was all it took. Danny let out a groan so loud, and I was sure the next-door neighbor heard it. He held me in place as he allowed his seeds to travel deep down into my love canal.

After taking a few moments to catch our breath, he pulled out and walked out of his jeans into the bathroom. I hadn't noticed the suitcase that was in the corner.

"There's a change of clothes along with body wash and shit in there," he mentioned.

I pulled the suitcase as I followed him into the bathroom. He ran the shower and allowed it to heat up as I sat on the toilet to release my bladder.

"When are you removing your birth control?" he asked me randomly. I paused because I hadn't thought about it. I did want children, but I was so focused on school and graduating that I had honestly forgotten that I had the IUD. Danny and I agreed that one day we would have children, but we never discussed when. I shrugged, although he wasn't looking at me.

"I never thought about when," I answered honestly.

"Time to start thinking about it. I'm ready to start a family. You're done with school, we're getting married, and we now have our home."

"Okay."

Even without a shower curtain, we took a quick shower. I kept thanking him over and over for the house. I couldn't wait to call Kayla and fill her in. Once we were done and dressed, Danny gave me a copy of the key, the address, and hand in hand, we walked out of the door and headed back to the city. Growing up, I always said I wouldn't move to Massachusetts because it was just too expensive. However, this house was beautiful, and I knew I wouldn't have found something like this in Rhode Island. Besides, we were moving to Quincy, and Providence was only about an hour away. I was pretty sure that Danny would still be doing business there, and I would be back often to visit my grandmother in her nursing home as well as Kayla.

I was excited about this new beginning with Danny.

If only I would have known, it would be short-lived.

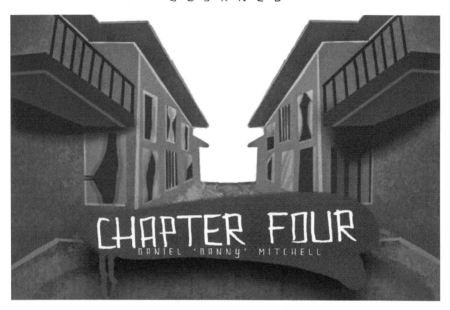

CHAPTER FOUR
DANIEL 'DANNY' MITCHELL

I had done everything I wanted to do on this special day for Mariah. Despite the loss we took some months back, business was booming better than ever for us. We ended up getting word that one of our workers, Monty, had a brother, Jamal, who was fresh out of jail. He wanted Monty to put him on, but Monty refused because he knew his brother wasn't a smart hustler. The nigga hustled backward, and Monty knew that was some shit we wouldn't tolerate. The nigga was flashy and spent money just as fast as he made it. The nigga was a walking fuckin' target, and that wasn't something I needed.

It wasn't hard for him to find out who Monty was working for. The moment he did, he gathered up his little fuck boys and basically started watching me and Brandon. When he saw we were back and forth to Mystic, he and his rugrats decided to hit it. Once Monty caught wind, he wasted no time popping his brother. Their mother had abandoned them as children, and they grew up in state custody. I knew he felt a kind of way about having to handle it, but I also knew he wouldn't have wanted anyone else to do it. One by one, we picked off each and every one of Jamal's minions until they were gone. We recovered about half of our work and had no idea where the rest of the shit was, but we chalked it up as a loss. We moved Monty up and gave him his own trap to build his own team. He wasn't a partner with us, but after how he handled the situation, he deserved a little higher rank than a trap boy.

I dropped Mariah off to her car and let her know that we had dinner reservations for later on tonight. I knew she would want to brag to her best friend about the house, so I would give her time for that and handle the business I needed to handle. My phone vibrated on my lap, and when I looked at the screen, my good mood was shot to shit. One of the biggest mistakes was on the other end. I sighed heavily as I contemplated letting the call roll over to voicemail. Before I could make the decision, the call ended. It wasn't long before the vibration started again.

"Yo," I answered on the second ring.

"Where are you?" Denise asked. I rolled my eyes and sighed heavily.

"Around. Why?"

"Are you coming back by?"

"I don't know. Why?"

"Damn, I was just wondering."

"I'll holla at you."

I disconnected the call before she could say anything else. I came to a stop at the red light and washed my hands down my face. I couldn't believe I had gotten wrapped up in this shit I was in.

SCORNED

I had met Denise about three months ago when I was out at the club with my guys. We were turning up and wilding out. Denise came through the section in this badass short, black dress that barely covered her bubble butt. She wasted no time twerking on my lap, bricking me right the fuck up. I had smoked several blunts and was about six shots in, so I was feeling nice. Denise had me wanting to bend her ass over right the fuck there, but I knew that wouldn't be a good look in a club full of people.

Once the song was over, I went and sat down on the couch in our section and grabbed a bottle of cold water that was sitting there. Denise came and sat next to me, leaving her hand resting on my leg. She leaned in and began running her tongue along my earlobe. Unbeknownst to her, my ear would have me ready to dive deep in some pussy in a matter of seconds. While I should have been thinking about Mariah, who was home studying for class, I was wondering what Denise's ass looked like outside of this damn dress.

"I got a room down in Warwick at the Hilton Garden Inn by the airport. Room 303. Meet me there in thirty minutes," she told me. She licked my ear one more time before grabbing my shit and standing up. She kept her eye on me as she left out the section. I would be lying if I said I was leaving here and going home. I took one more shot before I dapped the fellas up and told them that I was heading out. I stumbled a bit, but once I got outside to the cool air, I started to sober up. I waited as the valet brought my Beamer around front. I jumped in and headed straight to the hotel.

As I got closer, I started to wonder if this was a setup. I didn't even know if this chick was setting me up, yet here my ass was traveling to her at the drop of a hat. I slowed down a little, but I never switched the direction I was heading.

1 1 8

Rhode Island was only but so big, so it only took me a split second to get to the hotel. Pulling in, I looked around the lot to see if I saw her walking in, but I didn't. I sat in my car for a moment before I climbed out and headed inside, going straight to the elevator. I pushed three and closed my eyes as the elevator began traveling up. I checked my phone and saw it was shortly after one. I knew by now, Mariah was sleeping.

I stepped off the elevator and paused. My mind was telling me to get the fuck back on the elevator and head home to fuck my girl, but the moment it drifted off to the stranger's big, soft ass, my dick sprang into action, and my legs began moving in the direction of her room. It was easy to find right off the elevator, so I knocked softly and leaned against the frame. After a few moments, she came to the door in a matching bra and panty set with a sheer robe on. My shit was now ready to burst straight through the seams of my pants. She had a clear gloss on her lips that almost looked as if they were wet. I stood there looking her up and down. Her body was definitely surgically altered, but she was bad as shit!

I sucked my bottom lip into my mouth as she stood to the side to let me in. The moment I crossed the threshold, she closed the door and wasted no time pushing me backward. She started attacking my neck and ear.

"Chill with the neck sucking," I told her. I was a light skin nigga, so a hickey would definitely be noticeable. "Can I at least get your name before I bang your back in?" I asked as she unbuckled my pants.

"Denise. Now stop talkin'," she demanded. Once she freed my nine-inch member, she dropped to her knees and placed the head in her mouth. She started moaning on my shit, making it wet as fuck. I hissed and bit my lip as I watched my rod disappear in her mouth. I noticed she was playing with her pussy. She then began speeding up as she sucked and hummed on my rod. I assumed she was on the verge of making herself

1 1 9

cum as she began to whimper, but she never stopped sucking. Between the slurps and the whimpers, I was close to releasing a load down her throat myself. And I did just that. She took in every single drop I had to offer, removed it from her mouth, swallowed, then opened her mouth so I could see she swallowed. She stood to her feet and let her robe drop. I pulled her to me and ripped her thin ass panties off. I began placing kisses along her stomach as she straddled my lap. Once she was on my lap, I planted soft kisses along her breasts.

My hands found their way to her back and unhooked her bra. Freeing her titties, I immediately attacked her Hershey kiss nipples. She threw her head back and let out soft moans. My dick was growing again right underneath her. In one swift motion, she slightly pushed herself up before dropping herself right on my shit. Bareback. Caught up in the moment, I didn't bother to stop her. She bounced softly on me as I attacked her nipples. She started clenching her walls, immediately making my toes curl.

"Chill out," I said as I paused from sucking her breasts. She pushed my head back into her chest, and I continued flicking my tongue across her nipples. She sped up, and I could feel my nut building up again.

"Fuck," she whispered. I pulled my head from her chest and watched her as her head was thrown back, and she never missed a beat. I sucked my bottom lip between my teeth, gripped her waist, and began pounding her middle. It didn't take long before I was shooting a heavy ass load deep in her love canal. She started clenching her walls again, draining my member. This nut literally took everything from me.

I tapped her thigh to signal her to get up. When she stood, I noticed her creamy juices coating my dick. I held on to my pants in the middle of my leg as I went into the bathroom to clean up. Reality then set in. Not only did I just cheat on my girl, but I raw dogged a fuckin' stranger. Internally, I started kicking myself in the ass.

"Yo," I called out to her as I wet a rag with warm water. She came into the bathroom and sat on the toilet. "I need you to take a plan B."

She twisted her face.

"Excuse you?"

"You heard me. You don't know me, and I don't know you. We don't need a child to come from this one-night stand. Grab a plan B. I'll pay for it."

"Whatever."

"I'm out, though." I laid the rag on the top of the shower bar, pulled up my pants, grabbed my things, and walked out.

Two months later, she called to tell me that she was five weeks pregnant and was keeping it. I had never snapped on a female the way I snapped on her that day. She may have been every name in the book besides a child of God. Daily, I thought about how I could break the news to Mariah, but I knew that would end up being the end of us. Every time I got the guts to tell her, I bitched out and decided against it.

Instead, I asked her to marry me and told her we could start a family. Mariah had been wanting children for years but agreed that it would be hard for her to be pregnant while going through school, so we decided to wait until she graduated. Unfortunately, she wouldn't be the one to give me my first, but as far as she would know, she would.

My phone began ringing again, and it was nobody but Denise. Here she was, only a little more than two months pregnant and already annoying the fuck out of me, so I didn't know how I was going to deal with this for the next seven months. I pushed her call over to voicemail and put her number on *Do Not Disturb*.

I pulled up to meet up with Brandon for our monthly meeting about our operation. I was going to talk to my nigga because I needed advice on this shit. I was on the verge of telling Denise not to call me until she gave birth, but if something happened during her pregnancy and I ignored her, I would feel like shit.

Regardless, I needed to get the shit under control because the last thing I wanted was to lose Mariah.

I wasted no time calling Kayla once we got back to Providence and got to my car.

"Helloooo," she sang into the phone.

"Girl! Where are you?" I asked her as I pulled away from the apartment I shared with Danny.

"Home. Why what's up?"

"I have some news to share with you," I smiled hard.

"You're pregnant?"

"No," I sucked my teeth. "I wish, though! Danny asked me to marry him, *and* he bought us a house!" I shouted.

"Shut up! Are you serious?"

"Yes! Oh my God! The house is gorgeous too."

"Where is it?"

"Quincy."

"Quincy? There's a Quincy in Rhode Island?" she asked, confused.

"No," I laughed. "It's in Mass. It's about an hour away."

"Well damn," she chuckled. "Who would have thought that Mariah, who never wanted to live in Mass, is moving to Mass?"

"I know, huh. Girl, wait until you see this damn house layout, though! The shit is gorgeous."

"I bet. Where you at now?"

"Heading your way. Danny just dropped me back off at my car while he handled some business. We have dinner reservations later, but I have a few hours to kill."

"Alright, I'm here." We hung up, and I kept stealing glances at my ring that was glistening in the sunlight. Danny did a hell of a job with this ring.

As I made my way to Kayla's, I couldn't keep the smile off my face as I began allowing ideas for our wedding to run through my mind.

I truly was the happiest girl on earth and could not wait to spend the rest of my life with the love of my life.

* * *

ONE YEAR LATER...

The last year had been nothing short of amazing! Danny and I were only four months from our dream wedding. Danny allowed me to spend whatever I wanted for the wedding of my dreams! Although stressful, everything was coming along nicely.

Tonight was the night of our housewarming party. I wanted to wait until I was done putting my touches on it to have the event. It was going to be small. I was only planning for a few of Danny's boys, a couple of his cousins, and Kayla.

I was putting the tray of meatballs on the table when I heard the front door open. I peeked around the wall and saw Kayla walking in with cases of sodas.

"Hey boo," she greeted, kicking the door closed behind her.

"Hey," I sang as I went to give her a hand. I gave her a cheek-to-cheek kiss and led the way to the kitchen.

"I swear, every time I come here, I fall more and more in love with this house. Danny did good picking this," Kayla admired.

"He really did. It feels just like home." Kayla and I made small talk as I finished in the kitchen, and Danny's people started to show up. By 8:30 PM, the housewarming was in full swing, and we were sitting at the table enjoying dinner.

Out of nowhere, the doorbell rang. I looked at Danny, who was just as confused as I was.

"I'll get it," I said as I stood and walked to the door. Peeking out of the nearby window, I saw a lady standing with a car seat on her arm. I was confused because I didn't know of anyone who had a baby. Immediately, I opened the door, thinking she was in trouble. "Can I help you?"

"I'm looking for Danny," she spoke.

"I'm sorry, who?" I was sure my face showed my confusion. I looked her up and down, and I had to admit, she was a beautiful woman. She had the baby car seat covered, so I couldn't see the baby inside.

"Danny. Daniel. Whatever you want to call him. The father of my child if you want to go that far. I need to speak to him."

"Who are you?"

"Is that important?" she snapped.

"It is when you're standing on my porch. Who are you?" I repeated.

She sighed, rolled her eyes, and shifted her weight from one foot to the other.

"Just tell Danny to come to the do-"

1 2 5

"Denise?" I heard Danny ask behind me. I snapped my neck so fast that I was surprised I didn't catch whiplash. "What are you doing here?"

"Since you won't answer me, I figured I would bring your daughter to see you."

"Huh?" I asked. My heart rate sped up, and I felt like I couldn't breathe. Did she just say, daughter? Danny's daughter? "What is she talking about?" Looking at Danny, I could see his jaw flexing and him running his tongue across his teeth. What stuck out the most to me was he didn't deny the fact that she said this was his daughter.

"Yeah, Daniel, what am I talking about?" she questioned, placing the car seat on the porch and crossing her arms across her chest. I tried so hard to keep the tears from falling, but I couldn't. He glared at the woman he called Denise before he took a deep breath and started speaking.

"According to Denise, we share a daughter."

"Ain't no 'according to Denise', nigga. Don't try and save face now," she popped off. "Look," she looked at me. "I didn't know about you until I dug more into who he was. My daughter is a product of a one-night stand, but I told him from the beginning when I was pregnant. He kept in touch with me during my pregnancy, but once I told him that Eva was born, he just stopped responding. He never came to see her, didn't sign her birth certificate or anything. As someone who has grown up with their father in their life, the least I want for my daughter is to have a relationship with her father," she spoke. She sounded genuine, but I wasn't completely sold on it. I kept glancing back and forth between the car seat and Danny, yet his ass was sitting there stuck on stupid.

"Wow, Danny." I couldn't control my quivering bottom lip. "After all that we've been through, this is how you do me? What was it? I wasn't fuckin' you enough while I was in school? The house wasn't clean enough? Speak up, muthafucka," I shouted, gathering the attention of the guests in the house.

"Let's not do this here, Mariah."

"Nah, nigga, let's do this here. Here we are four months from getting fuckin' married, and your side bitch is standing on my fuckin' porch, telling me she got a baby by my soon-to-be husband."

"Now, I haven't disrespected you, so don't disrespect me," she said, twisting her neck.

"Fuck outta here. You disrespected me the moment you walked your ass up on my porch. Shut up," I told her, never taking my eye off of Danny. "You know what, I'll do you one better. Take this," I said, sliding the gorgeous engagement ring off my finger and tossing it in the baby's car seat. "And these," I continued to remove my keys off my keyring. "You can have him, this engagement, and this fuckin' house. Fuck the both of you."

I turned around and stormed inside the house. I went upstairs and packed my stuff in tears. I heard a slight knock on the bedroom door before I heard Kayla's voice. Thankfully, she didn't ask any questions. She simply began grabbing my things. I knew I wasn't going to be able to take everything, but what was important was going, and the rest, I didn't give a fuck what he did with it.

I couldn't believe that he had done this to me. I sniffled and silently cried for the almost two hours it took me to grab all that I could. As I was leaving, I noticed Danny had brought the woman and the baby inside of the house and was holding the baby on his lap. I caught a quick glance and had to admit, the little girl was absolutely beautiful and was a spitting image of Danny, so there was no DNA test needed. This child was his, and it hurt that much more. Watching them both sit there with each other turned my pain into rage, and before I did something I regretted, I stormed out of the house and out of Danny's life for good.

CHAPTER SIX

DANIEL 'DANNY' MITCHELL

It had been two months since Mariah walked out on me, and since then, she has ignored the fuck out of my calls and texts. I had gone by Kayla's house almost daily to try and see if I could catch her, but it seemed as if she wasn't staying there. I had been spending more time at Denise's apartment, ultimately getting to know her and spending time with my daughter, Eva. Denise expressed several times that she wanted us to get together and be a family, but I wasn't interested in that. I was simply here for my child.

Tonight, Eva was fussy because, at four months, she was already teething. I had her lying on my chest as I laid back on Denise's couch. She said how she desperately needed a peaceful shower, so I told her to go ahead and take her time as I kept the baby. Thankfully, Eva had calmed down and had fallen asleep, sucking on her hand.

I hadn't realized that I had fallen asleep until I felt Eva stir on my chest. Glancing at the time, I realized it had been more than an hour since Denise had gone and taken a shower, yet I could still hear the shower water running. I knew the water had to have been cold by now. I stayed still for a moment to ensure Eva was still in a deep sleep before carefully moving her and placing her into her bassinet that Denise kept in the living room.

I stretched, then headed to Denise's bedroom, where her bathroom was. Opening the door, I damn near pissed myself when I saw Denise sprawled on the floor with a pool of blood surrounding her. I stepped backward and bumped into something. Immediately turning around, I came face-to-face with a hooded figure. I immediately started taking steps backward into the room, which probably wasn't a smart idea. I glanced over my shoulder to make sure I wasn't going to step on Denise's dead body.

"It wouldn't matter if you stepped on her or not; she wouldn't feel it," Mariah spoke. I froze and stared as she removed the hood from her head. Mariah looked different. Her eyes were cold and dark.

"Mariah, what did you do?" I asked.

"Don't play fuckin' stupid, Daniel. You can clearly see what I did."

"Mariah…"

"Stop calling my fuckin' name," she snapped. I watched as she pulled something out of her pocket and noticed it was a knife.

"Don't do this. You're going to regret it."

She chuckled, and it was almost sinister.

"You know, I thought I would regret it, but honestly," she shrugged. "I don't. You took everything from me, so now, I'm taking it all from you. I'll raise that little girl to be mine while you and her homewrecking mother rot in hell."

"Mariah, wait. This isn't even you. What happened to you?"

"What happened to me? What happened to ME? You fuckin' happened to me, Daniel! Everything was great!" I could hear her voice cracking and knew it was only a matter of time before she cried. I was going to try and use it to my advantage to get myself and my daughter out of here alive. "Why did you have to go and cheat, Danny? Shit could have been great for us! The beautiful house, the perfect married couple, the beautiful children, and the lap of luxury. But you ruined it! You ruined all of that the moment you decided to stick your dick in her. Why?" She dropped to her knees and began bawling. I slowly kneeled down in front of her and wrapped my arms around her. I rubbed her back and began apologizing profusely.

"I'm sorry, Mariah. I am so, so, sor-" I paused when I felt an intense pain in my back. Immediately, I felt blood filling my mouth. What I tried so hard to stop was happening. Mariah had stabbed me. From the way that my mouth was filling and her having a degree in nursing, I was almost sure that she had punctured my lung.

"Fuck your apology. It didn't mean shit when you said it months ago, and it doesn't mean shit now. Fuck you, fuck Denise, and fuck everything you guys stood for. Rot in hell, bitch." She pulled the knife out before ramming it through my back again. I tried to speak, but every time I did, I coughed and began choking. I watched in the dim light as Mariah slowly backed out of the room. In that moment, I asked God for forgiveness for all that I had done in my life, including fucking her over. Life is never promised to anyone, but I never thought my life would end at the hands of the one I loved. However, with all the wrong I had done to her, I knew my karma was going to bite me in the ass. I just prayed she took good care of my little girl. Regardless of how fucked up her father was, she deserved the world.

Before long, everything slipped black, and life as I knew it was over.

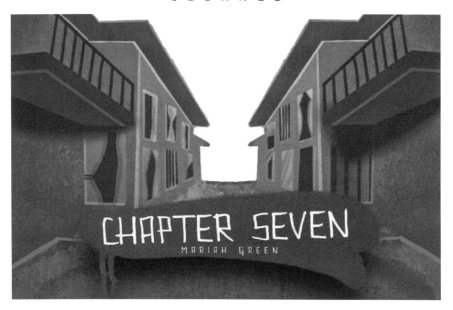

CHAPTER SEVEN
MARIAH GREEN

So, you see, I wasn't always paranoid, but with what I had done, I definitely had to watch my back. Within thirty-six hours, Danny and his side bitch's body was found. They did have an Amber Alert out for the baby, and because of that, we hardly left the small apartment. If we did, I kept her face covered. As of right now, it was simply considered murder and kidnapping. I kept in touch with Kayla as if all was normal. I told her after the situation with Denise and Danny that I had to get out of Rhode Island. I had lied and told her that I had moved to Texas and was starting over. She understood and always said she would come and visit, but I wasn't holding my breath that she would. Even if she tried, I wouldn't be there to greet her.

Thankfully, it didn't take me long to get an apartment here. I paid the first few months' rent upfront, which I think helped the situation too. The first few days here in the Apartments, I literally stayed holed in my house. I had all of my food delivered to me and hardly even opened windows. My neighbors knew I had a baby, but none of them had seen her.

I had done a lot of researched and purchased the necessary items to create entirely new identities for me and Sariah, which is the baby's new name. I drew up fake birth records and created a fake birth certificate for the baby with me listed as the mother under the name Nicole Marshall. So far, everything was working in my favor. I personally was hoping that Sariah's looks changed somewhat, and she stopped looking so much like the baby blasted across the television everywhere.

These last few weeks here have been smooth, but now with the police lurking outside, everything I thought I was leaving behind was on the verge of blowing up in my face. I looked toward Sariah's bassinet again and saw despite the noise, she was still sleeping.

"We have your apartment surrounded. Come out with your hands up."

I peeked out the window and saw guns all pointing up to either my level or the level above, but from my angle, I couldn't tell. I took a few more deep breaths and said a silent prayer. I knew I had fucked up in life, but I damn sure never thought I would be caught so soon.

I stood to my feet on shaky legs and walked to the door.

This was it. I did all I could to escape the life I had in Rhode Island, and now it was ending. LAPD was here for me, and my run was over.

Or was it…

PROLOGUE

The flashes from all the cameras had her mesmerized as they stopped on the red carpet to talk to yet another well-known blogger. Aquarius tried hard to pay attention to what the beautiful girl was saying but she was high off the shrooms she had taken and the flashes from the camera were doing something to her. She felt like she was getting higher by the minute. She regretted taking them before she left home. She did not want to smell like the exotic weed she smoked while she was at the awards ceremony. Aquarius could not handle alcohol, so that was out of the question. She had to have something in her system to help her calm down. Public appearances with her social anxiety made her a basket case if she was sober.

"Aquarius, what are you wearing tonight? Did you design you and Shooter's ensembles? Will it be a part of your upcoming collection?" The blogger for the *Shaderoom* asked Aquarius question after question. It appeared as if Aquarius was looking at her, but she was looking past her at the flickering lights. They looked like fairies circling the blogger's head. She had not heard a word that was said to her.

"Baby, Vanessa is talking to you." Shooter said startling Aquarius out of her reverie. He noticed the glassy look in her eyes and knew that his girlfriend had ingested more than she could handle. He had recently introduced her to taking shrooms because she smoked too much weed. He was trying to get her away from using it excessively. He only indulged in weed and shrooms during the off season. Shooter noticed that his creativity increased, and he was a lot calmer when he did the shrooms.

"I'm sorry Vanessa. Can you repeat that?" Aquarius noticed the photographer right over Vanessa's shoulder snapping pictures of her and her man. She hoped that he had not caught her at any awkward angles or her making any faces. She suddenly had the urge to burst into laughter, but she resisted as she answered Vanessa's question about her clothing line. Aquarius felt Shooter's glare, she looked up at him and smiled. He did not return the gesture. He seemed to be upset with her.

Aquarius grabbed his large hand in hers, squeezed it and mouthed "I'm sorry baby" when he looked down at her. She watched him shrug his shoulders and smile at her as they walked into the Fox Theater.

Tonight, he was being honored as "*Philanthropist of the Year* " by the *Boys & Girls Club of Metro Atlanta*. Shooter did a lot for them. The *Boys & Girls Club* was the only constant thing he had in his early childhood life, and it was at the *Boys & Girls Club* that he was introduced to basketball. This was his first public appearance besides his basketball games since his mother passed away from complications from Covid-19. She usually would be the one at his side on the red carpets. He made it a big deal for her. He had promised her that she would forever be his date and he stuck to his word.

Aquarius did not mind Shooter's mother accompanying him and walking the red carpet with him to his events. Her anxiety was so severe that she did not even want to attend the events much less, walk a red carpet. When he did make her come along, she usually was already seated by the time him, and his mother made it into the venues. Now she was front and center with him and high as a kite. Shooter was simply happy that all the people who he had spoken with avoided the subject of his mother. He did not want to become emotional tonight, but he knew that he couldn't avoid his feelings or the truth. His mother was gone, and grieving is something that you can't run from no matter how much he tried. He was really missing her right now.

Their bond was tighter than it's ever been. It seemed since Shooter's mother's passing, he was displaying his love for Aquarius more. He constantly spoiled her with more affection and even more thoughtful gifts. They left the award show right after he received his award because he was overwhelmed with emotion. He choked up twice during his acceptance speech. There wasn't a dry eye in the room when he was finished. Shooter dedicated this and every accomplishment that he made in his life to his mother. He vowed that he would build a new basketball complex at the Boy's and Girls Club in his neighborhood in his mother's honor. They rode in silence in Shooter's blacked out bullet proof Cadillac Escalade. Aquarius was cradled in Shooter's arms like a newborn baby.

CHAPTER 1

She stuffed the duffel bag with as much as she could from her master bedroom closet that was filled with designer clothes. In another place and time this fairytale that she had been living would have never ended. Things were better than they ever been, she should've known something was going to happen. She moved around the house as fast as she could. Aquarius had turned security cameras off so she wouldn't be seen packing and hauling items to her truck. She sniffled loudly as she fought back the tears that had been threatening to fall since she made up her mind that this is what she needs to do. This was only the beginning; she knew that once this shit really hit the fan there wouldn't be anywhere for her to hide from her harsh reality.

Aquarius caught a glance at herself as she walked past the huge mirror in the foyer. Her left eye was swollen shut; she knew she probably would need surgery on her nose. It was perfect before he slammed his fist into it. Bitches had surgery to look like how God had made her. Looking at her face in the mirror triggered the tears to fall uncontrollably. How could the person she was in love with hurt her so bad? Aquarius will never forget the look in his eyes when he burst into their bedroom. Shooter looked like he was possessed. He didn't ask any questions. He immediately jacked her up by her sleepshirt and started beating on her.

It took a minute for it to register what was happening to her because she was in shock. Aquarius usually traveled with him everywhere even the out-of-town games. But she stayed home because she had a big photo shoot. She hadn't done anything wrong; she hadn't been anywhere. Aquarius didn't even talk to anyone besides the people helping her with her photo shoot.

As the punches rained on her, she wrecked her brain trying to think of what brought this on. She didn't try to fight back. She didn't run. And although she knew she didn't deserve it, Aquarius took the beating from Shooter like she did. He beat her in silence. All you heard was the grunts coming from him, she didn't even know what this ass whooping was for. When it became obvious that he wasn't gonna stop and the pain had become too much to bear anymore, Aquarius kicked him in his groin. She jumped off the bed and ran into the bathroom and locked the door.

Her face hurt and she was scared to look in the mirror. She stayed crouched down in front of the door and she cried silently to herself. She heard voices come from downstairs, he wasn't alone. Aquarius had no idea who Shooter had brought home with him. Who in the world was with him that didn't stop him from what he had just did? She couldn't decipher how many people it was or who it was. She listened closely and she heard Shooter say *"yeah, I beat dat mutha-fucker ass. She ought to be happy that I didn't kill her. This shit can ruin me. I gotta figure out a way to get ahead of it. It got to be a way for us to stop this from*

1 4 1

circulating. I don't care how much it cost. Man I told you I didn't know about this shit."

Aquarius heard footsteps then the garage door go up and down. She heard the loud engine of his Hellcat truck as it roared when he left. She waited in silence for 10 minutes before she came out of the bathroom. It seemed like she was walking in slow motion, her body hurt from the body blows that he started to give her after her nose poured blood everywhere.

She reached for her phone on the bed and didn't care if blood got everywhere. She texted Shooter first. She really didn't have anyone to turn to honestly. Aquarius had made him her world. All she had was industry friends here in Atlanta. She wouldn't dare call any one of them and let them know what happened to her. The blood poured from her nose like a faucet and she started to feel lightheaded. She wiped the blood covered cellphone on the duvet and then texted angrily. '*What in the hell is wrong with you? How could you do this to me Shooter? I'm not no fucking punching bag. If one of them nigga's on the court made you mad, you should've beat their ass and paid the fine. You have never put your hands on me and we are not about to start this shit now. You got me fucked up. Are you drunk or high?"*

She loved this man and felt like they were made for each other. She didn't want to do anything drastic. For what he had just done to her, she could ruin his life forever. Aquarius couldn't go to the hospital because as soon as she pulled up looking like this, the authorities would immediately get involved. As much as she tried to stay under the radar, she couldn't because of her business and her man being the number #1 draft pick for the Atlanta Hawks. Shooter was the hometown hero.

Aquarius phone vibrated and her heart rate sped up when she seen Shooter's name with the text message alert. She was afraid to open the message. She knew she had to just in case he was on his way back home. She held the phone up to her face for recognition. It was a screenshot of a side-by-side photo of a little boy and a cropped photo of her that was taken last week. There was a name, city and state with $100,000 and money bag emoji under it. She dropped her phone and burst into tears. Shooter always knew the truth, but the world didn't.

CHAPTER 2

Aquarius never expected to return to *The Vista's*. In fact, it was her worst nightmare. So much of her trauma had happened here. She was a firm believer in the fact that she could not heal in the same place that hurt her. She did not have anywhere else to go and no one to turn to. Everything looked the same as when she left fifteen years ago. Outdated, dingy, and poor were the words that came to her mind then and now.

Regret hit her as soon as she got out of the Uber Black. She had a plan, she just had to work it. Aquarius' heart felt like it was about to leap out of her chest. Her palms were sweating, and her temple jumped as she clenched down on her teeth as she looked around the front of the building. She only had her Louis Vuitton backpack, a duffle bag and a Chanel purse. She did not bring a lot of stuff with her. She planned on going back to Atlanta when this blew over. She tried to dress down and cover up so that she would not draw any obvious attention to herself.

But she was unsuccessful, all eyes were on her as she stood on the sidewalk watching the uber drive away.

The courtyard was filled with people and music could be heard from different apartments that had their windows open to let in some of the fresh air. Kids were running around, guys were shooting dice, a couple older women sat in folding chairs on their stoops and some teenage girls were practicing dance routines. Aquarius did not want to be recognized or her black eyes to show, so she kept the big Louis Vuitton sunglasses on and her head down low as she walked up the sidewalk toward the building. She spoke barely above a whisper as she returned greetings to the older women that spoke to her as she walked through the entrance.

This building had been in her family for years and it was guaranteed to be the refuge for one or more of her family since her great-grandparents purchased it over sixty years ago. Her older cousin Yolanda who she called her aunt was the apartment's manager. She was the first person in the family to accept Aquarius as she was and treat her like a human instead of a freak of nature. No matter the distance or the time that passed when Aquarius called, Yolanda dropped everything to help her. She needed that since both of her parents were gone. She called her after Shooter jumped on her and Yolanda told her to get on a flight. She told Aquarius to get as much shit as she could first.

"Auntie it's bad, really bad. Shooter jumped on me, and I'm scared. I have never seen him like this before.

"You better get out of there before he kills you and you better not leave empty handed either. I will see you when you get here". Yolanda replied.

Aquarius knocked on the door marked *LEASING OFFICE* because it was closed.

"We are closed for lunch." Yolanda hollered from the other side of the door.

"It's me Auntie, Lil' Bit." She responded quietly using the nickname everyone in her family called her because of her very petite stature. She looked around nervously to see if any of her family was around. She really didn't want anyone to know she was here. Aquarius could afford a hotel, but she couldn't risk the employees or the guest revealing her whereabouts. Shooter probably had people looking for her everywhere, except for The Vista's. She had no place to run.

CHAPTER 3

Shooter paced the floor deep in thought. Both of his cellphones were in his pocket going crazy between rings and notifications. He had played his first game since he had returned to the court after his mother's death, and he had scored his career highest. He kept looking at the seat where his mother would usually sit, and he saw her there. Whenever he had a game *FedEx Forum*, his mom was sure to come. He loved when they went to Memphis because they would always go to eat at this barbecue place that had been there for years. His mother went to college in Tennessee, so she knew the town like the back of her hand. He felt her presence In the FedEx Forum as soon as he walked in the door. Shooter knew that it was her angelic presence that made play so amazing tonight.

He was on a natural high when the game was over. It was the best that he had felt in a long time. Shooter thought to himself that maybe that is what he needed to focus on to keep the depression from grief creeping up on him. His new goal would be to top this feeling, top this score every time he played for the rest of the season. He wished that Aquarius was there with him. She was preparing for a photo shoot for the launch of her clothing line. She had been putting her stuff on hold for so long to help him while his mother was sick and then help him after she passed away. It was time for things to get back to as normal as possible. Shooter had encouraged her to go ahead with the shoot when the famous photographer that she had booked previously was in town working with other clients. Aquarius didn't want to, she kept saying that she needed to be at his first game back on the court. He told her to work on her stuff instead, so she stayed behind and missed his most amazing game of his career.

Shooter was excited to get back home to share with his girlfriend his outstanding night and listen to her tell him about her day. They would probably stay up all night making love and looking at highlights on ESPN and Sports Center. He was happy the owner of the team had chartered a private plane back to Atlanta for the team. Shooter would be able to sleep in his own bed next to his girl tonight. He hated being away from Aquarius. She was his comfort and peace when he wasn't on the court. It took everything in him to make her do the photo shoot because he wanted her there. He just didn't want to be so selfish.

His manager Melly had received the same text he did, and he misunderstood it. He rushed over to Shooter's house because his phone was going straight to voicemail. Melly knew Shooter was fragile. He watched him pace back-and-forth as he searched his mind for the words to say. He didn't ask her whereabouts but he inadvertently searched around the house, looking for Aquarius. They had been together since his first year in college. He concluded as he drove over to Shooter's house that the baby in the picture was a child that he and Aquarius had early and gave away to a family member to raise while they continue their education. And maybe all this was just coming out because Shooter's mom had passed away.

"Y'all still young. We can just say that a family member was raising the child while y'all finished college. The both of you have been very active in the child's life behind the scenes. The death of your mother made you want to have your child with you, especially since the two of you are about to get married." Melly felt like this was a good plan and It was believable.

"Man, what the hell you talking about?" Shooter's best-friend and assistant Big Shaq said as he walked into the den smoking a Backwood stuffed with weed. He looked at Shooter's manager like he was speaking a foreign language. His story was farfetched, but it was more believable than the actual truth, which he still couldn't believe. Big Shaq had all kind of questions that he wanted to ask Shooter. He knew that he needed to wait until he cooled down. He overheard him beat Aquarius' ass. If he tried that shit with Big Shaq he was gonna get his ass beat.

Big Shaq didn't know what would hurt Shooter's career more, him beating Aquarius or the secret being revealed. He didn't want anything concerning them coming out. His life depended on Shooter's success. They had to fix this mess before it got any worse. Shooter was already on the edge dealing with the loss of his mom. Unfortunately, the only person who could help him was the person who all this shit was about, Aquarius

"I'm talking about the picture of Aquarius and your kid that was sent to me. We could tell the world that your mother has been raising the child all this time, keeping him out of the spotlight. It's okay, y'all are young. Y'all both grieving, it will be accepted. Stop pacing, have a seat. You want me to fix you a drink?" Melly got up from the seat and headed toward the bar and fixed them both a drink.

In another time and place Shooter might be laughing at this ridiculous story. This story really wasn't ridiculous, but it was a lie. The truth is what was ridiculous and so fucking unbelievable. He couldn't even bring himself to tell the truth. He took the glass of 1942 that his manager had poured him straight to the head. He's gonna need more than a shot to help him get this out.

Aquarius never hid anything from Shooter. In fact, she told him the truth from the beginning. Well not the jump, but before anything had happened between them. She gave him ample enough time to walk away. What she didn't know then was Shooter was already in love with her and there was no turning back. The way he connected with her; he never had connected with any other person before. If it was between the two of them, he was down for life. Well life had ended as he knew it when he received that text message. Here he was about to start yet another life in less than a month. Ain't this some shit?

CHAPTER 4

Aquarius grabbed the photo of her and Shooter from her purse and placed it on top of the chest that held all her belongings. Everyone probably would think she was a fool if they knew that her love for him had not changed. Call her stupid but she had only experienced a love this pure from her mom. They were the same sign born on the same day. Since her first conversation with him, she felt as if he they were connected on a spiritual level. Because of this connection, she didn't feel as if she had to hide her truth. She told him everything on their second date. He had the choice to get up from the table and leave. He didn't, he looked away and then stared in her eyes deeply and said *let's just take it day by day, be friends. This might not go anywhere, or it might go to the moon. Let's just go with the flow.* Well Aquarius wasn't her first name for nothing. She could go with the flow better than anyone, she knew that this man was her future. It just felt like her mom had sent him to her.

Aquarius saw Shooter every day since the first day that she met him. Whether it was for fifteen minutes or was for eight hours, she saw him. And he saw her, beyond her beauty, beyond her fly clothes, beyond her nice car, beyond her intelligence and talent. Shooter saw her heart and soul and that is why what he had done to her, hurt so bad. Aquarius felt like he was doing this because he was under pressure from their secret being revealed to the world. She heard the voices downstairs in their home, maybe his friends encouraged Shooter to beat her. Shooter wouldn't have never done this under any other circumstances. She knew him, she knew his heart. Just thinking about all of this made Aquarius burst into tears. Her face hurt, her body hurt, and her heart hurt.

Aquarius hadn't felt this type of pain since her mother passed away. She felt so alone and so lost. She didn't know what to do next. She didn't feel like talking about what happened, she just wish it didn't. Why did they have to be public figures? If they weren't celebrities none of this shit would matter. The knock at the door startled her. It could only be one person, her aunt. She opened it without looking out of the peephole, a big mistake. A huge young man was on the other side of the door staring at her. Her heart start to race and she immediately thought that Shooter had found her. She tried to shut the door on him, but his foot was preventing it. The look in his eyes scare the shit out of her. He wasn't looking at her, he was looking through her. Tears ran down her face. "Please don't hurt me, I haven't talk to anyone."

He was staring at her like she was crazy but still had not said anything. She didn't know what to say either, she just looked at him as he looked at her. Time seemed to stand still as he pushed past her and walked inside the apartment. She wanted to scream for help. Aquarius didn't want her life to end her, especially not like this.

1 5 2

He looked around with his dark pop eyes with long eye lashes. "Where yo trash?" The big guy asked Aquarius as he held his hand out.

Aquarius stepped backwards and exhaled a sigh of relief loudly as she leaned against the wall. She swore her life had flashed before her eyes. Yolanda walked through the door and pushed the big boy to the side like he was a light as a feather.

"Chase move your big butt out the way. Make sure you get all this trash out of here before it starts stinking up this place." Her aunt told the young man pushing him to the side.

Aquarius opened the small fridge and got all the food she had ordered but played over since she been here. Her appetite had not come back yet. She just wanted to be at home with her man. "I'm happy you came up here because I was low-key scared as hell. I didn't know who he was. I didn't think Chase was this big auntie. Isn't he like twelve? Aquarius looked at her younger cousin who looked like he could be at least 18 years old. He didn't talk much because of a speech impediment. She hadn't seen him in five or six years in person. He was the size of a college defensive linemen.

"I figured you wanted to get rid of some of the Amazon delivery boxes and all these to-go boxes. And FedEx just delivered just delivered your phone and iPad." Yolanda handed Aquarius the large, opened box.

Aquarius rolled her eyes when she took the box from her. She had her aunt to order it in her name because she didn't want anything to be traced back to her. She was trying her best to stay under the radar. Shooter had long money and a long range.

"Don't call, text or email that boy. We already know he has someone watching your condo and your design studio. Let him keep thinking that you are still in Atlanta. He probably didn't even think that you would jump on a private jet so you couldn't be traced. Him and his goons running around Atlanta hunting you down and you are clear across the country baby." Yolanda has been in L.A. for over twenty years, but her New Orleans accent was just as thick as if she still lived there.

Aquarius wanted to call him like hell. She wanted to hear his voice, hear him apologize and promise he would make it right. But that was wishful thinking. According to her aunt who was also a clairvoyant, Shooter had someone looking for her to hurt her more and silence her. No one in the world would think that she was hiding out in The Vista's. He couldn't risk her truth coming out, it would ruin him. The beating alone will have him kicked out of the league. They would say it was a hate crime even though he loved her.

"Just look at what he has done to you. That was the tip of the iceberg. He can do so much more to you without getting his hands dirty. He doesn't even have to leave his house. We have witnessed it happen before, time and time again with celebrities. We only seen the ones that were caught or found out. Money makes things happen and people disappear. Shooter has a lot of money and people who get paid because of him. With him being who he is, a fool will do it just to be closer to him. I know it's a lot to have to hide out, but we are keeping you alive."

Her aunt was painting Shooter out to be a monster. No matter how long they have been together or how many good things he had done for Aquarius, all those things were overshadowed by the ass whipping he gave her. "So, I supposed to hide under a rock forever? Auntie I have a life. A life that does not revolve around Shooter. What am I supposed to do about my career? This isn't fair. I haven't done anything wrong." Aquarius was ready to get back to work. She has her clothing line that was launching. She needed to start preparing for the different fashion weeks. She already had her spot in New York and Paris fashion week. This was the worst time in her life for this to be happening.

"I feel as if something bad is about to happen. You need to stay here and lay low. We will figure something. My spirit won't be able to rest if you are away from me and something else bad happens. I'm slipping and your mother's spirit is riding me. I must protect you. You have your iPad, your computer, your phone and sewing machine. Your fabric is being delivered throughout the week. Let your frustration fuel your creativity. When this is over with you will have your best work. It's okay to be still for a while Lil' Bit." Yolanda walked close to her and hugged her tightly.

Aquarius couldn't hold it in. "Ouch!"

Her aunt jumped back quickly "He hurt you all over? Take your shirt off. Let me see."

Aquarius moved slowly taking her shirt off. She had not looked at her body yet to assess the total damage, but she damn sure felt it. There were no full-length mirrors in the barely furnished apartment. The sound that came from her aunt startled her and let her know that she was in even worse shape than she thought.

"His ass needs to be in jail. He needs to be under the jail because he is too big to be putting his hands on you like this. That's why he is looking for you, so he can silence you. We need proof! I'm about to take pictures of all this shit, just in case Shooter ass wanna get funny. He can play with you. But he can't play with me because I got something for his ass. It's gonna take more than some money to keep me off him if he comes after you. Her aunt snapped pictures of her from all angles on her iPhone.

Aquarius didn't even want to see the pictures. The look on her aunt's face was enough. This was taking a toll on her mental. She just wanted to smoke and go to sleep for a long ass time. She cried when she closed her eyes and prayed that God will speak to her, for her mother speak to her; that some type of resolution will come to her because this wasn't it. She refused to be like this much longer. She couldn't help the situation and she didn't do anything to deserve whatever happened to her. Aquarius didn't plan on calling Shooter, but she definitely was going to call somebody. "Can you send me some Backwoods back up here. My head has start to hurt. I need to go to sleep."

"Your head hurting 'cause your little ass ain't eating and you smoking all that weed. You need to take your ass to the emergency room cause your ribs are broken"

Aquarius knew something was wrong, but she didn't think her ribs were broken. "I can't do that. What if someone sees me? How am I gonna go to the hospital and they not use my insurance? He is probably waiting on a notification from the insurance company right this second so he can come get me. Shooter knew he fucked me up enough for me to seek medical attention. I don't care if I am all the way across the country, I ain't going to the hospital. I'll be okay. It ain't like they can put a cast on a broken nose or some broken ribs. They will heal."

"Okay but what about your damn nose? It's definitely gonna need surgery. It's fucked up bad. What are you gonna do about that? Your face makes you so much money. Girl you better not go back to that nigga. Get some rest. I'll be back to check on you later. And don't forget what I said." Her aunt reached in her pocket and pulled out a pack of backwoods and a pack of white runts and gave Aquarius both.

Shooter was tired of talking and even more tired of listening. Between Melly and Big Shaq going back-and-forth telling him what he needed to do, he was fed the fuck up. He was mad at himself because he handled this situation like a real fuck nigga. He made Aquarius look like the bad guy because he had a lot to lose. But next to his mom he had just lost his most prized possession. He closed his eyes and started to intentionally breathe deeply. Shooter tried to quiet his mind and be still as possible. He wanted his mom to whisper to him and give him instructions on what to do next.

He knew his mama would be so disappointed in him. If she was alive this wouldn't have never happened. Shooter told his mom the truth when he first started falling in love with Aquarius. His mother's simple instructions could be used as a life hack for all things. "Just follow your heart baby." All she cared about was thar he was happy. Now here he was alone, being blackmailed, possibly facing criminal charges and the biggest scandal in the NBA all because he listened to some else and didn't follow his heart.

Big Shaq burst into the den talking loudly. "We should've checked the house when all this shit first went down. All your shit is missing. Your lil' girlfriend took all your jewelry, some money and your watch collection. Your bedroom safe has been emptied. You are going to have to call the cops now."

Shooter's manager didn't want the cops involved and neither did he. He had people searching everywhere for Aquarius. He felt like if he could talk to her and apologize to her, she wouldn't tell anyone that he had beat her. He knew he did a lot of damage. He had people watching the hospitals and urgent care for her too. She was bound to turn up somewhere because she was injured.

"Man quit sitting around here sulking. You need to get up and wash your ass and you need to see what all is missing. Your jewelry alone was worth at least two million dollars and that's not including your limited-edition collection of watches, that's another million and a half. How much money did you have in the safe? Anything of value in there besides the money?" Big Shaq paced back and forth angrily like it was his shit that was missing.

"I am not calling nobody until I find out who is trying to blackmail me. I got to dead that situation first. I would give them the $100,000 if I knew that would be the end of it. I'm not about to be paying $100,000 to any and everybody, every other week. You pay one person then another one is going to come out of the woodwork." Shooter's frustration was written all over his face.

"You need to be worried about if your folks gonna come out the woodwork. You said yourself that you at least broke her nose. I saw all the blood upstairs. She might be in the hospital under Jane Doe with a lawyer at her bedside waiting to drop a bomb on your ass. She is a brand; uses her face to make money. You got to be stupid if you think she not gonna fuck you up. It isn't that much love in the world. That girl is going get your ass!" Big Shaq had his own people looking for Aquarius. Shooter was too much in his feelings to realize what was going to happen.

"He sure does need to be worried. He is literally in the same spot, wearing the same clothes since yesterday. Have you eaten? Have you bathed? Don't you have basketball practice tomorrow and a game the day after? If nothing has happened by now, it's not gonna happen. Come on man get up. Shake this shit off! You are not the first man to get your heart broke and you won't be the last. As far as the blackmail shit goes, they haven't made a move and they haven't called anymore. We're gonna let this shit be. We got bigger fish to fry. You cannot let this sidetrack your career. You already missed half the season because of your mom. You just got back on track. Let's finish the season out on top." His manager had a key to his house and all his alarm codes. Shooter never heard enter him into a room and never hurt him leaving. It's like he always just appeared out of thin air.

Shooter's phone started to vibrate; it was unknown caller. He was hoping like hell that it was Aquarius. He just wanted to know if she was okay. His best friend had him shook when he spoke about the blood loss. Shooter would regret forever hurting the woman he loved. He answered the phone. There was a silence on the other end. "Aquarius, is this you baby? I'm so sorry. Please forgive me. Come home. Are you OK? Where are you? I'll come get you wherever you are. I'll come to you. Stay there, just send the address. Say something Aquarius. Aquarius!"

Shooter's feelings were hurt when he heard the laughing on the other end of the phone. Whoever it was, used something to disguise their voice.

"It's not Aquarius. You ready to pay me my money? Shaderoom, Baller alert and Hollywood unlock are on standby waiting for this information. I got the account number for you to wire the money, you ready?"

"How can I be sure this is gonna be the end of it? You gotta give me some type of guarantee. How can you prove that if I give you the hundred thousand this week, you are not gonna be asking for another hundred thousand next week? Nawl 'cause it ain't no guarantees! I'm good."

Melly jumped up from his seat and snatched the phone from Shooter. "No, no, no! Wait a minute, wait a minute, wait a minute! Give us until the first thing in the morning to arrange the transfer with the bank. Call back at ten a.m. We'll have the money ready to wire to your account. This is his manager. We're going to dead this situation immediately."

"Okay I will be calling no later than 10 AM. Be ready or Shooter is going to have more to worry about than where his precious Aquarius is. Oh, and by the way for another $100,000, I'll tell him where she is right now." They hung up the phone abruptly.

"Bruh, I know you ain't thinking about paying them. If the shit comes out, tell them that you didn't know anything. That money could be going toward building the gym for The *Boys & Girls Club*. You better not be thinking about giving them a hundred thousand more to find out where Aquarius is. Hell, she probably took more cash than that from your safe, not to mention the three and half million dollars' worth of jewelry that has disappeared." Big Shaq threw his hands up in frustration. He then looked over at Melly and said "Please talk some sense into this man. I'm tired of talking about it."

"Two hundred thousand dollars in cash, three and a half million dollars' worth of jewelry? Did she take your watch collection too? Oh, it's over with! We're gonna call the police and say you found out that she has been stealing from you. You confronted her about your things that were missing, and we haven't seen her anymore. You are a way bigger celebrity than she is. You made her a celebrity. Aquarius is in possession of your stolen money and jewelry. She could've been in a car accident and broke her nose and blamed it on you. There is no proof that you did anything to her. I'm gonna call my friend at the police department and get him to come over. We can file a report and get a warrant issued." Melly exhaled loudly. This was just what he needed to spin the story in their favor. He had to get Shooter out of his feelings and back on the court. He walked out of the den with the phone to his ear as he made a call to his police connection.

"I guess this is why he gets paid the big bucks. That story is believable. We are gonna go with it. Let's get this shit over and done with." Big Shaq has always been Shooter's soundboard when he was going through something, even when it was involving Aquarius. He wasn't used to seeing him so helpless.

"I just supposed to be a police ass nigga. Aquarius has not done anything wrong. She didn't call the police on me so why am I about to call the police on her?" Shooter knew he was antagonist in this story no matter what Melly or Big Shaq was saying to him.

"Nigga! She didn't call the police on you 'cause she got over three million dollars' worth of your shit. Hitting her was unnecessary and I'm sorry I suggested it. You barely listen to what I say anyway so I didn't expect you to go upstairs and beat her like that." Big Shaq felt guilty and he knew he probably wouldn't be able to look at Aquarius again without feeling guilt.

Shooter got up from the plush sofa and stretched. He was ready to take a shower and finally change clothes. He didn't see a way out of the shit he was in. He wished his Momma was still here. Now without Aquarius as well he was out here with the wolves. He was a firm believer in women being the backbone. "Order me something to eat. I'm about to take a shower." He said to no one in particular, he didn't care who did it.

"Make it quick, the cops are on the way." Melly said as he started walking back into the den.

"Cops? I thought you said you was calling your friend who was a cop. Not the entire precinct. I don't need a whole bunch of cops coming to my house. It's going to draw too much attention. I thought we were trying to keep this on the low. Sometimes doing nothing is better than doing a whole bunch of bullshit." Shooter walked out of the room and stomped up the steps frustrated. He didn't know what the hell to do.

CHAPTER 6

Aquarius woke up in so much pain. She wished she could take her head off her body because it hurt so badly. She could barely lift her head from the pillow and her entire face hurt whenever she tried to inhale. She was going to have to go to the hospital because something was very wrong. She had not left the apartment since she arrived. She was being very precautious. She didn't want to be seen in her current condition and she did not want to be noticed.

She jumped in the shower. Aquarius did her best thinking in the shower. As she let the hard hot water hit her skin, she visualized all her problems going down the drain with the water. Never in a million years did she think she would be back in The Vista's. Aquarius visited Los Angeles often and always saw her aunt, but she stayed away from The Vista's. This time she didn't have no place to run. She got out the shower and looked at herself in the mirror for the first time. Tears poured from her eyes when she saw her reflection. Both of her eyes were black, and her eyes had broken blood vessels in them. Aquarius' small nose was swollen three times it's normal size. She couldn't believe that Shooter did this. She was grateful that L.A. was still under a strict mask mandate in all public businesses. Her walking around with the large blacked out Chanel sunglasses with her face covered and a mask on wasn't out of the ordinary here. In Atlanta, Aquarius looked like she was about to rob the place.

She dressed quickly and picked up her cellphone to get an Uber to take her to the hospital. Knowing she couldn't be too careful; she created an account in her aunt's name. Aquarius' breath left her body as she walked down the steps. All the hurtful memories of her childhood flashed before her eyes. She had saw one of her cousins when she first got here. This particular cousin named Ro, wasn't as bad as all the others. He didn't pick on her or try to fight her, he just stared at her like she was an alien. He grew up to be very handsome. He looked like the average guy their age where you can't tell if he was a hustler or rapper. Aquarius walked past him with her head down and prayed that he didn't recognize her.

As she walked towards the awaiting Uber, she saw her cousin Ro again. This time he was with a young lady and a little girl. The young lady looked in her direction twice as if she noticed her. This filled Aquarius with unease. She couldn't risk being noticed. As the Uber pulled away from the front of the building, she noticed her little cousin Chase staring at her in the vehicle. It was something about Chase that made the hair on the back of her neck stand up. Aquarius knew he was only thirteen years old, but he scared her. Something wasn't right about him. She just can't put her finger on it.

Aquarius arrived at Kindred Hospital faster than she expected. Her anxiety was through the roof, and she was afraid. She kind of wished she would've asked her aunt to accompany her. She didn't ask her because she didn't want to keep hearing about how horrible Shooter was. She walked slowly through the door of the emergency department and immediately wanted to walk out. She didn't leave because it was not crowded. It was only two other people waiting to be seen. She went to registration desk and didn't know what too say. She stammered over her words when she was asked what she needed to be seen for. Aquarius told the older lady that she had been a car accident and that her nose was broken, and she also thought that her ribs might be broken too. When she was asked for her identification and insurance, Aquarius told her that her wallet was left in the damaged car. Tough time calls for desperate measures and she was proud of herself for her fast thinking.

She had only been sitting in the waiting area for less than thirty minutes before she was called to the back to be seen. Aquarius was escorted into an exam room by a beautiful young lady about her age with freckles and ginger colored hair. She used to always want to have freckles and red hair when she was younger. "You are so pretty. I always wanted red hair and freckles growing up." "Thank you so much. I love It now, but I hated it then. You know kids can be so cruel." The young lady replied.

"Girl, you don't have to tell me." Aquarius instantly thought of her horrible childhood spent at the Vista's. Her family tormented her and allowed others to do as well. Her mother moved them there for a fresh start and it was the worst thing she could've ever done. The family insulted her mother for her decisions on how she raised Aquarius. Her cousins bullied her and mocked her until she was suicidal. No one knew what it was like to live in her body or the turmoil she felt day to day.

Aquarius' mom moved them to Los Angeles after her father passed away. She had promised Aquarius that everything was going to be better. They were finally free, but they literally moved from one prison to the next. She had no help because she was the only child. Her father made it known after she was born different; he didn't want to try for any more kids. Her father wanted a son, and her mom wanted a daughter. Until the day she was born they thought they had a son. Aquarius was born with an intersex condition called androgen insensitive syndrome. Her mother fought tooth and nail with her father for them to wait until she was at least five years old before surgery. Her dad wanted a son, come hail or high water and he got what he wanted in the beginning.

As she transitioned from toddler to preschool age, Aquarius mother noticed that she was naturally more feminine than masculine. Her voice and mannerisms were very girly from the beginning. But her daddy was not budging on his son and right before she turned five years old her father got sick with prostate cancer and all her mother's focus went to keeping him alive. Her father eventually passed away and they moved to Los Angeles with nothing but some dreams. They moved into the family-owned apartment complex The Vista's. Her mother used to always throw it in her father's face that her family owned an apartment complex. She could hear her mother's voice right now as she thought about her *"Nigga I got somewhere to go. My family own a whole apartment building in Los Angeles. Me and my daughter will never be homeless as long as we got "the Vistas". What your family got besides that rageddy ass bootleg house?"*

Aquarius thinks that her being born inter-sexed caused the divide in her parents' relationship. Her mother fought with her father over the way she was treated until his death.

She had zoned out as she mentally walked down memory lane. The nurse was calling the name Aquarius gave them when she checked In. It wasn't her real name. She didn't respond until she lightly touched her on the shoulder. The nurse was ready to examine her, and the fear took over. She took the dark oversize sunglasses off, pulled her face mask down and looked her in the eye.

The nurse gasp loudly in shock when she saw Aquarius face. She immediately put her hand over her mouth. "Are you in danger? I can get you some help." The nurse knew that this wasn't from a car accident. There was no way her lip wasn't busted, or teeth messed up if this was from a car accident.

Tears fell from Aquarius eyes as she shook her head. Deep down in her heart she didn't think that Shooter would hurt her again. He reacted under the fear of what others would think about him when her truth came out. He was her first love, her best friend, her soul mate. Aquarius knew for a fact that he was hurting right now for hurting her. At least those are the things her heart was telling her. They were building a future with each other. They had it all planned out, everything except for this. While she wanted to go back home to Atlanta and everything to go back to how it was before, she knew things would never be the same.

"Are you sure that you are safe? We have resources here to protect you. I can tell without an X-ray that your nose is broken, and you have a deviated septum. You will need surgery immediately so that it doesn't start to heal like this. We are going to get you an M.R.I. to make sure this didn't cause any internal damage inside your nasal cavity. Can you stand up so I can look at your ribs before they take you over to radiology?" The nurse watched the Aquarius stand up slowly. She winced in pain when she lifted the shirt over her head. It was obvious to the nurse that someone used her as a punching bag. She was bruised black and blue. The nurse had to report this.

Aquarius replied, "Yes I am safe." She saw the shock and sadness on the nurse's face as she looked at her bruised torso. So many things could've went wrong when Shooter lost It. He could've punctured her breast implants, caused internal injuries, or did some damage that couldn't be undone. She didn't do anything wrong and even if she did, she didn't deserve this. Aquarius racked her brain trying to come up with why beating her was Shooter's reaction to the truth being revealed. The more she thought about it, the more her disdain for him grew. It was her truth, a part of her. What was he trying to do, beat it out of her? He accepted her as she was years ago. It's a problem now cause the world is about to find out that NBA superstar Shooter Jones is engaged to someone who was born intersexed.

She had made it up in her mind that she was going to need surgery to fix her nose since she first looked at herself after everything happened. Los Angeles had some great plastic surgeons so she would book a consult the following day. Aquarius couldn't stand to look at herself in her present condition. The wheels in her mind turned as the wheels on the wheelchair rotated when she was being escorted to radiology. She knew by now that Shooter had discovered the money and his prized jewelry collection missing. Aquarius took it because she was upset, she had her own money and jewelry. She didn't know what she was going to do with it. She wasn't a thief, but she wanted him to be upset as she was. Her aunt told her not to leave empty handed, so she didn't.

"Momma why you are busting into my bedroom like that?" Dominique asked his mother as he closed his laptop swiftly.

"'Cause I can! Did you go fix the toilet in that apartment downstairs yet?" His mama made sure he did all his daily tasks before he got on that computer doing whatever the hell he was doing.

He was living at home this semester because he couldn't afford to live on campus during the summer. His scholarship only covered his housing during the fall, winter and spring semesters. Dominique was attending summer classes to graduate early. He was happy he was home helping his mother. If he was not home, he wouldn't have come up with his money-making plan. Ever since Dominique was a little, he could fix anything, he always been good with his hands. He was one of The Vista's maintenance people, he had access to every apartment. All the people in The Vista's loved Dominque, he even worked on some of their cars. He had never been formally trained, but there was nothing he couldn't fix.

"I was checking to see if this assignment that I submitted was accepted. The Wi-Fi has been acting up and it had to be turned in by ten a.m. I will fix the toilet by noon." Dominque waited for his mother to close his bedroom door before he opened his laptop again. He opened the Text Now app and sent the picture he had just snapped.

Dominique heard his cousin Ro talking to his mom. His mom had not mentioned anything about their cousin being here at The Vista's. He was going to see how Ro felt about her later when go to for their evening session of playing Madden and smoking. Ro was like the big brother he never had. He didn't treat Dominique different like everyone else did and he didn't use him to fix things either. He wanted to tell Ro about what he found out and his plan, but he didn't.

People treated Dominique like he was a freak cause he was so smart. He was going to go back to school in the fall and never come back to The Vista's until he was rich enough to take care of his mother and brother. In a couple days he would have enough money to survive until he graduated and got a job at a research firm and continued his eduction. Dominque knew he could only go so far in this environment. Just like his famous cousin had to get the hell out of The Vista's to live her best life, he knew he did too. Him and his cousin had one thing in common, both were considered the misfits.

* * *

Aquarius mind frame had changed in a matter of hours. It was time for her to start living in her truth. She couldn't care less about how it affected Shooter 'cause Shooter didn't give a damn about her. If he did, he wouldn't have almost killed her. She had to look at herself in the mirror at the end of the day and at the beginning of the day as well.

Right now, Shooter had her looking like a monster. The nurse walked back into the exam room; this time accompanied by a young doctor.

"Hello Miss Smith, I'm Dr. Kuma. It is good that you got here when you did. You didn't mention any breathing problems, but your lungs are bruised. A slight bit more pressure during your accident, would've punctured your lungs. We are going to need you to stay here a couple of days to get the swelling down and monitor your lung function with a respiratory therapist. Tomorrow morning you will see the the ear, nose and throat surgeon to repair your nose. I will come back to see you before my shift ends. Nurse Morgan is gonna take good care of you down here until you are assigned a bed upstairs." The doctor left the nurse in the exam room with Aquarius.

"Dr. Kumar one of the nice doctors. All the younger doctors are nice, it's the old ones that get on my nerves. Are you hungry? I'm about to take my lunch break, I can bring you something back from the cafeteria."

Aquarius figured that she might as well get something descent to eat before she was assigned to a hospital room. She needed to put something on her stomach because once she got in her room, she wanted something heavy to put her sleep. Her brain needed to rest for more than three or four hours at a time. "I will take a tuna sandwich, a Caesar salad, a fruit salad and a green smoothie please." Aquarius was hungry, but she wanted to have something to eat later. She reached for her purse and pulled a hundred-dollar bill off a large roll in her Chanel bag.

"Your lil' butt can eat. But I got you Aquarius." Nurse Morgan said using her real name as she walked out the exam room before the shocked young lady could respond

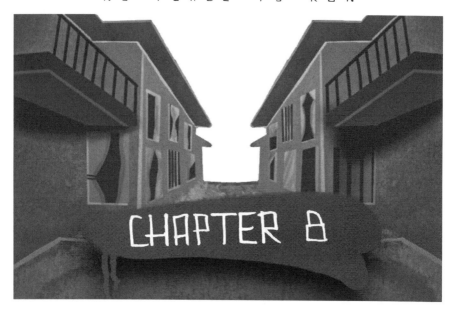

CHAPTER 8

"You can't tell me I ain't the GOAT!" Big Shaq said loud and proud as he walked into Shooter's bedroom unannounced. He stopped in his tracks when he saw all the dried blood on the bed and the floor. Shooter was curled up on the couch watching ESPN. He looked like he had lost his best friend.

"What have you done now?" Shooter looked at Big Shaq's eyes staring at the blood. He didn't even want the housekeeper to clean it up. He had planned on doing it himself. The nice old lady who cleaned and washed his laundry four times a week was one of his mother's church buddies. Shooter wouldn't want her to see this mess or look at him in a different light.

"I got my people to track down who making the extortion calls. See that is why you keep me around. I get my hands dirty in the trenches." Big Shaq was proud of himself. He would lay his life on the line for Shooter, and it had nothing to do with the money he paid him. They have been best friends for almost twenty years. He was more like his brother than anything else. They both were only children, and their tight bond brought their mothers togethers as close friends as well.

"Nigga I keep you around because you are my brother. But good job, because I was just waiting for Melly to get here so we can do the transfer. Now we don't have to send nobody shit. So, tell me who blackmailing me so I can pull up on they ass with my Goon squad?"

"Well, you going to have to jump on a plane to do it. It appears to be some computer geek at UCLA. I got my people working on finding out more about them right now. But I have their IP address, so we can literally go to their door."

"A college kid? Are you serious? What have I done to them for them to try to ruin my life? Not give an autograph, didn't accept them into the basketball camp? Yeah, hit up a few of the homies and call the pilot and tell him to get the jet ready. We are going to Los Angeles." This news brightened Shooter's morning. He jumped up from the couch and snatched all the covers off the custom chrome California king sized canopy bed. Blood had soaked through to the mattress as well. He would order a new mattress before he left for Los Angeles so when he returned home, he could sleep in his bed. Aquarius designed this bed; he would never get rid of it.

"I got the L.A. homies already on standby. We can just take Pop and the twins with us." Big Shaq had already hit up all their west coast people before he came to tell Shooter.

As always, Melly was walking in on the end of the conversation. "What is in L.A.? Did I miss something?" He always tried to be super aware of everything his client did. Shooter grew up on the streets of the Westside of Atlanta and he was still very much affiliated with the streets everywhere, especially when his best friend/assistant was around. Even though Big Shaq and Shooter denied it, Melly knew that they both was a part of Crips.

"I did what I usually do... come to the rescue." Big Shaq said smiling with pride.

"It's the least that you could do. But what did you actually do and why do we have to go across the country to do it? Melly was always suspicious of the way that Big Shaq came to the rescue.

"Who said anything about you coming? I found out who blackmailing us, and I know where they are. We bout to go and pull up on them real quick and show them that they pick the wrong motherfuckers to be playing with." One thing about Big Shaq, he was trained to go, no matter the time or place. That's why he was a very valuable asset. It's just sometimes cleaning up his messes was weren't worth the trouble.

"Man get the fuck out of here! You serious? I need to put you on my payroll too. I got some people in L.A. In fact, I was just talking to them about this shit. We can have they ass locked up in no time." Melly was a lawyer first and he was in a fraternity. He had a lot of connections in the business, politics and law. He was just talking to his frat brother DeAunte, a field supervisor for the F.B.I. about how to pursue charges for the extortion.

"What in the hell you doing talking to police in Los Angeles about my shit? I told you from the jump I didn't want the cops involved like that. You went ahead and had four cops show up here to file charges on somebody ass who I beat. Now you talking to police on the other side of the country. What part of I don't want my business in the street don't you understand Melly? I know you have a way doing things. But I ain't with all this police shit. You literally have told five people that didn't know anything, basically everything. I can get kicked out the league, lose my endorsements plus much more if one of these people start

1 7 4

running their mouths." Shooter was beyond furious. Melly was putting so much at jeopardy trying to do things the legal way. Shooter came from the school, you don't call the police until you can't do anything but call the police.

"Man, she stole millions of dollars worth of your shit and somebody else is blackmailing you. I'm trying to fix this shit the legal way." Melly was trying his best to stir Shooter away from the thug-gangbanging basketball player persona that the media was tried to portray him as when he was first drafted.

"Aquarius has not even gone to the cops yet. She still trying to protect me. I beat her up badly. You see all this blood nigga?! You know how small she is? I know I fucked her up. She can keep the money and the jewelry. I just need to know she is alive and okay. And as far as the blackmail shit, I don't give a damn about that either. I ain't paying that shit. Fuck all this shit!" Shooter was frustrated, upset and he missed his woman.

"You don't care if the world knows about your sexuality?" Big Shaq was stunned at Shooter's outburst. He had changed his mind within a matter of minutes. Melly just didn't understand how things worked with them.

"Are you fucking kidding me? I ain't gay nigga. Aquarius was born with a pussy. All of this is my fault 'cause I shouldn't have reacted the way I did. Get your people to find my lady. Fuck all that other shit!" Shooter walked out the room without letting them reply.

CHAPTER 9

Aquarius woke up with the same nurse at her bedside checking her vitals. The nurse had dropped her food off and never came back. She had been wondering since the nurse left how did she know her real identity. She was so nervous she could barely sleep throughout the night and ended up requesting pain medication that was guaranteed to make her fall asleep. She expected to wake up with the authorities in her face.

Aquarius was sad that Shooter had not found her yet. He let her go so easy. He didn't know or care if she was dead or alive. She wondered what would have happened if she stayed at the house after he beat her. Would he have come home regretful, or would he try to beat her some more? Would he have kicked her out the house? Tears fell from her eyes as she thought about how alone she felt.

She felt the nurse looking at her. "Are you not going to say anything?

"What do you want me to say Miss Jones? I don't have to ask any questions. I read your admittance papers. If you want me to know the truth you will tell me. Do you need anything? What level is your pain at? Are you comfortable?"

"I want some normal. Can you bring me some of that? Do you have a time machine that you can put me into and take me back to last week? How did you know who I was?" Aquarius tried her best to sit up in the bed

"Miss Jones you have been featured on a lot of the blogs. You have over two million Instagram followers, one million followers on Tiktok as well as a half a million Youtube subscribers. Your nose is swollen, and your eyes are black but that doesn't stop you from being your beautiful self. I knew who you were as soon as you pulled your facemask off. I have been following you since you made the Mayor of Atlanta inauguration dress when you were in college. You are so talented. I know you are dropping your own clothing line soon and this is the last thing you need." Nurse Morgan knew much more about Aquarius than she let on.

"Tell me about it. I really need to be home in Atlanta working. I had just had one of my big photo shoots the day this happened. Life sure has a way of throwing you a curveball." Aquarius was ready to be back in Atlanta. She just couldn't imagine a life in Atlanta without Shooter.

"Or a basketball." Nurse Morgan said unconsciously. She regretted the comment as soon as it left her mouth.

Aquarius was shocked. "I don't need anything else. You can leave now and please don't come back. I'm sure this isn't your designated area. You were just working in the emergency department when I came in yesterday. Thank you, I appreciate your help thus far." She was ready for the nurse to get out her sight so she could cry in peace.

As soon as the nurse exited her room, Aquarius exhaled deeply and screamed loudly. She didn't give a damn who came in her room. She was trying to figure out what she had did wrong to spark this downward spiral of events. Aquarius overthought everything and looked at everything as a sign. She was ready to go home. She didn't want to return to The Vista's. The energy just wasn't right. Being there made her remember too much of her childhood battles. Since she was scheduled for surgery in the morning, she decided now was the best time to do what she had to do. She got out of the bed and went into the small bathroom.

Aquarius looked at herself in the mirror and didn't recognize the person staring. The bruises around her eyes were even darker and contrasted heavily with her bloodshot pupils. The small bridge of her nose was missing. Her nose now looked like a just a glob of skin on her face. She wet her hands and smoothed her hair down the best she could. Aquarius didn't have a comb or brush, so this was going to have to do. She grabbed her iPad from her backpack and hopped back in the bed. She propped herself up and opened the keyboard. She exhaled loudly and went to the camera on the iPad.

She knew that if she didn't record right now, she might not record it all. Aquarius press record on the screen and started talking.

"Hello and welcome to my YouTube channel. I know I haven't been over here in quite a while. But I will never forget where the real ones are. I just want to thank you guys for supporting me from the very beginning and I'm back. I'm going to start bringing you guys some amazing content and dope vlogs. I miss you guys. Don't be alarmed this is Aquarius Jones and my YouTube has not been hacked. I know I don't look like myself. Everything happens for a reason so I'm gonna chalk up what happened to me as a sign that it is time for me to live in my truth. I say to the

person who did this to me, the only surprise you have is that I took back my power.

Twenty-four years ago, I was born in New Orleans to a loving couple whose world revolves around each other. My birth built up a wall between these two people that never came down. My dad wanted a son. My mother wanted a daughter. Both was hurt and disappointed when I was born. I was born intersexed. This is a condition when a person is born with reproductive organs or genitalia that doesn't categorize them as male or female. My mother let my father decide and I lived the beginning of my childhood as a little boy. I never felt like a little boy. I don't think God wanted me to be a little boy. I never grew into a little boy physically or mentally. I was always the smallest boy in my class. My face was round. I had the soft feminine voice and long eyelashes and full lips. I felt like a little girl. I want to play with a girl toys. I wanted to play with the little girls in the neighborhood. I want to dress like a little girl.

My father dragged me to the barbershop every week to get my haircut. I would get my haircut and then go home and cry in my bedroom closet. My father tried to make me play football. I hated it. They tackled me too hard. I couldn't catch the ball. I couldn't throw the ball either. I sat on the bench and pouted. I was distracted by the cheerleaders. I wanted to join them. I knew all the cheers and chants by heart. I was mesmerized watching them throughout the football game. I got a spanking when I got home for not playing like he wanted. My mother and father argued. My mother threatened to take me and leave. My father replied, "Get the hell on, I didn't sign up for this shit anyway." He left the house following the argument and I listened to my mother weep for an hour straight. I knew I was the reason. Things only got worst." Tears fell from Aquarius eyes as she remembered living in the home filled with tension because of her.

Aquarius sniffled loudly and continued looking at the iPad camera.

"I'm good guys. I have been in therapy for years. Healing isn't something that happens overnight, it's a process. But back to what initially bought me here. I have had a hell of a week. Someone started to blackmail me with threats of exposing my truth. I was attacked, hence the reason why I am recording this video from a hospital bed with broken ribs, a punctured lung, a broken nose with a deviated septum. I must have plastic surgery to look like myself again. Some evil person wanted to tell my truth from their point of view. I'm here to tell you, a stranger can't tell you a bitch ass thang about me. I am a woman, but I spent the beginning of my childhood being raised as a little boy. I will insert a picture in this video of me as a little girl dressed up like a little boy. There was only one picture because my mother didn't force me to be what my father wanted me to be. My name is Aquarius Jones, my mother named me Aquarius Jones at birth. I was born with a vagina, a uterus, ovaries, but I also had a very very large clitoris that doctor told my parents was a penis and. My breast was small, but I had some and a great plastic surgeon helped me get them like this. I no longer have a large clitoris, that was removed as a child. I attended elementary, middle school and high school as a girl. My mother gave birth to a daughter and raised a daughter. I'm not a freak of nature. I'm not pretending to be somebody I'm not. I was born a little different that's all. The people that needed to know knows and Ii they say they don't, they are telling a motherfucking lie. Thank you for coming to my Ted Talk, and please keep me in your prayers for a safe surgery and fast recovery. I'm so grateful for your support. I will be back soon and I'm gonna vlog my next photo shoot for my upcoming clothing line." Aquarius tried to joke and be lighthearted in the end of the video because she knew the topic was heavy.

It felt like the weight of the world had been lifted off her shoulders and she not even uploaded the video. The tears fell freely from her eyes as she thought about her mother and how she fought so hard for her. Aquarius finished editing the video and she added a handwritten note that she had just scribbled on her iPad. 'Anything don't kill me, make me better. MOTIVATION!

Aquarius picked up her cellphone to call her aunt to let her know her condition and that she was about to have surgery.

CHAPTER 10

Yolanda had not heard from Aquarius and she was worried. She left in the Uber on yesterday headed to hospital. When Yolanda woke up, she did not feel right. Usually when her spirit was unsettled like this, something bad usually happened. She was worried about her niece and her safety. Their bond was always very special. It was no surprise when Aquarius' mother asked Yolanda to take care of her before she passed away. It was hard to watch over her across the country. She knew that Aquarius was ready to escape The Vista's as soon as she could. Attending college in Atlanta was her way out. Yolanda knew that when Aquarius left for college she was never coming back.

She was happy when her niece told her about her boyfriend Shooter who was an only child as well. His mother loved her and accepted her. It made Yolanda worry less because Aquarius had someone to look after her. Now years later, they're both are rich and famous. Shooter's mom had just passed away. Maybe she has been Aquarius safety net all this time and now he could treat her how he really wants too. Yolanda was scared for her niece. Shooter had unlimited resources. There was no telling what extent he would go to keep her silent. Yolanda really wanted to call him and give him a piece of her mind but then he would know that Aquarius was in Los Angeles. She had only met him once at Aquarius' graduation. He appeared to be well mannered, and he was very loving and affectionate with her niece. She never expected him hurt Aquarius. Yolanda was a very good reader of people. She made a lot of money because she could see things.

Her oldest son Dominique walked into her bedroom without knocking and startled her. "Boy what in the hell you want?" She hollered at him. He had been acting strange ever since he got home from college. Yolanda hoped he had not start doing drugs. He only hung around a bunch of rich white kids at school.

"I was looking for you to ask is there any work you need to be done before I leave to go to the library?" Dominique had come into his mother's bedroom to look around because he thought she was already in the leasing office.

"Go change the lock on the unit downstairs that moved out yesterday and then check back with me before you leave." Yolanda had given Aquarius the last of her weed. She would have to call her nephew Ro to see if he was in the building to get some to hold her over until later. Her phone started ringing with an unfamiliar phone number and she pressed ignore. The same number called again on Facetime, and something told her to answer.

"Auntie, I'm sorry I'm just calling." Aquarius said to Yolanda before she could get anything out. She knew her aunt was ready to cuss her out.

"Honey I was about to put out an A.P.B. I woke up feeling unsettled about you baby girl. You okay? How are you? What did the doctors say?" Yolanda's words came out fast. She was startled at her niece's appearance. She looked even worse than she did the last time she seen her.

"I have a deviated septum; my ribs are broken, and my lungs are punctured." Aquarius heard her aunt sniffling on the other end of the phone.

"I'm so sorry baby. You don't deserve this. You should think about pressing charges. Shooter can't get away with this. Your lungs are punctured? Aquarius you could've died. I'm so happy that you went to the hospital when you did.

"I am too, I am happy that I listened to you. I didn't think I was messed up this bad. I have surgery later today. I just wanted to let you know that I finally did It. I'm not going to let anyone else control my narrative. It's my truth and I'm going to be the one to tell the world about it. I recorded a video and uploaded it to YouTube so if Shooter paid them people, they just got some free money. I feel like a weight been lifted. I feel so free Auntie. Thank you so much for never turning your back on me. I love you. Don't worry about me. God and my mama got me."

"Oh my God! You did what? With your face like that? I'm on my way to the hospital right now. You know that everyone is going to automatically think that Shooter did this to you. He is gonna try to track you down for real now and try to silence you. Just let me smoke me one and take a shower. Do you need anything?" Yolanda had to get to the hospital as soon as she could. Aquarius had opened a can of worms and she feared what the end results was going to be.

"I'm not sure how long I'm gonna be here. Can you grab me some underwear and personal hygiene items?" Aquarius didn't know how long her recovery process was going to be in the hospital. She needed to get home to Atlanta to finish working on her collection. She planned on taking her aunt Yolanda with her.

"Okay I got you. Where did you put that weed I gave you, it was my last? I definitely need to calm my nerves before I come down there." Yolanda was hoping her worry wasn't evident in the conversation. She didn't want her niece panicking before surgery. She knew she needed to be present to keep an eye out for her. She was more worried about her safety from Shooter than going under the knife to fix her nose.

"I don't know. Look on the bedside table. I didn't even get to smoke it. I will send you my room number. See you when you get here." Aquarius was happy that her aunt was coming to be with her. She didn't want to be put to sleep without someone to represent her. Shit happens and she didn't want to be one of the people that the shit happened to.

Yolanda rushed to jump in the shower so she could hurry to the hospital before they took Aquarius into surgery. As she was putting on her clothes, she heard a knock at the door. She hurried to the door thinking one of her sons may have left their house key.

"What you got going on Auntie? Who is the girl that you got put up on the top floor? I've seen you coming and going in and out of that apartment. I saw when they first got here. I tried to get a glimpse but when I turned around, they had disappeared. I told you about being on your superhero shit without letting me know. I'm the person you call in to be the muscle after you have done something crazy. I like to have a heads up. You remember what happened last time? Yolanda's oldest nephew who was more like her little brother, than her nephew was always coming to her rescue as she was his. Ro knew how to make to some shit shake when it needed to. He had all kinds of people on speed dial, from the robbers to the shooters to the celebrities and the big homies. Everybody fucked with Cali Ro.

Yolanda really wanted to let Ro know what was going on, but she had to check with Aquarius first. She didn't even know that Ro had seen Aquarius. He has been caked up with his first love and acting like a family man since he come back from Texas with her and her daughter. "I'm gonna tell you later. I got to go and take care business. Keep an eye out on your lil' cousins, especially Dominique. Dat lil' nigga been acting weird ever since he got home from school. You know he hang around all those white kids up there at that college. Ain't no telling what he got going on."

Ro couldn't help but laugh. His aunt was always cracking on people, but it was always truth in her words. Ro thought that it was just him because he felt like Dominique had been acting off too. He hoped his lil' cousin hadn't got caught up in partying like those white boys. "You ain't lying. He always got his face in that MacBook or on the phone whispering. Maybe he got a little girlfriend or something. He definitely acting really sneaky and stand offish. I'm on high alert anyways because of my ol' girl. I got to keep her safe."

"Oh well, we don't have anything to worry about with your hawkeyes on watch. I want to talk to you when I get back. I will call you later." Yolanda watched her nephew leave and knew that she had to tell him about Aquarius and Shooter because he could help protect her too. Instead of jumping on the faulty elevator she took the stairs to the floor directly above her to Aquarius' apartment. She let herself in with the master key and as soon as she opened the door, she saw locked eyes with her son Dominique who was sitting on the loveseat with Aquarius' brand-new MacBook opened.

"Boy I'm gonna beat your got-damn ass. What in the hell you doing in this girl apartment on her computer? You have lost your fucking mind." Yolanda lunged toward her son with her hand raised. She didn't know what Dominique was doing, but she knew he didn't have any business doing it and not in here.

Dominique jumped up and dashed out of the apartment with something small in his hand. Yolanda didn't have time to run after him. She had to hurry over to the hospital before Aquarius surgery started. She had heard horror stories. She really didn't want the doctors thinking they could do anything and everything other than what they were supposed to do because she had no love ones there with her. She planned on getting to the bottom of what ever her son had going on when she returned home. She hoped like hell that he had not taken anything of value from her niece's apartment.

Yolanda scanned each room quickly to see if she noticed anything out of place. She picked up the pack of weed and the Backwood that she had given her niece. She was happy that Aquarius had not smoked it because she was gonna definitely need it. Yolanda opened the drawer and pulled out a couple pairs of underwear, socks and a sports bra. She opened another drawer and pulled out a body suit and a short set. She shook her head when she saw the price tags. Her niece gonna made sure she spent some money. Yolanda often got on her about how much the gifts cost that she purchased for her. Money was not an option when it came to Aquarius. Her mother lived by that rule. She would spend her last on her daughter. She left behind a pretty penny for Aquarius to be taken care of and Aquarius didn't even know the amount.

She put everything in the duffle bag she found in the closet and locked both locks on the door before leaving. Yolanda was pissed off at her son, but she had to go and take care of her niece first. Instead of waiting on the slow ass elevator, she took the steps and went out the back door to her car. She planned on calling Ro soon as she checked in with Aquarius. Yolanda was going to need his help with Dominique.

CHAPTER 11

They were tired because they had not slept since all the chaos started. It seemed like all of them were asleep before the pilot made it out of Georgia. Melly was the first to awake and as usual he was hungry. *Ruth Chris* was ordered for the flight. He summoned the flight attendant to bring him his meal and to make him a drink. He needed it. Being Shooter's

manager was deeming to be more than he anticipated since his mother's death. Deep inside he felt as if it was only going to get worst now that his girl was gone. The two of them together kept Shooter under control.

Melly called his frat brother who was a field supervisor for the FBI for some assistance once he found out that the blackmailer was in Los Angeles. DeAunte had warned him when he left the law firm for sports management that it was more than just securing deals and he never lied. Melly wasn't used to this lifestyle. Even though he was raised in Atlanta, he grew up sheltered. His father was a pastor, and his mother was an attorney and law professor. His upbringing was very structured. He had friends that grew up in the hood. He made friends with them playing little league sports. He met Shooter playing AAU basketball in seventh grade. Melly's father made him play sports all year since he was an only child and he wanted him around other kids.

Years later, Melly had linked back up with Shooter. He was his first client in his newly formed sports management company. Since he had been representing him, Shooter had been in incident after incident. Melly was not getting a break and it seemed as if it has gotten worst since Shooter mom's death. He wasn't prepared for the aftermath of what was going to happen because of Aquarius. Shooter was a ticking timebomb and the two people who could diffuse it was not there. Here they were flying across the country for God knows what and he was trying to get in front of whatever bad was going to take place. The fact that Shooter listens to Big Shaq before he listens to him isn't good. Big Shaq is a street nigga who still was. Very much active in the streets. Melly was afraid that once they get to the west coast, all their gang affiliates were going to show up and there was going to be violence.

* * *

Shooter woke up and looked over at Melly who was knocked out with his mouth open. His tray table was filled with the remnants of the food and drinks he had earlier. Everyone else was sleep as well. They were scheduled to land at Van Nuys airport in less than thirty minutes. He could not believe that he had seen or heard from Aquarius. He was worried because none of the people he had searching for her had a clue where she could have disappeared to. Shooter was so ashamed of how he had behaved. He couldn't believe he did her like that. It was like he was having an out of body experience. The look of shock when he first struck her, to the look of fear she had when she balled up trying to shield herself from him. He knew she would never love him the same again.

Shooter planned on having a few words with the person that was blackmailing him before Big Shaq got his hands on him. On the call they had offered to tell him where Aquarius was, and he planned on getting that information without coming out of his pocket. He had a game in two days, but this right here was his biggest priority. Everyone would just have to understand that. Shooter planned on returning to Atlanta with his lady and with peace of mind. She was now the only thing that seriously bought him peace besides being on the basketball court. He was afraid what might happen to him without Aquarius and his mother. They kept the monster living inside of him under control.

He was starting to believe that he needed to attend the counseling sessions that everyone around him had been recommending since his mother passed. Shooter went to therapy when he was a child. After the therapist that he was seeing moved out of state and he started playing basketball, it seemed like all his issues disappeared. At least it felt like the problems disappeared. He couldn't get a handle on his emotions, and it manifested into anger. If he could let his anger hurt the only woman that he ever loved, there was no telling what he would do to a stranger. Shooter was scared that one day, someone would trigger him on the basketball court and in a split second his career would be gone down the drain.

The flight attendant's voice flooded the plane instructing them to make sure they were seated with their seatbelts on. The flight began its descent, as Shooter looked out the window at the beautiful hills of Los Angeles. The skies were clear, and the weather was warm. He knew that Big Shaq was not going to want to go straight home after they finished handling business. They both loved L.A. especially Big Shaq.

He was considered a Big Homie on the west coast too and he took full advantage of It. He keeps his banging quiet at home in the A, but in L.A., Big Shaq banged hard.

Melly had arranged for them to have transportation waiting for them when they landed. The blacked-out Chevrolet Suburban was parked with the keys in the ignition. Big Shaq was still quiet because he had just woken up. He hopped behind the wheel and prepared to chauffeur them around his second home. He was familiar with the area that the apartment building was in. It was not the best part of town, and he wasn't strapped. He needed to make some calls. He was already going in the blind, but he wasn't going unarmed. Big Shaq sent a message to his homies and told them to meet him there.

Melly rode in silence. He texted DuAnte that they had landed and was headed to the destination. He was trying to be safe more than sorry. Extortion was a federal crime. He had his client's best interest in mind when he reached out to the authorities. They had crossed the country and his client was a very famous basketball player that was clearly not in his right mind. Melly seemed to be the only one thinking clearly and it was his job to do what he had to do to secure Shooter's career legally. He didn't know what Shooter had planned when he got to where they were going. He had been silent since they got on the plane. Melly hated silent Shooter. Nothing good ever came from Shooter being in his head. He received the text he had been waiting on. "They should be there shortly, and I will get there around the same time as you."

Shooter exhaled loudly and said, "You think she gonna take me back?" Asking no one in particular. He felt like the blackmailer knew where Aquarius was hiding. He was ready to confront him, get the address and jump back on the plane to get to her.

"I hope she hasn't spent any of your money or sold your shit. Cause if she has, I wouldn't take her ass back. We in Atlanta bro, it's more where that came from. If you gonna take that type of loss, take Aquarius as a loss as well." Big Shaq could have one hundred of the baddest in the country posted at the house before they got back to Atlanta. He really wanted his boy to get this shit out his system and be done with it. If it took him coming across the country to do it, then so be it.

"She can have that plus so much more. You didn't see what I did to her." I'm just happy she hasn't gone to the police or social media. My life would be over." Shooter didn't want to argue with Big Shaq, he had never been in a relationship for over six months. He was a big trick who thought that the world revolved around him.

"You should've gone to the police about your money, jewelry and watches. Those watches cannot be replaced. You had one of the best collections in the country. If I, was you, I would check the pawnshops and jewelry shops in the city to see if your stuff turns up so that you can recoup it. You are being extorted by someone on the other side of the country, that is a federal offense. You need to get some help from the FBI. That would take the heat off what you done and shine more light on what was done to you. You will walk away like the victim and the good guy." Melly said to Shooter who was strolling through his phone acting as if he wasn't listening to the two of them talking to him.

Big Shaq's answered his cellphone over the Bluetooth. He recognized the number even though he didn't have a name saved. It was his Big Homie. "Hey Big, my guys just pulled up to The Vista's, that is the name of the apartments that you sent me the address to. It's cops everywhere. My people still in the area, hit me up and let me know if you need them. I'm not about to put my guys in the line of fire. I don't know what you got going on, we don't do this type of shit here in L.A."

Melly remained quiet, he looked over at Shooter who remained stoic as he stared ahead. He wanted him to be happy that the police were there so that things would not get out of hand. Then he would say that he was responsible for getting them involved. He could see the red and blue lights flashing before they made it to the apartment complex. He was not expecting it to be so much chaos. Squad cars and unmarked vehicles were everywhere. There was uniformed police and some men in suits who he assumed was the FBI. Melly instantly regretted calling DeAunte. He knew he counted at least seven marked police cars. There was two vans and some SUVs as well. You couldn't get close to the apartments because they were surrounded with the authorities.

Shooter knew that Big Shaq didn't call the police, he had called the goons. He looked over at Melly who was nervously chewing on his bottom lip. He knew that he had done something. "Bro I know you ain't did what I think you did."

CHAPTER 12

Aquarius was so happy that her aunt made it before she was put under anesthesia. She felt better having surgery with her here because anything could happen. The nurse had not made any more appearances, so she knew that she had got the hint. Her iPad was going crazy with notifications from YouTube and Instagram. She was sure that someone from the blogs had probably seen her hospital vlog. She was not checking it, she did not want to hear or read any negativity before she had her surgery. She thought to herself that she probably needed to take the apps off until after she recuperates. Aquarius knew for certain; you don't miss out on anything when you are healing. "Thank you so much auntie for jumping up and coming down here. Now I can go into surgery with no worries."

"Baby girl you have nothing to worry about. You know your mama and daddy sit high and they are looking after you all the time. I would've been here sooner if I knew that you were here. I'm not gonna leave your side." Yolanda felt bad that Aquarius had been through so much at such a young age. She wasn't even twenty-five years old yet.

"I'm so happy you said that. I want you and the boys to move to Atlanta with me. I have enough room in my condo and if not, I will get us a house. Aren't you tired of *The Vista's* auntie?" Aquarius was afraid to return to Atlanta alone.

"I can't just up and leave like that. I'm the property manager and Dominique is in college. This is my home."

"You didn't want to leave New Orleans, but the hurricane drove you out. What is it going to take for you to leave *The Vista's*? You have seen way more nightmares than me there. I hate I had to come back. I didn't have no place to run. You said that you loved Atlanta when you came out to visit for my graduation. Don't worry about the money. I can pay you twice, make it even better three times more than you are making being the property manager. Just come back with me. Give me a month to recuperate and get back on my feet. School is out now so you really don't have to worry about the boys.

It wasn't the money; it was the fear of change and unpredictability. *The Vista's* was like an Army Base and Yolanda was the General. She dictated who lived in *The Vista's* and she called the shots. Yolanda was always prepared because she knew what was always going on. "I can go back and help you until you get back on your feet. I'm not going to promise you anything. You know I hate you being there by yourself, but my life is here.

"What life Auntie? This ain't living! You are just existing." Aquarius said as the nurse came in to let her know that they were ready to put her to sleep.

Yolanda knew that her niece was speaking was truth. She was grateful that they had been interrupted. She kissed Aquarius forehead and watched as they pushed her out the room in a wheelchair. Energy was everything and the energy in *The Vista's* was toxic. Nothing grew in *The Vista's* but everything bloomed once it left. Yolanda let her son go away to school because she seen how her niece progressed once she left. The thought of Dominique reminded her that she needed to call her Ro so he could check on him. Yolanda had to find out what type of shit Dominique was on. Ro always helped her keep the boys in line for her.

She sat in silence thinking about her niece's proposition. Yolanda knew she needed a change of scenery if only for a little while to get her mind right. It was like something inside her believed that she didn't deserve better than *The Vista's*. She barely left since the pandemic. She had become the live-in warden and the residents were her prisoners except they could come and go. Money wasn't an issue, she had quite a lot saved, and she was going to get more when Aquarius turned twenty-five years old next year. Her aunt wasn't broke, she just lived like it. She planned for her daughter's future. She also rewarded Yolanda in allotments for caring for her. Yolanda wanted Aquarius to be humble so she never revealed to her anything regarding her inheritance or the allotments that she would receive. She only knew about her college tuition being paid for. Yolanda knew that this made Aquarius work hard because things weren't handed to her.

The vibrating phone startled her; it was her nephew Ro calling. "I was just about to call you. You really need to..."

"Auntie, where you at? The building is surrounded by cops, there is even choppers in the sky." Ro cut off his aunt mid conversation. He was out of breath and peeping out the window.

Yolanda stood up from her chair so fast it fell backwards. She instantly thought the worst. She panicked because they could be coming for her, her niece, her nephew, his girlfriend or her son cause she didn't know what the hell he had going on. So many thoughts were going through her mind, but she couldn't get them to come out her mouth. They had to be coming for Aquarius. There was no way that nigga Shooter was going to let her get away with stealing his shit, even if he beat her ass prior to.

"They there for Aquarius." Yolanda blurted out somewhat sure of herself. She didn't even think about all the criminals that were living on the premises.

"Wait a minute. Why are they here for Aquarius? She in Atlanta." Soon as he said it, he thought about the person who he seen coming and going that his aunt was hiding. Ro never thought that it was his cousin, he swore she never would return to *The Vista's*. Ro didn't blame her. He knew shit was hard for her here. He stayed rooting for Aquarius from afar. He wanted to exhale but he was still holding his breath. He looked over at his lady and knew what he had done could be the reason why the authorities were outside. He didn't say anything to his aunt. Ro signaled for his girl to go ahead. They had an escape plan and he was about to put it into use. It was better safe than sorry.

* * *

1 9 7

Dominique was hiding inside of the maintenance closet. He was scared. He was just about to leave out the building and head back to his college campus when he saw police at all the exits. He didn't want to be home when his mom got back. His heart was beating so hard he could feel it in his ears. He had really fucked up. All he wanted was enough money to pay for housing, clothes and transportation while he was in school. His scholarship covered his tuition and books. He wasn't trying to walk around the campus looking like a million bucks but his classmates were the children of one percent and he was the small, black nerd from Crenshaw. Dominique didn't want to stick out like he didn't belong, but that is what he did. He didn't want to beg his mother for more than what she was doing. It seemed like she was literally giving all she had to make sure that Dominique was okay at school.

He wanted to be able to take care of his mother and his little brother. He vowed to get them out of this hellhole known as *The Vista's*. Now he was about to go to jail, and this was going to break his mother's heart. Dominique didn't want to be a hustler like his cousin Ro'. He knew he was destined to do great things and he just had to get through school. Him blackmailing his cousin and her boyfriend wasn't killing anyone. Her boyfriend had plenty of money, he had spent more on a car than what Dominique was requesting. This money was lifechanging for Dominique but a drop in the bucket for Aquarius and Shooter. Tears fell from his eyes as he thought about how he was about to be dragged away in handcuffs for this federal offense. He took comfort in knowing that his mother wasn't at home to see him being carried away.

Dominique wiped the tears and closed his eyes to pray. He had no place to run...

TO BE CONTINUED

I hope you enjoyed Aquarius and Shooter's story. They will be featured in the next full-length novel by Sevyn McCray. This will be her first release since Love & Trap Houses Atlanta 2. I'm back bishes!!!

FLOWERPOTS

BY DRUSILLA MARS

PROLOGUE

JULY 2, 2022

You think living in the Magnolia projects in New Orleans was some shit just imagine living somewhere all your life and a hurricane just come and snatch that shit like nothing. We traded the south for, the dirty south to up north now the west going from state to state because my man Easy have connects all over. These last two years we been living in Cali. On our South-Central shit, for real.

The Vista is a sweet spot for Easy and I to lay low and for him to hustle, as always. It was a vibe, and I loved every minute of it just remind me a bit of ghetto fabulous project living. We only lived the luxe life when we were in the five-star hotels to get away, and then it was back to reality because we really just passing through. We haven't lived anywhere more than three years since 2005.

"Ahh shit, Choppa, watch them damn clippers around my ear." Easy stated jerking his head away from me. I was caught up in my thoughts while cutting his hair. Since 2008 when we lived in Atlanta Easy had let his hair grow into beautiful long healthy locs. Now they're all over the floor after being cut a couple hours ago. It was one thing about me and hair, I could do it.

Fuck, I'm a little distracted today and he want me in his head especially since I was the only one that started them, washed, treated and styled. I had those dreads looking like God himself used my hands to make them look the way they did. Cutting the locs I started felt like it was cutting a part of me as they fell and for him I knew it felt like a weight lifted, considering the circumstances.

"I got it the best looking way I could."

"Shit, you done worked the clippers plenty times over." Easy stated standing up and looking in the mirror.

Knock Knock Knock

Both of us looked toward the camera and noticed it was one of our regulars. It was Ro, one of our fine ass neighbors and regulars so we eased up and Easy opened the door with the towel still clipped around his shoulders. "Ooooh man, you cut your hair off, bro?"

"Yeah man, I needed to change it up like always." Easy said rubbing his hands together while he went over to the couch and sat down going under the coffee table and pulled out the box filled with weed and all the shit to get you right.

I went on to clean up while they made the sell. "That's some new shit?"

"Yeah, got wax, crumbles and liquid too." Easy answered. "Me and Choppa tried the crumbles and maaaann it had us so loaded we forgot the the fucking AC was broke in this bitch."

"We was stupid loaded until that sweat started rolling down my titties." I laughed while putting the locs in a bag. Easy said he wanted to burn them.

"Let me get some of that then and my usual, Shon been bugging out I might have to get her something new to try." He said handing Easy the hundred-dollar bill. Just like I knew, this dude wasn't coming to our door for anything under a hundred dollars, Shon too. Easy set him a package together and he was on his way.

"What the fuck?" I heard Easy say. I turned to see him looking at the camera and unmarked cars lined up around the perimeter. It was easy for Easy to get a view of things he is not allowed to and then again, we never did follow any rules in any apartment.

"Oh fuck, they know Easy, they know." I said my tone was almost in a whisper as if they could hear us.

"We done been in bigger jams, Love." Easy said. "They got you, they got me." I don't know there were so many cars and people outside and there is really no way out this motherfucker.

EASY

FOUR DAYS AGO

Choppa counted out twenty-five grand in blue faces on the round glass table before me and Spider, better known as my Cali plug. He was locked up with my cousin Nardi for five years in the feds. Nardi is the reason I chose to bring my hustle to the west coast because he knew I could do a lot with a little. My circle is nonexistent it's just me and Choppa I only have associates. My family went their way, and I went about mine with my woman beside me.

"It's all there," Choppa let out as she sat back in the chair. I knew it was all there I had counted it already ten times before we came.

Spider smiled and looked at me and extended his fist, we bumped, and he stood. "Be right back." When he left the room, it only took a minute for him to return with a duffle bag. I knew that wasn't what I paid for by the looks alone. His smile was mischievous, and I figured he was up to something.

"Man, what the fuck is that?" I asked with a smile.

"Listen, Nardi looked out for me in the feds, and he told me when I see you to bless your game. That was his only favor." Spider replied opening the bag. He pulled out vacuumed sealed pounds of weed and a few jars of crumble and wax shit that I had heard a lot about. "The thing about being in a legal state is nothing is off limits." Spider gloated.

"Shiiit, I see." I told him.

"What your cousin did for me is more than what is in this bag. He really saved my life on some real shit cuz," Spider stated with conviction. Nardi grew up in the wild Magnolia projects and he was thorough as they came, and we all ran together just so happen before Hurricane Katrina Nardi got pinched on a trip to Texas and was picked up by the feds.

"He one of the last real ones left out here." I spoke.

BAP. BAP. BAP.

Spider's brain and blood splattered all over the table and Choppa was holding the Glock and let it rest at her side. "Too bad you was a sewer rat more than a spider." She stated and grabbed the duffle and slid it over to me.

"Go through and see what else this nigga got and let's roll." I told her and scooped the money in the duffle Spider gave me.

Nardi had sent word that when Spider get served his due date, then Nardi will be paid hefty and so will I. It was no honor in these streets and none for a snitch like Spider who had gotten a fellow dope boy put away for twenty-five years. My cousin looked out for him because he saw a price tag attached to him, so it was only right to keep niggas off his head until his release six months ago.

Choppa returned with another bag full of weed, money and some more shit.

2 0 7

"Let's go." She said heading for the door.

"Hold on," I told her and walked through and found the room where the cameras were and took the system apart and stuffed the recording box into the lighter bag. "Now, let's roll." I spoke. We headed out the house and put the duffles in the trunk of the old Honda Civic and got in. I let my locs cover my face and Choppa had her mask on and we casually left his cul de sac where Spider lived.

We rode approximately ten minutes, and our car was still parked outside the body shop, and I whipped into the lot and hopped out. Choppa was bobbing her head to *No Friends* by EST Gee and Yo Gotti. When I turned the car off, "Grab the fifteen grand and then go get in a car." I told her.

Choppa's thickness slid out the car smoothly and closed the door and then I noticed Shawty coming out the office. The lot was filled with cars that was either halfway painted or just parked. "Yo, N.O," He said walking over to the car.

I opened the door and Choppa walked to our ride and I turned to Shawty, "Oh, you know I got ya together." I told him rubbing my hands together as I went to the trunk and gave him a pound of weed and bundles of rolled hundreds. "Send that to Nardi, he expecting that ASAP. And that there greenery for you."

"*Love*, bro." Shawty stated with conviction. I know he wasn't expecting anything but it's only right anybody in the play get a cut somehow that's how I was brought up in the game.

"My cousin speak highly of you and that's a hard thing for that nigga to do." I informed him. I watched the street and handed him the key to the car he'd let us use. Many underworld niggas came through Shawty's spot to get a hot car to pull a move and they paid him well. When you return it, he either changes everything or breaking it apart for something else.

Nardi being in the feds had gained him a plethora of people who owed him favors he was well known in the federal pen and highly respected. From what I hear and what I know he is a real stand-up dude and a vicious villain.

"Yeah, he is man that keep his word and always tell me to make sure I take care of you and I'm happy you here." I felt weird hearing both niggas say the same shit about how Nardi speak about me. He's the only one from our family that I keep in distant contact with because of the way I move and what I'm into out here.

"Fasho, we was brought up to never put each other in a bad situation." I said as I grabbed the two duffels and headed to his car. "I'll check with you in a few days."

"That's right." Shawty said after smoothly putting pound under his shirt. "Alright bro, do that because I will be talking to Nardi and seeing about this other lick he been talking about."

I stopped and turned around at the sound of favorite word, "What other lick?" I asked intrigued by his words.

"Some white dudes from Colorado coming in with an organic strain, grown from some shit that came from Jamaica and I hear it's the best shit smoking." Shawty explained. "Spider had good shit, but he was stingy, but these dudes travel by vans from Colorado and word is they have about two hundred or better in each van." Shawty was the eyes and ears of all money-making opportunity and criminal activity in the area.

The trunk opened and put the bags in and scanned the block. "What Nardi got to do with that?" I asked. "They can drive pounds like that?"

"One of the white dudes who own a share have a brother in prison for murdering his girlfriend about fifteen or so years ago and they locked up together." Shawty explained, I was all ears. "The brother in prison is a racist cracker and he sent a ol' massa ass nigga to get a pack from Nardi and call himself not paying him back."

I tugged at my beard as the conversation was getting better. "He don't like nobody playing with his product."

"Shit no, say the white boy been in there popping big shit since his brother got that money and flaunting it in his face."

I laughed. "So Nardi on the chess board thinking about what he can do to the cracker pockets."

"You already know. He say he letting him laugh and keke and the whole while he baking a cake." Shawty stated. "In fact, he wanted me to run it to you about getting the first pick at getting it done."

"Dirty work and take the pack?" I quizzed.

Shawty nodded.

"Tell that nigga my prices went up and call me." I said before walking around the driver side.

"Gotcha bro." Shawty said sliding back in the lot. Choppa already had the car running when I got in and I put it in drive and pulled off.

"What he talking about?" Choppa asked.

"Two hundred pounds up next and some white dudes. Dirty." I replied.

"Hmph, from him or Nardi?"

"Nardi, you know that's the only one I'm getting my hitlist from." I stated.

I felt Choppa's hands run from the root down, "I know, Bae."

We drove over to the condos we rented a few times and parked the car and popped the trunk. Choppa and I both got out at the same time and headed for the trunk to get the duffles and transferred them into our Honda Accord to head to the apartment where we lived.

"Shit, this motherfucker is heavy." I realized as I tried to hunk it in the trunk.

This time Choppa was in the driver seat. I got in and we coasted until we got to our shack at the Vista.

"It's so goddamn hot I know this motherfucking maintenance man didn't come fix this air yet." I complained as we walked to our apartment. I noticed Whisper walking to the elevator and shook my head because that shit barely worked. "Girl, you better hope that raggedy motherfucker move."

She smirked. "I'm over it let me catch these stairs."

"That's your best out baby," I told her as we headed to our apartment. I put the key and when the door opened heat greeted us and I was pissed off because we didn't have to put up with this shit every day or every other month seems like.

"Fuck, I'm sweating from the heat out here and now it's heat in this bitch too." Easy complained as he went into the small bedroom and put the duffle on the bed, and I turned the box fans on to circulate the air a little. He took his shirt off and showed off all his ink work. He is a fanatic when it comes to his body art everything was a representation of his life and interests.

2 1 2

I opened the bag I had in my hand it was the shit Spider showed us and Easy had laid out money, ten pounds two jars of crumbs and more money- hundreds only. "No wonder this one was heavier."

"Yeah, I found that in the back room of the house." I told him as I looked at the names written on the tape.

"What you bussin' open first?"

I was overwhelmed looking at all the flavors, "London Pound Cake mixed with some of that crumb shit."

"Ouuu, go hard then." Easy said walking behind me and grabbing and caressing my titties and ran them down to my pussy. I bit my bottom lip and smiled as I pushed my against his dick. "Hmph, let me go shower and you handle that."

"What we eating tonight?" I asked.

"What we have?" He asked. "Fuck, it's so hot in this bitch I can eat a turkey sandwich or something." He said and I laughed because he was not lying.

"We have steak and chicken in there." I told him. "I can do a poboy or something with that." I suggested.

He moved past me and over to the closet to pull out Nike shorts and a towel while I put all the shit away besides what we were going to smoke.

I went to the kitchen and pulled out everything I needed for our dinner and got started. I turned on HaSizzle *"Getcha Sum"* and I was shaking my ass all in the kitchen with the beat.

"Aye, somebody knocking Bae," Easy hollered from the room.

I stopped cooking and went to look at the camera and spotted Ro. I smiled inside he was a fine motherfucker, and it was always a pleasure to serve him. "What up." I asked opening the door.

He smiled and slid me a blue hundred-dollar bill. I laughed, "Come on in." I told him and Easy came from the bedroom with his shirt in hand and gun tucked in his shorts.

"What up Ro," Easy greeted with his hand extended to bump fist.

"Shit, getting me and Shon something to get high to." Ro replied he was a real smooth nigga and his people ran the building and dude always kept us informed about anything suspect to fallback from. "What up E!" Ro greeted.

"Shit, hot and hungry." Easy said. "Aye, man holla at your people bout this shit for me."

"I gotcha." Ro assured.

"How Shon doing?" I asked while fixing Ro's package. "Bae, check the steak in the oven for me since I done started this already."

"It smells good in this bitch, bro." Ro complimented and scrolled in his phone.

"We had fried steaks the other day and some bake chicken thighs from the night before, so I'm basically warming it up and gonna cut it up and make a poboy out of it." I stated shrugging my shoulders. "Them steaks was tender as a bitch."

"Fuckin right." Easy agreed. "These can come out because we don't want to dry it out." He added pulling them out and setting them on the counter.

I finished up with Ro and he was out the door. "So, what's this shit with Nardi now?"

"White dudes who grow they own shit gonna have about two hundred or more pounds coming in soon. I'm going over there tomorrow and run it with Shawty."

"Bae, I think we can maintain with what we have now from Spider and get into something else." I reasoned while getting our meal together. Instantly I could feel a little tension.

"Choppa, you already know when I said we was coming to Cali I have some shit to do for my cousin. That's the only family besides you that I even *fuck* with, and you know me and Nardi can't talk right now because I'm here and I'm making some moves for him and you know we communicating through other people." Easy explained. "We can maintain; however, I got shit that was already in play and you know. Not only to maintain bae but go out the country and shit. Right now, I'm making big ass moves to do everything we both want to do."

"Okay, I was just saying. I know he's your cousin, we don't want to be doing this for too long or get ourself in a fucked up situation behind you cousin and his prison rivals."

"Look, for now on baby you just stay here and sell the weed and let me do what I gave my word on." Easy told me so nonchalant. "I understand what you saying and how you feel I have to do what I have to and I'm not explaining that shit anymore."

"Okay, fine." I said not wanting to argue. Maybe one day he will see that his soul will not rest with all this shit on his conscious that Nardi is putting him in now. This is not my first kill and I'm sure it won't be the last and each one is etched in my mind. I feel like any day now they will one day find me and haul me off to prison. My fucked up mentality mixed with Easy's we were better off without putting this energy or stress on our families.

Hurricane Katrina couldn't have come at a better time. It was a time to get some money from the government and make money. We reaped full benefits from housing to financial assistance and food stamps for a long time. Hustling has always been in us so wherever we lived we had either plates or weed rolling out the door and sometimes it was both. Sometimes we had to get dirty and get the fuck out the state because we were real life hood rich Bonnie and Clyde. I would pull a trigger quicker than Easy and I guess that's what made me feel like we shouldn't do this anymore.

I plated our food and fixed our drinks while he twists up a backwood and cone. Easy stood up and opened the door and the weird dude who looks like a nerd, or some shit stepped in. Easy served him while I sat our plates on the coffee table and turned the music down. "Alright." Easy said and the dude left.

"That motherfucker is weird."

"Easy laughed. "That man just trying to get high like us, ya heard me." He said locking the door and sitting down on the sofa beside me.

Neither one of wasted time diving into the sandwich and we smashed it pretty quickly. "That was so damn good." I said leaning back on the sofa.

Easy's phone ring on the table and it was an unsaved number, he grabbed it and answered. "What up." I couldn't hear the other person. I got up and grab our empty plates and brought them to the small kitchen. "Alright, I'm on the way." Easy said getting. "You rolling Choppa or you gon chill?"

I smacked my lips, "Yes, but wait." I told him and poured a shot of Henny and downed it. "Whew."

Easy went to the bedroom and returned with my gun and purse. "Don't forget the blunt." He told me. I grabbed all the things and was on his trail to the car after he locked the door. We swiftly got to the ride and Easy cranked the car and I lit the blunt before he pulled out the small ass lot. "I thought you was staying in your lane and shit."

"I am, I will stand down when I get ready and today ain't the day." I replied.

Nardi is a shot caller in the federal prison system for Louisiana and it represent. They couldn't stand for him to touch down on any compound. The last three years they had him California and from my knowledge from Easy is Nardi had gotten plugged in a lot of connects who were in on trump charges but still running shit on the streets. It's Nardi and Easy's mission to get the bag and blood along the way. Easy had only given me just enough information but as days went by and things happened it all started to unfold. I just don't my man out here by himself.

The weed was getting a hold on me, and I rolled the window down to catch some of this fresh air. Easy tried passing it back and I tapped out.

"Ahaha. Yo ass can't handle this shit." Easy joked as we pulled out front Shawty's home. I instantly was on alert because they never had a meeting at the house it was always at the shop.

"I'm done with that." I laughed as I peeped the neighborhood. California was everything I imagined it would be except this goddamn heat. The sun don't play no games.

We sat out front while Easy finish smoking the blunt.

"You ready?" Easy asked as he tossed the roach smooth out the window.

"Yeah." Easy opened his door and I followed, and we both walk up to the house with him behind me. Easy reached around me and knocked and a few seconds later Shawty's wife open the door.

"Hey," She greeted.

217

"Hey, how you doing Angela?" I greeted with a smile.

"I'm good girl, Shawty said meet him in the back yard." Angela stated. "I was in on Zoom with my old colleagues." She said.

"Oh alright." I said and moved past Easy.

"Hey there Easy, he in the back waiting on y'all."

We headed to the back and it evident Easy has been here before without me. Angela and I met and always talked when she would be at the shop with Shawty. She's a schoolteacher and tutor on the side and everything a bitch like me not, but we have a cordial and friendly bond. She is just as hood as me because she's from South Central and still have her ghetto vibes.

Shawty had a garage in the back and Easy entered. They slapped hands and Shawty looked over to me, "what's up Choppa." He spoke.

"Hey there Shawty," I replied. The garage was set up like a true man cave.

"Let me steal this one from you," Shawty stated pointing to Easy. "You can help yourself to anything at the bar, turn the TV whatever." He told me.

"Pour me a shot of henny, bae." Easy said as I casually just walked behind the bar and fixed both of us a cup of Hennessey. I gave him his straight and mixed mine with coke.

The two left out the garage and left me to play with all the toys in the man cave. I snuggled into the red plush recliner I relaxed with my drink and positioned my gun in place just in case.

"Nardi gave me the information about the lick, and he want you to get it done." Shawty got right to the point. "Two vans and it's two drivers no followers or none of that. It's three hundred pounds in both vans." He explained. "I got a spot to bring the vans and I have a ride set up for you to and from."

I thought about what Shawty said. "Change of plans. I got a spot for the vans, and I'll let you know when to pull up." I stated.

"Come on Easy bro, this shit is big."

"You don't think I know that." I scuffed. "I'm putting me and my people life and freedom on the line and if it's as much as you say it is why would I place it in your hand to know *everything*." I told him. "Nardi know I don't do snake business, talk to your big dog about what we discussed and holla at me." I told him.

"Aright, I feel you. I just don't want any blow back from Nardi about negotiating his plan."

"Yeah, well…it's your assignment homie." I told him.

2 1 9

Shawty sighed and shook his head. "Easy, he is counting on me to get you to do it this way because these dudes are dangerous just as much as they are racist."

"You can plead all week long but if Nardi want me to do it, it will be on my terms. He knows my work is thorough." I stated. "Hit me back when y'all in agreement."

Shawty seemed to feel defeated by my demands however he didn't know what he was asking of me and my girl and whoever we hired to get this shit done. Why would I let a nigga like Shawty set the play and Nardi is aware I don't take shit lightly. Never did let no nigga set a trap for me and I won't start. "Well alright, I'll let him know that and it can go from there then because I'm just the messenger and I do what I can for him and y'all know one another better than I do, so that's what it is." Shawty said.

I extended my hand to shake. "It's all good business when you fucking with me Shawty, I'm sure my time here has shown and proven that." Then I let his hand go.

"I know bro, you been one hundred with me." He agreed. "We good, Nardi really don't trip long as it gets handled."

"Exactly. You learning." I chuckled.

"Definitely." Shawty replied with a smile. "You want a drink or something?"

"Nah, I'm good." I declined. "We bout to take us a lil walk or something and enjoy the rest of the night."

"Ahhh, yes, it's beautiful tonight and not as hot as earlier."

"Shit yeah." I agreed. "I appreciate you being the middleman for me and cuz but we can't get caught slipping on the same line until all business is handled."

"He already told me Easy."

We headed back to the man cave and Choppa was sitting back with a cup in her hand and she smiled when she seen me enter. "You ready, ma?"

She nodded and stood up. "I done poured a lot of Hennessy in this because I feel so good." She said with a mischievous smile and handed me the cup.

"Nah, I'm good, bae." I said and turned to Shawty. "Hit me up Shawty when you get the rest of the information on the date them niggas coming through so I can put the shit in motion."

"Oh, I'mma have that soon as the morning come." Shawty stated with conviction.

"Perfect." I said as Choppa and I walked out to the car. "Peace." I told him as we headed to

the beach to take a walk.

****

"Get the fuck out!" I heard a female screaming outside and I looked out the window peeling the cheap curtain Choppa hung a week ago up, and when I saw who it was, I went back to sit on the sofa smoking my backwood. It's after three in the morning, and it was always something with that girl and her old man. The shit was a repeat episode of the young, stupid, and the restless. They didn't get tired of fighting and fucking because the bitch stayed pregnant. We haven't been here that long and feel like we done witnessed this chick entire life of babies and drama with the same no-good nigga who only want to buy half grams and waste a nigga time. I still look out because she does put him through it even when he is trying, but it just ain't good enough.

"Who is that?" Choppa asked coming from the bedroom with only a thing and bra on and a cup in hand.

"Crazy man and his old lady."

"Again?" She asked going into the kitchen.

"Yeah." I replied blowing out the thick cloud of smoke. I heard her cracking the ice tray to get some ice. "Fix me a cup with some kool aid in it." I said.

"Yo ass got thirsty when I came in here?" She snapped back.

"Yeah," I laughed. "I really did on some shit. And it don't matter when the fuck I get thirsty when I say fix something, just do it." I told her. She laughed but I was serious in that moment. Sometimes she had a habit of talking back to a nigga and I been letting her ass slide, and I do my best to laugh the shit off but shit like that bothers me.

"You ain't been to sleep yet?" She asked handing me the cup.

"Not yet." I replied as she sat beside me, and I passed the blunt over to her. "Been catching plays all night." I said pulling the box from under the table out. "Go in the back and count that." I told her handing the box to her. Since she's been asleep the door was busy, and my phone was jumping for sells and I wasn't turning anything down. Though I had bigger plays over my head I still enjoyed the chaos of the traps and the Vistas felt like a trap just like all the ghettos we lived.

The one thing I don't like about California is the damn heat... it's the sun following us around. It was eight at night and Easy and I were laying in wake of the vans to pass through, and it is still hot as the fuck. Easy blew out a cloud of smoke and it simmered around the car before he passed the blunt to me. "We have about twenty minutes." I stated looking down at my watch before hitting the weed. Instantly I started choking.

Easy flipped the headlights and the car across the street hit theirs and we gathered our bag filled with guns and supplies. I hit the blunt again hard and passed it to Easy who held it between his lips and slipped the gloves on his hands and I followed suit. The first flick meant twenty minutes and the second hit mean boots to the ground. Down to the last minute we held our smoke ritual before hitting the lights and then we proceeded out the car dressed in all black.

Easy had a crew of guys he used on jobs and so far, they hadn't let us down. They too had on all black and ready for whatever. I checked the street, and we had a mile to walk and not get noticed, it was complex because of the long walk however the preparation had to be on point down to the second. We walked down the street as unnoticed as possible until we got to the spot we needed to be and lay in wait of the vans to pass by.

The watch struck twelve and we got into position to ambush in the middle of the street. Easy was laying out in the middle of the street like he had passed out with a half pint of gin in his hand like an alcoholic. I wanted to crack up laughing while one of his men was acting like he was trying to wake him up. Suddenly, headlights were approaching, and I heard the whistle that it was our target. The first van halted at Easy and partner in the street and blew the horn for them to move two of us walked into the street and I raised my gun and hit the passenger rider in the head twice. I walked around to the driver side with another one of the men and the man driving was scared as fuck, fear was in his eyes as if he knew the ending is near. I read the words on the side FLOWER POTS, I grinned inside at the simple but clever name for a weed company.

The second whistle indicated that we had got the first van and all others proceeded to get the others. The driver window was shot and one of the men grabbed the driver out and jumped in to put the van in drive. The driver tried to run away screaming and I hit him in the back and walked over to him and shot him in the head twice. No witnesses left behind a few more shots rang out and I hopped in the driver seat with Easy on the bloody passenger seat.

"Let's go then." Easy stated. I put the van in drive, and we were headed to the garage to get the business clear.

The drive was wild, and the adrenaline pumped through me as I pulled up to the garage, we heard the sirens in a distance. We all parked and hopped out the vans. Everybody pulled their masks off, and they unloaded the vans of bud into the back of an air conditioner company van. I was pleased with the efficiency of the crew and once they were done Easy paid them a fee and vowed to keep in touch. These guys admired Easy and the way he conducts business, and so do I he was so smooth in everything. It was like his hands were always clean and I would prefer it that way.

They all piled in a SUV and headed back to their ride as Easy, and I headed to Shawty spot to drop the van off. Shawty sat out front on the porch smoking as we pulled in and got out the van. "Heyyyy." He greeted.

"What's up," Easy spoke handing him the keys.

Shawty pointed to a duffle sitting next to him on the ground and he picked it up and handed it to Easy with a wide smile on his face. "Nardi is super excited about this one."

"I bet he is." Easy stated unzipping the bag revealing blue hundreds all the way through the bag. It was definitely easy money made tonight.

A car pulled up in front of Shawty's house and Easy looked at Shawty and extended his hand. "Alright homie, pleasure doing bidness wit ya."

"Always, did you grab you something to chief on back home?"

Easy answered, "Nah, I bring it all back."

Shawty went to the back of the van and Easy looked at me, "get in the car bae," he said handing the bag to me. I did as told and watched them closely as they went to the back of Shawty's house and returned five minutes later. Easy was laughing and got in the car as I slid over.

I didn't know the cleanup side of Easy's business deals all I knew was the plan of the mission. He kept a lot of those details to himself, and I loved that. I leaned over and put my head on his arm and rested until we returned to the car. We got out and hopped in the car and headed to the apartment and suddenly I started to feel queasy, and my stomach turned flips. I hated that feeling of emptiness afterwards.

When we pulled up to the apartments, we noticed our neighbor standing outside smoking a cigarette sitting on the hood of her car. It was busted up as fuck and looked like it had one more bump to hit before it fell apart. "She need to let them people come pick that bitch up for $200." Easy let out and I giggled a little. "I swea' ta gawd." Easy looked over at me with a handsome smile and I reached my hand over and rubbed his chin. "Take the bag inside and I'll be back, bae, gotta drop this motherfucka off." Easy told me.

"Okay, hurry back." I told him as I got out the car and headed to the courtyard to get to our apartment. Tonight, it was warm, and it was quiet for once I didn't see my girl Jamaica or the homie Shooter sitting out tonight which was unusual for them. I walked to our door and put the key in and entered and locked it behind me then headed to the bedroom and slid the duffle bag under the bed. I undressed and ran a shower as usual I cleaned up decent and got out then went to find something really quick to cook until Easy make it back.

When I made it back home it was three hours later, and Choppa was sitting up on the sofa with a mad look on her face. I knew she was gonna be awake and pissed because I didn't come right back. "Why you not sleep?" I asked.

"What the fuck Easy, you think you could have told me you had some other shit to do while you were dropping the car off."

"Choppa, it's all good, love, don't get yourself worked up for nothing." I said and the look already said she wasn't having it. I went to the bedroom and to the bathroom and took the clothes off and sat on side the bed.

"How the fuck you say don't be worked up for nothing and it's not nothing…it's you not coming home when you said you was." Choppa was livid. She wanted to catch me in some cheating shit, but that wasn't me to do that to her.

"Listen, bae, lay down and get you some rest. You don't have anything to worry about." I assured her.

"Unhuh." She said as she climbed in bed.

"You made any money since you been back, I see you turn the red lights on." The LED lights we put up were for anybody in our building to know red meant don't knock and green meant knock.

"Well, I didn't feel like being bothered after all that, Easy." She replied. I left her in the room with her attitude because truth be told I didn't want to be bothered either. I had doubled back to Shawty's house and stole the AC van and hid it at a partner of mine's storage garage. It would all fall on Shawty for not moving that van like he was supposed to. What Shawty didn't know was Nardi had already put it in my ear to stiff him too, all in one night, killing two birds with one stone.

I heard some music playing and Choppa was rapping along with Money Man *"Boss Up"* and I started rapping with it too. It took my mind off what tomorrow may bring wondering what Shawty next move will be. Once I finished showering and dressed, I pulled my hair back and went into the front dressed only in Nike shorts and turned the green lights on to let them know shop is open since I wasn't sleepy and seem like Choppa wasn't either, though at times she needed music to sleep.

The door was active soon as I turned the light on, and Choppa hadn't come out the room as the music played. I checked in on her and she was knocked out sleep as I knew she would be. I was up until the sun came up watching some shit called the Umbrella Academy, I heard Choppa stirring around in the bedroom at seven o' clock. I turned the TV on the morning news and got up to make some coffee. We normally go to Hilltop Coffee and get us some, but I figured after last night it was good to make it at home.

Choppa entered the kitchen, "Good morning." I greeted her wrapping my hands around her waist. She was soft and thick in the right places; I pulled her close to me and inhaled her essence. She snug into my arms like a baby and leaned her head on my chest.

"Good morning." She said back.

"You feel like making breakfast?"

She nodded her head and I let her go. "You was up all night again?"

"Shit yeah and smoking like a Navajo chief." I told her.

She laughed, "you need to start getting more sleep, Easy." She stated. "Go lay down."

"I know bae, I be having all type of shit on my mind." I told her.

"You spoke with Nardi yet?"

"Nah, but I should be speaking with him soon." I replied heading into the bedroom to lay down. "I left the light on too. We need to get off all this shit we got right now."

"Alright, I'll be up. I need to wash our clothes and clean up this hot motherfucker anyway." Choppa answered.

Before my head hit the pillow I was out like a light.

It was after five in the evening when Easy woke up again. He would exhaust himself so bad until the point he had to wait to crash out when he did get some rest. I had done a good bit of making plays all day and watched the news to make sure what happened last night hadn't made the news and luckily it hadn't as I knew it would.

"Roll something up." Easy said as he got up and went into the bathroom and closed the door. He had a routine when he wake up sleep, shit and shower. I rolled the blunt and put it in the ashtray for him.

When he came out he was naked and then he slipped into some shorts and a tank. He entered the living room and picked up the ashtray from the table and lit it before heading to the front door. "You made breakfast?"

"Yeah, ate and everything. Tried waking you up but you was sleeping down and didn't move." I replied.

Easy laughed as he opened the door and instantly the smell of BBQ rushed inside our apartment. We were so wrapped up in what we had going on we totally forgot about it was a holiday weekend, at least I did. Instantly upon the smell I was filled with nausea and my stomach was queasy I wanted to throw up. "Oh, they got it going on out here, bae."

"I know I was just talking to Whisper, and she seemed a little out of it and Shon was on some other shit. I don't know what's going on with everybody today." I replied.

"You saw Shooter, he said he wanted to holla at me bout something."

"Oh, talking about dude from Atlanta?"

"Yea." Easy answered.

"He left out the courtyard about an hour ago." I stated.

I could hear everybody outside and stood in the door while Easy sat in one of the chairs we kept outside and lit his blunt. "I want to cut this shit off my head, bruh."

I was taken back by his request. "What?"

"I'm getting tired of it." He said, his tone was he wasn't negotiating my fuss if I had one and I do.

"Alright." Going along with it, he passed the blunt to me and I hit and passed it back. I watched as Shon and the others were all standing out and around including a lady, we all called Grandma she was the sweetest but also had an edge about her. She had some granddaughters who lived with her and one in particular I liked so much named Jamaica. Me, her, and Shon would smoke from time to time when we could, and it was rare I hung with anyone but these two at the Vistas was prime stock.

"Come on, let's go get started on my hair I wanna get right before the fourth come." Easy said heading back inside with the chair. I couldn't believe he was doing this shit. He went grabbed the scissors and started cutting them out and if I had ten mouths, they all would be on the floor. I couldn't explain the hurt I felt about this and him bringing his ass in later than expected made me wonder what the fuck is really up with this nigga.

It took him all night to get the dreads cut out and he wanted me to cut the shorter pieces off and taper it down. I was feeling like a nervous wreck in the inside, but I had to hold my shit together until whatever it is gets revealed.

Easy's phone rung and it was Nardi burner number I brought the phone to him, and I left them to talk. When he finished talking, he came out the bathroom with the scissors and clippers. "Man, we got some bad news here," Easy started.

"What?"

"Shawty was killed this morning."

"Huh? So Nardi didn't get his money?"

"Oh, you know Nardi got his." Easy replied. "Shawty wasn't gonna be long term anyway." He went on. "Shit, you want to finish this tomorrow?"

"Yeah." I answered. "So, you mean Shawty dead and you sure this won't blow back on us?"

"Choppa, baby I'm sure." He told me.

"How you know for sure, Easy?"

Easy stood up and looked at me, "Woman, listen, I put all this shit together out here, I know everything that's happening. The only thing you need to worry about is where to go to next when we leave here."

"See, Easy, you making a lot of plans without me," I pointed out. "When did we decide to move?"

"The day we came in this motherfucka, Chop." He replied with a stern look. "This is not home, we don't have a home, remember, never get comfortable. We are home for each other." He scolded. "Act like you know, I told you about making friends and getting attached and shit."

I sighed and stormed into the room and slammed the door. "Stop slamming them raggedy ass doors before the fucking building come down." Easy shouted and I couldn't help but laugh at his stupid ass. No lie, I was ready to go after last night something about it seemed off and I couldn't help but think that shit was going to bite us in the ass. I spent the rest of my day and night in bed and let Easy do whatever it is he wanted. I was in a funk, and I needed my little space I did have in the apartment.

The sun had no fucking business keeping it one hundred with us on this good ass day. I rubbed my head a Choppa was getting ready to cut my hair and some of our neighbors looked at me like I was a new tenant. The pits were once again blazing, and a few tables were set outside in the courtyard while Shon fine ass helped put some stuff out. This definitely felt like back home in the projects where everybody pitched in and did something. It was like one big ass family, or some shit and I loved it over here especially Cali as a whole, but I knew, and Choppa knew that it's short lived for us. We had done a lot of shit here and got away and soon enough we didn't want anyone connecting the dots on us. If the maintenance man could do his job a little better, I may reconsider but it didn't look promising. I need to talk to Ro about it and see what he can do because I know with some cool air pumping through Choppa, and I can commit a little longer to The Vistas.

I went back inside when I heard my phone ring, "Yo."

"Aye Cuz, what up." Nardi spoke in the phone.

"What up," I said sitting on the couch.

"Man, this white boy going crazy bout his brother in here." Nardi stated with a menacing laugh.

"That's his problem." I stated.

"Exactly." Nardi agreed. "I got my people to get that from the spot and he want you to meet with him on Rodeo and pick your money up for that one and we good and squared away." Nardi said. "You know I was gonna bless your game."

I laughed, "Yeah I already knew that cuz, you always did."

"I had to get that nigga Shawty out my business because he was being too nosey wanting to know where you live and that sent up a red flag for me and I blacked out on that."

"Right, fuck his soft ass." I stated.

Nardi laughed, "I ain't going to lie he was doing his shit with me for a while and with you but lately he started moving kinda funny and I have to make adjustments before I let any motherfucka come and fuck up our shit and any other shit."

"Shit, I understand, completely." I told him.

"What y'all got planned for today?"

"BBQ and some good old times, smoking and drinking." I replied. "I sent one of our neighbors to the store yesterday to get us some liquor."

"That's what's up, well cuz, y'all enjoy and tell Choppa I said what's up and I'm praying y'all get some babies soon." Nardi laughed.

I laughed too, "I sure will tell her ass." I said, "Alright fam, talk to you later." We hung up the phone.

Choppa came out the room with the short and body fitting dress on that hugged her natural curves exposing her tattoos on her arm and leg. She is so perfect in my eyes and her beautiful brown skin and thick lips gave me hope in natural women. Choppa was the epitome mixture of beauty, class, ruthless and ghetto. She was loyal to the bone and had my back through whatever and I respected and protected her to no ending, she'd earned that from me. One day soon I pray to make her an honest woman.

"They are jamming out there," Choppa said as she strutted to the open door of this fucking matchbox and looked out waving. "Wheww shit and hot as fish grease out here too." She added. "Goddamn, can we get some air traveling in here."

"Shit, my thoughts exactly, are you ready to hit my hair up?"

"Not really, but let's get started I guess." She answered.

****

Later that evening
4:52PM

"Oh fuck, they know Easy, they know." Choppa said in a nervous whisper as if they could hear her.

"We done been in bigger jams, Love." Easy said. "They got you, they got me." He assured. There were so many police cars and undercovers filing in as they had knocked over the smoking BBQ pit and tables with the food on them and got in position. Easy snatched the lights off from around the window as he had a blunt in between his lips as if he couldn't do anything without smoking.

Choppa went to the bedroom and looked out and noticed the agents had the building surrounded. She started to panic feeling closed in. "Bae, hold it together, please." Easy said trying to calm her nerves.

"Easy they may have had cameras on the van or a tracking device or something. Maybe someone told. Those niggas you work with could've said something." She stated.

"You are overthinking, Bae." Easy tried his best to get Choppa to think rationally and he understood her worry but with Easy everything is always clean.

"Nardi could have set us up, a motherfucka who don't have nothing to lose."

"CHOPPA!" He stated with a scold look on his face. "Fucking chill and let this shit play out." Easy told her as he watched the police officers walk back and forth then one stood in front of their door.

Easy took a deep breath because he didn't know what type of games was being played around here. "Check the back window and see if anybody by the kitchen." Easy said.

Choppa went to the kitchen window, "they have a car, but nobody is in it."

"Get the duffle with the money in it and stand by that window, put your tennis on."

Easy slipped his Vapormax on as he watched the cameras, he had calculated a blind spot and soon as they hit the window, they had to make a run for it to the car he kept parked around the corner. It was a hard task. Just then all the power went out in the building, and they heard a few loud screams and a loud bang. Easy and Choppa looked out the front window and all they seen was officers filing up the stairs.

Choppa gasped. "No, what the fuck?" she said in disbelief witnessing who they were there for.

"That's wild, I wonder what the fuck happen."

"This gotta be fake." Choppa let out. "A mistake or something."

"Aww man, that's wild." Easy said. The lights popped back on and Easy quickly opened the duffle he kept the weed in and revealed a vacuumed seal pack with **FLOWER POTS** stamped on top.

CHAPTER ONE
GRANDMA LU

"Arei! Jamaica! Get up!" my voice boomed through the tiny government subsidized apartment I shared with my two teenage granddaughters. The kitchen was a mess and there was no way, I would be cooking breakfast in a nasty sink-filled kitchen.

"What's up Granny?" Arei rubbed her eyes as she leaned on the door jamb connecting her room to the kitchen.

"Where is Jamaica?" I questioned lighting the cigarette that dangled from my lips as I repositioned the plants in the window.

"She should be in her room," Arei rebutted wiping cold from her eyes, visibly tired.

"Go to her room and see if she's in there,"

Some time passed before the both of them walked into the kitchen. Looking Jamaica over, I could tell she was up to something. She was by far one of the unslickest, try to be slick all the time muthafuckas I knew. She was just like her mammy, but we'll talk about her ass later.

"Why the fuck is my kitchen dirty and why the fuck ain't y'all handling business? Jamaica what happened to the one you said you had?" I questioned flicking ashes from the tip of my cigarette into the ashtray. In the background I could hear the front door quietly closing as Jamaica tried to talk over it.

"Grandma what had happened was…"

"Grandma what had happened was my ass! Who the fuck did you have in my house Jamaica?" Standing up to peer out of the window, I saw some lil nigga pimping through the courtyard. "Next time you bring your ass in here you better have some rent money lil' nigga!" I spat causing him to look up at the window and take off in a light sprint.

"What the fuck I tell you about sneaking them lil' nappy headed ass niggas in my house? Ain't nothing going on but the rent up in here so where the fuck the money at? I know he gave you more than a wet ass Jamaica Marie!"

"Granny what are you talking about?" Jamaica tried to kiss me on the cheek but was met with my hand. I didn't know where the hell her lips been.

"Back your ass up!" I pushed her away. "Y'all need to clean up this kitchen but before you do that, we need to find some girls. Money getting tight around here. We ain't been handling them like we used to,"

"I don't see how money tight Granny," Arei added her two cents. Just last month we had four girls. The going rate ain't low for thick hotties with exotic looks," she turned on the hot water preparing to wash the dishes.

"If I tell ya ass it's tight goddamnit it's tight. Don't question me!"

"Alright Granny go off, cause I'm not about to argue with you," Arei shook her head and commenced to washing the dishes that had littered the sink all night long.

"I was going to cook for you heffas but since you want to sass me and you want to be a little slut," I pointed at Jamaica who was now sweeping the floor, "Cook your own goddamn breakfast and go find me some girls!"

CHAPTER TWO

AREI

Granny ass be tripping, I started off today's entry in my journal. I don't know why in the fuck she thought it was so easy to lure girl's home under the guise that we're their *friends* and want to *help* only to have them sold off to the highest bidder to do God knows what. Some of the girls we brought to granny over the last couple of years actually came from families that gave a fuck about them. There were a few that were out bad, but just because we come from the hood don't mean we fucked up!

Hell, we weren't even fucked up in a technical sense. Sure, we were living in a government subsidized tenement, but we lived good. Had the best of everything thanks to grandmas under handed dealings. I was starting to feel a way about what she had us out here doing though. Like who would have their sixteen, and, seventeen-year-old grand-daughters out in South Central recruiting young girls to be trafficked? As soon as I graduate high school and go off to college, she, and Jamaica can have this shit.

244

After finishing my entry, I peeled myself up from the bed and looked through my closet for something to wear. It was the weekend and me and Jamaica were going down to Hollywood Blvd to see what or should I say who we could find so Granny could get off our asses.

*　　*　　*

Walking up and down the strip as if we were tourists, I kept my eyes open for anyone that seemed out of place. It was nothing to run across homeless girls or runaways on the boulevard, but we were looking for a certain type. Someone that could clean up well and be pleasing to the eye.

"I'm bout sick of this shit. I'm going to call Ray to come and pick me up. I'm tired of walking this bitch like a woman of the night," Jamaica scoffed.

"Damn… just leave me out here to work," I rolled my eyes and stepped out into the street to cross over to the opposite side. That's when my eyes fell upon just the right target. She was caramel complected, tall and slim-thick. She carried a backpack as she paced with her head down looking at her phone.

"Bingo! Hold off on that call," I put a little speed to it and bumped into the girl on purpose as I stepped up onto the curb.

"I'm so sorry," I apologized and noticed that she was crying. "Are you ok?" I feigned concern.

"My fucking boyfriend who I moved here to live with just put me out. I'm stuck with no way back home to Chicago," she sat on the bottom stair to Buffalo Wild Wings and bawled her eyes out. Jamaica gave me the look and I knew for sure we were about to finesse her ass into going home with us.

"Look, we were about to go inside to get some wings. We live with our grandma and I'm sure she would be ok with you staying with us, for a night or two while you figure something out," Jamaica quipped.

"Ain't no way we're going to leave you out here alone. Hollywood ain't safe for nobody," I offered a caring smile.

"Thank you cause being homeless on the street ain't the move." She, tried to smile through her tears. "I'm Jalisa by the way," she extended her hand.

"I'm Danni and that's my cousin Sherelle," I gave Jalisa our fake names.

Over wings and mixed drinks, thanks to our fake ids we got to know Jalisa a little bit better. We found out that she was a twenty-year old aspiring model from Chicago that met her *boyfriend* after he slid in her dm's on Instagram. One year and a one-way plane ticket later he left her ass stranded on Hollywood Blvd. Her family tried to talk her out of flying across the country for some nigga and have since cut her off since she didn't heed their advice.

Granny was going to be elated that we're back on business. Too bad for Jalisa, that we were setting her up for the okie doke. Like I've always done time and time again, I silently prayed for her as I did every girl we delivered to the unknown. With a smile, I paid the tab and we headed home.

CHAPTER THREE
JAMAICA

"You have a collect call from Corrine. To pay for the charges press five or hang up to deny the charges…" the automated voice boomed through the phone. Rolling my eyes, I pressed five and greeted my mother.

"Hey ma,"

"You don't have to sound so dry. I'm in here for you!" she had the nerve to cop an attitude and throw her reason for being behind bars in my face.

"If you had left the nigga when I first told you he violated, you wouldn't be in there," with nothing left to say I passed the phone to my grandmother who had the nerve to talk shit about the way I responded to her child. Both of them could kiss my ass!

In case you couldn't tell, I didn't fuck with my mother too hard. I was the product of a teenage mother that ran the streets and fucked with dope boys. One of her boyfriends used to put his hands on me. And by put his hands on me I mean down my pants and under my shirt.

The first time it happened I was nine years old. When I told her, she told me to keep it to myself. It wasn't until I was twelve that he thought it was a good idea to put his thang in my mouth, she walked in on it and used his gun to shoot him point blank in the head. I guess sucking his dick was far worse than him feeling me up.

The judicial system was a joke, rather than go easy on her for the crime, it was her third time getting locked up and you know how those California three strike laws went. Add to that the drugs and cash that was in our apartment when the cops came. For years I resented my mother. Her killing ol' boy didn't make me feel good nor safe. Instead, it freed me of having to look the woman who wanted to brush the shit he'd done to me under the rug in the face. Hence me living with my grandmother who's been a shady ass old lady all of my life.

Grandma done been in all kinds of shit from selling dope, running numbers, hoeing, and now trafficking. She was an old G from way back and since she was up in age and couldn't run around like she used to, she used me and Arei to do her shit. It was alright by me but Arei wasn't built for this life. Trust, if she found an out, she was going to take it. But for now, she abided by grandmother's rules.

Retreating to my bedroom, I slammed the door and picked my phone up off the dresser before lying across the bed. I didn't want to be bothered and since Arei and Jalisa were gone in the car we shared, my room would be my only safe haven at the moment. Opening the Instagram app, I keyed in my freak of the week, wife's username and went straight to her stories. Video and photos of them on their little date night flashed across the screen. Even knowing he was with her I texted his phone anyway.

My pussy so wet just thinking about you.

You should come scoop me tonight.

Three dots in a bubble appeared indicating that he was typing, then it disappeared. He didn't leave a reply but I was fully aware that he saw my message. Going back to the previous screen I went back to spying and making myself feel worse than before, but I couldn't stop looking. Ray and his wife were really cute together, and although I knew she was the love of his life, I couldn't help but enjoy the time he and I spent together. When it's just us, he makes me feel like I'm the only girl in the world. He dotes all over me and showers me with gifts and love. Even if it isn't real, I'll take it over receiving no love at all.

"Jamaica Marie Wilson!" Grandma yelled busting into my bedroom.

"You rang?" I looked over my shoulder and continued to lay on my stomach and look at my phone.

"I swear you one disrespectful little bitch! You look at me when I'm talking to you,"

Rolling over onto my back I stared at her blankly. Just because she could see my face didn't mean that I was listening to anything that she had to say.

"I'm going to need for you to respect your mother a little bit more. She gave up her life for you and left me to care for your ungrateful ass. You going to keep up the bullshit and I'm going to put your ass out on the street ya hear me!" she wagged a thick finger in my face.

Momentarily I stared her in the eyes before responding "You always come spewing idle threats. You know if I leave you ain't going to have nobody to bring you any girls then what you going to do?"

"I got Arei... don't think you do that much around here except for eat, sleep and shit. You ain't carrying your weight,"

"Whatever grandma," I stood up from my bed. "Arei got one foot in and one foot out. You bet not let her find out she not really your granddaughter because she's going to leave your ass high and dry,"

Leaving her with the doo doo face, I brushed past bumping her shoulder. I needed some weed in the worse way. Good thing Big Easy and his girl Choppa had it on the first floor. Car to get around in or not, I was getting the fuck out of this apartment and far away from grandma.

CHAPTER FOUR
GRANDMA LU

That lil' bitch Jamaica made my ass ache. If I had to choose between her and my daughter Corrine, I'd trade her ass in a New York minute. It seemed as if all the anger and hostility she had pinned inside for her mother, she unleashed on me. True enough we didn't have a normal grandmother/grandchild relationship, but I ain't never been a normal mutha fucka. I came from a long line of hustlers and was taught to get it by any means necessary. My mama hoed with the best of them, and so did I in conjunction with a whole lot of other things. One thing about me I was going to get it how I lived. I knew no other way. But for this heffa to threaten me about telling Arei I wasn't her grandmother for real was unacceptable and could lead my ass straight to prison.

Haleigh was the one and only girl trafficked that I held a soft spot for. Her parents kicked her out of the house because she had fucked around and got pregnant while she was just fifteen years-old. She was friends with my daughter Corrine and would come to our house all of the time. I gained a liking for the smart, pretty girl with the curly red hair.

2 5 1

She lived in my house from the time she found out she was pregnant all the way up until she gave birth. Then it happened... I went out to Vegas and my gambling ways got the best of me.

I spent my entire weekend on the roulette table until I'd lost every dime I had, literally. As luck would have it, I had Haleigh and Corrine with me. I was teaching them how to work the men at the table by way of finessing them out of cash. That's when I met Fabian, he was a young Italian mobster that had his hand in just about everything. He had a hard on for Corrine and even asked how much it would cost him to have her. Strapped for cash, I wasn't willing to let my daughter go but I did give him Haleigh. Fabian and I formed a lucrative friendship that I hid from people in the outside world. I felt bad for selling Haleigh off for profit, Fabian never told me where she was, but he let me know that she would be busy making his family money for years to come.

My way of making amends with my sins, I kept Haleigh's daughter and raised her as my grandchild. Ironically, she was now helping me put girls in the same world as her mother. Many nights I prayed that she was alive. And although I sometimes felt bad, if I had to choose between my child and someone else, Corrine would win every time.

Breaking out of my thoughts, I retreated to the living room. Firing up a cigarette, I inhaled deeply, filling my lungs with the smoke from the cancer stick. Picking up the phone, I dialed Fabian and let him know that I had a new girl and once I got her as comfortable as possible, he could pick her up. Jalisa was about to make me at least thirty grand richer. At the rate Jamaica is going, I should swap them out, but her ghetto fabulous ass wasn't going to bring me in too much. She shaped funny, her eyes wide-spread and her hair nappy as sheep fur. She better be damn lucky she ugly. Even still, she can count her goddamn days.

LE'VONNE

*

"Good morning, Jalisa. How you feeling baby?" I questioned whisking a pot of grits as she walked into the kitchen. Playing up the doting grandmother role was a bit tiring. I'd rather be kicked back in my recliner watching game shows but here I was cooking breakfast and being extra loving for the second week in a row now.

"I'm good. Do you need any help?" Jalisa questioned throwing balled up paper into the garbage can. I could only imagine what she had been writing and decided to toss.

"Naw baby. You just sit down and don't worry 'bout that," I laid it on thick. "How's my granddaughter's treating you? good?"

"They're very nice to me. Thanks for allowing me to crash here for the last week," Jalisa texted away on her phone not bothering to look up at me. "What's this address? Jason wants to come talk to me face to face. I'm hoping we can work this all out,"

The horror of someone knowing that Jalisa was at my apartment sent me into fight or flight mode. Wise enough not to show the alarm I used my cunning ways to talk her out of giving this Jason person any vital information for when she comes up missing. Thinking fast, I asked Jalisa if she could make some dish water. Obliging my request, she stood over the sink. As she plugged the drain and ran hot water into one side of the double-sided sink, she continued to text away on her phone and said something about sending her location. With my wide hips, I turned and bumped her harder than I needed to, knocking her iPhone into the sink filling with water.

"Noooooo!" Jalisa squealed on the verge of tears. "I cannot be without a phone," she stomped her foot, and I sang sorry's filled with fake regrets. She was going to have to go tonight.

"I'm so sorry baby. I'll have the girl's take you to South Bay mall to get a new phone," I took the water filled phone from her hand and shook the water out as if I was trying to save it.

"Try putting it in a bowl of rice to dry it out," Jalisa instructed.

Gathering the items, I called out to Jamaica. When she came into the kitchen, I gave her the look and told her that I needed her and Arei to take Jalisa to South Bay mall for a new phone. After telling me she had to change first, that gave me enough time to set everything up with Fabian for an immediate drop-off.

CHAPTER FIVE
AREI

The time had finally arrived for us to deliver Jalisa to Fabian. No matter how many times we'd done this, it never got easier. Like what is my afterlife going to be like when I stand before God? There has got to be a special place in hell for each of us. Jalisa didn't deserve whatever her fate was going to be. None of the girls did. From the conversations she and I had, it was obvious that she came from a loving family. Her one mistake was flying to California for a nigga and now she was being sold off to the highest bidder to do God knows what.

When Jamaica finally got dressed, the three of us left the house and headed towards South Bay Mall. Taking the scenic route, we made a few stops before going as a means to kill time so that we could bump heads with Fabian, and he could take his latest girl.

"Danni, run to the Shell gas station on Vermont and El Segundo really quick," Jamaica referred to me by my fake name. Through the rearview mirror, I spied her texting away in her phone. This must be the drop-off spot.

Diverting from the route, I obliged Jamaica's request. There was a U-Haul van parked behind the Shell. An olive-skinned man wearing dark shades sat in the driver seat thumping cigarette ashes out of the window. Slowly driving into the parking space next to the van, I once again said a silent prayer for Jalisa. She was none the wiser to what was about to take place. It was a known fact that the security cameras on this particular location were never in working order.

Jamaica got out of the passenger side of the car and walked towards the gas station. I waited approximately thirty seconds before pretending I needed to go inside as well. Jalisa opted to stay in the car. Her feelings were hurt about the phone. Being parked in the rear, saved us the trouble of being seen by too many prying eyes, walking or driving by.

Fucking around, we walked aisle to isle like we were looking for something to buy. While Jamaica searched through chips, I searched through drinks. Choosing our drinks of choice, I met Jamaica at the register just as the U-Haul truck pulled out of the lot and into traffic heading East on El Segundo Blvd. After paying for our items, we slowly walked to the car.

"I wonder what they going to do with her?" I spoke more to myself than to Jamaica

"Not our problem," Jamaica rebutted uncaringly.

"Why you gotta be so heartless?" I challenged.

"I'm not being heartless. As long as it's not us I can't get too invested in caring," Jamaica admitted. "Grandma Lu ain't the most trustworthy person and as long as we keep bringing her girls, it won't be me or you in the back of a U-Haul,"

Snatching the driver side door open, I slid in behind the wheel and rested my head back on the seat. Jamaica's words put something on my mind. Would she actually sell us off to the highest bidder if the price was right? I definitely needed to start working on a master plan.

Sticking the key into the ignition I brought the car to life and slowly pulled out of the lot heading back towards the house. The drive was a quiet one with Jamaica texting away on her phone and me deep in thought.

CHAPTER SIX
JAMAICA

"You couldn't do better than The Patio Motel? You usually take me to your house so why not today?" I questioned taking in the meager accommodations.

"There are renovations being done at my house so this was the best I could do. You here with me though so why you tripping?" Ray inched behind me and wrapped me up in his strong arms. His semi erect penis poked my butt and I pushed back on it.

Walking out of his grasp, I pulled my tank off exposing my small perky tits and slid out of the biking shorts I wore. Completely naked I assisted Ray with getting undressed. I had some news to share with him, but I would wait until after we made each other feel good. Both naked, I pushed him back onto the bed and dropped down to my knees swallowing him whole just like he'd taught me. Ray wasn't my first, but he was the one that taught me how to really please a man. Sucking him to eruption, I swallowed every last drop. With his dick limp, I was going to suck it back to life, but he stopped me.

"Gimme a minute. Let's kick back and smoke first," Ray suggested.

"I can't smoke," now was the time to let Ray in on my secret. Finding my purse, I pulled out the ultrasound picture I got just one week ago when I found out I was expecting. Passing it to Ray I awaited his response with bated breath.

"What's this?" Ray looked at the ultrasound photo he held in his hand as if it was diseased or something.

"I'm pregnant," the words hung in the air as Ray took me in, looking me up and down.

"So, what you telling me for? I ain't the father," he hurled the thin paper at me as if it was a frisbee.

"Wow! This what we doing? You fuck me raw. Nut all in me every time we fucked and now that I'm pregnant you want to deny our child?" Tears formed in my eyes but there was no way in hell I was going to let them fall. Crying was a sign of weakness, and I was far from a weak bitch.

"I thought you was on the pill or something? Why you let me fuck you like that if you weren't on birth control?" Ray spoke incredulously.

"So now this my fault? You sound crazy as hell,"

"Yeah! This your fault! You should have told me we weren't protected!" Ray paced back and forth. "I hope whoever the daddy is help you out because I'm done,"

"Oh, you done?" my eyes narrowed as I balled up my fist ready to pounce. "You stuck with me for eighteen nigga! I hope your wife ready to be a good step mama,"

Without warning, Ray's massive hands were around my throat, and I was being choked out in the corner. With all my might, I swung my fist at Ray's head connecting, causing the grasp he had on my neck to loosen. We tussled knocking over the lamp on the bedside table. Guess he didn't know that putting his hands on me would awaken the beast I kept tucked deep inside. Being abused as a kid, I promised myself that no one would ever hurt me physically and I stood on that. Kneeing Ray in the nuts, I was able to get him off me long enough to rain down a few stomps as he rolled on the floor holding his man meat. In a hurry I slipped back into my clothes and flip flops. Noticing Ray's shorts, I picked them up and went through his pockets. On one side he had forty dollars, a lighter and a bag of weed. In the other he had a rubber band knotted around a wad of bills.

"Oh, so bitch you be low balling me!" with rage building I kicked Ray one final time, taking the knotted bills with me. He could split those forty dollars and weed with his goddamn wife. Hustling to the car I wanted to get far away from this situation for more reasons than one. I couldn't see Ray letting me just beat his ass nor taking his money without wanting to get some get back at me.

As I opened the car door and slid behind the steering wheel, I noticed Ray groggily coming out of the main entrance struggling to put his clothes on. Bringing the engine to life, I backed out of the parking space narrowly missing a hooker and her John. Through the rearview mirror I could tell that they were cussing me out, but I didn't have time to be petty and argue back. Instead, I pulled out of the Patio Motel parking lot onto Redondo Blvd and blended in with the southbound traffic.

* * *

When I got home, I went straight to my bedroom and locked myself away from everyone. Taking the knot of money out of my purse, I counted it out and found myself two thousand dollars richer. Ray was blowing my phone up, so I had to place him on the blocked list. Considering he wasn't willing to acknowledge the child we made together, I took the initiative to bring his wife up to speed.

Opening the Instagram app, I went to my messages, tapped the compose icon and typed her name in. There was no need to write a long, drawn-out message. Instead, I uploaded a picture of my ultrasound, let her know that her husband was the father and that I'd been fucking him for almost two years. I also threw in that I was three months shy of my seventeenth birthday and her funky ass husband thought I was nineteen. Knowing we'd probably be going back and forth after the bomb I'd just dropped I went ahead and blocked her.

The tears I'd been holding back won the fight and began to fall from my eyes one by one. With my anger and frustration building I silently cried into my pillow. I didn't know what I was going to do. I don't know why I thought Ray was going to be excited about our baby. He already treated me like a secret and only came around when he wanted some ass. I could've easily taken the bum bitch route and put the baby on someone else but that wasn't in my character. One thing for sure, two things for certain Grandma Lu was going to lose her shit! Unless of course, she looked at the baby as another check. Either way, I didn't want my baby to feel used and useless like me. With a heavy heart and even heavier eyes, I cried myself to sleep.

At some point the sun had long ago set and darkness covered my bedroom. Rolling over in the full-sized bed, I felt wetness underneath my body causing me great alarm. Reaching out for the lamp, I felt cramp like pains in my stomach. As the light illuminated the space a large crimson red spot came into view. Jumping up from the bed, I just about ran to the bathroom leaving a trail of blood behind me. In the closed space, I hastily removed my clothes and jumped into the shower.

Once again, the tears began to fall. Crying was a weak bitch trait and it infuriated me even more that I'd cried twice in one day. A bitch like me hasn't cried since I was a little ass girl, and I didn't like it one bit. Snatching my rag off the shower rod, I squeezed Dove body wash onto it and began to scrub my body down. As I wiped between my legs, I pulled the rag back and noticed a large clot. I'd officially lost my baby. In my mind, I could wash up and head to St. Francis Medical in hopes of saving my child, but it was too late.

A gut retching scream came from deep within as I screamed out in pain. Not from the pain of the cramps, or even for Ray saying fuck me even. The opportunity to love somebody and have somebody love me back was literally floating down the drain.

CHAPTER SEVEN
GRANDMA LU

I was sitting in my room smoking a joint and listening to Suga Free, when I heard Jamaica screaming like she was a goddamn fool. Snuffing out the weed, I put my main man on pause and snatched my bedroom door open, noticing a trail of blood on the floor. *'I know this lil bitch ain't bled all over my clean ass floors!'* I spoke to myself as I stalked to the bathroom with the stealth of a Gazelle.

"Why the fuck you dripping blood all over my floors like you've lost your goddamn mind?" Looking at the blood-soaked clothing on the bathroom floor, I noticed it was too much blood for it to be her period. Hoping the fool hadn't slit her wrist and changed her mind about dying, I snatched the shower curtain back and found my granddaughter, holding a rag with blood clots in her hand.

Breathing a sigh of relief, I couldn't help but talk the shit I was known for, "I know like hell you ain't in my shower miscarrying or did you get yourself a botched back-alley abortion?" When she didn't answer, I began to shake her hoping to get a response. She must have been in shock or something. "Answer me goddamnit!"

When she finally snapped out of her haze, she told me that she was having a miscarriage. This goddamn girl was going to be the death of me! I wished Corrine was here to take care of her own child because I didn't sign up for this kind of shit. Even in my hoe days, I knew better than to get knocked up. Shit, if love hadn't found me and slammed me on my neck, I probably wouldn't have even had Corrine. I didn't want no damn kids!

"Arei!" I called out needing her aide and assistance. In no time she was standing at the bathroom door asking what was going on. Instructing her to run down to the corner store and get some super overnight pads, I guided Jamaica out of the shower and dried her off with a nearby towel.

"Sit on the toilet until Arei come back," closing the bathroom door I walked back to my bedroom, careful not to step in any of the blood that was now half dry on the floor, in my Daniel Green slippers.

I needed to calm down in the worse way. Rather than refiring up my joint, I settled on a Newport. Lighting the tip, I inhaled deeply and took the nicotine to the head before blowing smoke out my nose like a bull. If I was a drinking woman and could handle my liquor, I'd be sipping something potent but that wasn't in my ministry. If I didn't need Jamaica, she would have been shipped off somewhere a long time ago. I was getting up in age and shit like this wasn't conducive to my mental health. Sure, I was with the shits, and a different kind of *grandmother*, but that didn't mean I didn't want more for the grandchild I was stuck with. I don't know why she couldn't be her ass like Arei. Arei was kind, pretty, mannerable and an overall good child.

Guess she got that in her DNA from her real family because that shit wasn't learned over here.

When Arei returned from the store, I had her give the bag of pads to Jamaica and mop the floor. Finally coming to a place of peace, Jamaica walked into my bedroom fully clothed like she was going somewhere.

"Where you think you're going?" I questioned slowly rocking in my chair.

"To the hospital what you mean? Why you not dressed," Jamaica held the bottom of her stomach.

"Girl you might as well go take a Tylenol and lie down somewhere. I am not about to take you to the doctor and have them white folks all in our business, thinking I raised you wrong. No ma'am" I shook my head and continued to rock.

"I fucking hate you!" Jamaica screamed and stalked out of my bedroom.

"The feeling is mutual," I screamed back. I know I said I needed her, but I changed my mind. It was time to get rid of her ass. She was more of a liability than an asset, yet I wondered if Fabian would be willing to take her off my hands. She'd definitely have to be invested in, if he wanted her to make some money. I just wasn't putting any money into making Jamaica attractive. That would solely be on him. On the other hand, how would Corrine feel if she knew I sold her only child off? It didn't take too long for me to contemplate my next move. They didn't get along any way and Corrine wasn't never coming home so...

The more I sat and thought about it, selling Jamaica off wasn't too bad of an idea. With her looks no price would be too small. Arei didn't need a sidekick and there would be one less mouth to feed. Reaching over for the phone I dialed up a number I knew by heart.

"My good friend Lucille," Fabian answered on the third ring. "You got something for me already?" he questioned.

"Christmas has come early. I brought you something back from Jamaica?" I spoke in code.

"Jamaica huh. Isn't that place near and dear to your heart, no?"

"Not really. Just a fun place to visit," my words hung in the air as the line went silent. "Hello… are you still there?"

"Yeah, I'm here. How much did you spend?"

"A little bit of nothing. Everything there goes for cheap,"

"I'm preparing for a trip out of the country for a little bit. I'll let you know when I return," Fabian's voice turned uninterested.

"You sure? I can bring it before you leave,"

"Yeah. I'm sure."

The line went dead, and I didn't know what to think. Was Fabian refusing Jamaica or was he really telling me to wait? Any way it went, I had no choice but to wait and see.

CHAPTER EIGHT
AREI

The bullshit that was going on in our apartment tonight was unreal. For the life of me I couldn't fathom why our grandmother would not take Jamaica to the hospital. The girl had just lost a baby for Christ sake and she worried about what white folks think! I tell you about niggas. It was shit like this, that had my ass planning an escape from the madness. I wish I knew more about my mother's side of the family or about my family in general. Only thing I knew about my dad was that he was killed in a drug deal gone bad, and the one picture I ever saw of him had long faded and tore apart.

I often wondered what my life would be if I knew them. If my father wouldn't have been killed, would my mother still have given me away? Where would we live? Would my life be normal? These were things I would never know so I shook the thoughts from my head.

"Come on, I'll take you to the hospital," I creeped into Jamaica's bedroom and found her crying uncontrollably. I knew what it felt like to feel abandoned, and I didn't want her to share in that feeling. I felt bad for her. Jamaica was one of the toughest people I knew so to see her so broken had me ready to beat grandma ass for her.

Although the sun had long gone down, it was still hot as hell outside. Everybody and their mamas were sitting around trying to catch a breeze that would never come. Assisting Jamaica down the stairs, our weird upstairs neighbor damn near knocked us over with his big ass man bag, rushing up the stairs.

"Excuse you!" I yelled behind him, but he kept going. He was so out of place. Like, why would a person that is on local television everyday live in a place like The Vista? He had to be doing some type of social experiment. There was just no way I'd willingly reside here.

Finally, inside the car, I put the key in the ignition bringing it to life. Turning the knob on the air conditioner, it blew out hot air. "You got to be kidding me!" I hit the steering wheel. We were sitting on hot ass leather seats in ninety-degree weather. Shit just keep getting worse by the minute.

Putting the pedal to the metal, what would have been a fifteen-minute drive was only seven. I prayed to God that the cops wouldn't pull us over the entire way. Had they, I just would have told them that Jamaica was miscarrying. It wasn't like I was lying. Parking in the emergency room parking lot we walked inside the hospital. Instructing Jamaica to sit down, I gave the lady behind the glass window Jamaica's information. Although she'd experienced a miscarriage, they still left us sitting in the waiting area for almost an hour.

"Jamaica Wilson," a short stocky nurse called out. From where we were sitting it was hard to tell if the person was a man or a woman. The closer we got it was quite obvious that she was a man transitioning.

"You can't come back," the nurse held her hand out to stop me from walking into the back.

"Why not?"

"Because you're not the patient. You can have a seat out here and we'll update you when we can," I wanted to say something smart in response instead I bit my tongue.

"Don't worry Arei. You can go back home, and I'll call you when I need to be picked up. I wouldn't want you sitting for hours waiting on me. You know how slow they ass be,"

"You sure?" I was apprehensive about leaving her alone. Grandma already pretty much said fuck the situation I wanted her to know she had someone in her corner.

"Yeah, I'm sure. Go home,"

Rather than going straight home I rode to Tam's and grabbed a bite to eat. The restaurant was crowded so rather than fight for a seat I opted to go back outside and enjoy my meal. Although it was still hot, it was a bit more tolerable than earlier. Busting my bag down on the trunk of the car, I stood in the parking lot feeding my face. As I ate my food, I couldn't shake the feeling that someone was watching me.

Taking the lid off of the strawberry shake, I dipped a fry into the thick concoction before placing it into my mouth. Turning my head slightly to the left, my sight landed on a pair of eyes that screamed familiarity although I'd never seen this person before in my life. Something about the eyes were comforting. It wasn't until the driver pulled out of the parking lot that the stare down came to an end.

Knowing how this trafficking shit go I decided to throw the rest of my uneaten food away and got back into the car.

The ride home was smooth sailing as an old hip hop mix played on the radio. Jamming to the tunes, I wasn't doing a good job of watching my surroundings as a car slammed into the back of me just as I was turning into the alley that led to the complex parking lot. Getting out of the car, I came face to face with those eyes again before something covered my head and everything went black.

CHAPTER NINE

JAMAICA

I sat in the hospital emergency triage for six whole hours before they finally released me. I called Arei to come and pick me up, I never got an answer. I didn't really want to go home anyway so I called this new dude Corey I been talking to, he came and got me with no issue and took me back home with him. He was around my age and had a whole lot of freedom because he had a young mama that didn't give a fuck. Or at least it seemed that way.

"So, what were you in the hospital for?"

"I had a miscarriage," I could have lied, but there was no reason for it. Shit was what it was. I was not worried about Corey or anyone else judging me.

"That's fucked up... you good? You need some Tylenol or something?" Corey questioned genuinely concerned with my needs. It felt good to know somebody gave a fuck about me. It's crazy, I've only known him maybe three months and he's shown more concern than folks who been around me my whole life. Guess it's true what they say about a stranger doing better by you than your loved ones.

"I'm not good in a mental sense but I'll be ok. Nothing I can't get over," I shrugged my shoulders and flipped through the tv menu trying to find something to watch.

"You don't have to be strong all the time. You can be vulnerable with me. We all got some shit with us and sometimes you need just one person to help lighten your load or at least be a shoulder,"

"Being strong is all I know,"

"I'm sorry to hear that. Let's smoke this blunt and chill,"

Later the next afternoon, after Corey and I woke up he took me home. I still hadn't heard from Arei and I was hoping that she was home when I arrived. Sticking my key into the door, the sound of the news enveloped me as I walked inside, locking the door behind me. Bypassing my funky ass grandmother that sat in the living room eating pistachios and drinking Coca Cola, I headed towards Arei's room only to have Grandma Lu stop me.

"So, you finally bring your ass home. I hope you wasn't out here making no other babies that might not be so lucky to die of miscarriage,"

With rage building I clenched my fists so hard that my nails pierced my skin. I wanted to beat her ass. She just didn't know how close she was to catching a fade. The copper like taste of blood coated my tongue as I bit it in a means to not snap. "You one miserable ass old lady, I swear!"

"Girl whatever! Where is Arei? I hope you don't got her out there trying to follow in your footsteps,"

Hearing that Arei wasn't home caused great alarm. It was unlike her to not come home— Ever! I should have known something was

272

up when she didn't answer or return my calls last night. She would have never left me stranded at the hospital. Rushing to her bedroom, I pushed the door open with so much force that the doorknob went through the wall leaving a hole behind.

"When was the last time you seen her? Did you call the cops?" I rattled off question after question as I looked around her room for any clues as to where she might be.

"Fuck would I call the cops for? She left out of here with your ass! What the hell you do to her? Where you leave her at?"

"You can't be fucking serious!" I threw my hands up in frustration. "I ain't did shit to her! Did you give her to Fabian? I knew it was a matter of time. The moment I'm not around your greedy ass sells her off!"

"Oh! hell no! I'd sell you before her!" Grandma Lu let her real feelings be known. For a brief moment regret showed in her eyes before she slit them at me.

"You should have done us both a favor and let the state take me in. Living in a foster home couldn't possibly be worse than being raised by you," with nothing left to say I headed towards my room. Taking a duffle bag out of the closet, I filled the bag with as much as I could and headed for the door. I'd take my chances on trying to get in a shelter or at least bumming on someone's couch. If I get caught up in trafficking, so be it. Long as Lucille ain't the one making money off of me.

With no tears left to cry I pulled out my cell and called Corey. He had no issue spinning the block to get me. Sitting out in the courtyard I tried my hand at calling Arei again. She answered on the third ring.

"Bitch where you at?"

CHAPTER TEN
GRANDMA LU

The bitch Jamaica done packed up some of her shit and left my house. There was no reason for me to be alarmed cause I knew she'd be coming back. She ain't have nobody that was willing to take her nappy headed ass in. If there were, they'd been available four years ago when I had to get her. She was right when she said she stood a better chance at being in the system, maybe she would have wound up with somebody that actually wanted a funny looking ass kid 'cause I didn't. Now as for Arei, where in the world could she be?

Hobbling my way back to the living room, I sat down in my recliner and fired up a cigarette before dialing Arei's cell phone number. The phone rang and rang until it rolled over to voice mail. Hanging up I tried again and got the same results. By the third time calling, the phone went straight to voicemail as if I'd been blocked.

"Now I don't know what's gotten into you, but you better bring your ass home right damn now Arei. I do not condone you staying out all night and I damn sure have an issue with you blocking me…" I couldn't continue my rant as the phone went dead on me.

Switching gears, I dialed Fabian's number. Although Jamaica called herself leaving, she would be returning. I was certain of it. Time and time again over the years she's gotten too big for her britches, pulled an I'm running away stunt only to come back with her tail tucked tightly. When Fabian didn't answer, I just hung up. He knew why I was calling, and I just knew he'd call me back once he could then I'd finally be rid of Jamaica.

Reaching for yet another cigarette, I found that the pack was empty. Rolling my eyes deep into my head I let out a deep sigh. I had no one to send to the store and if I wanted to smoke, I'd have to go my damn self. With no other choice, I went off in search of proper attire to wear outside. Might as well get the grocery shopping over with since I would actually have to leave the house. The weatherman said it was ninety-seven degrees and Lord knows that wasn't my type of weather, but I lived in Cali and just had to deal.

Taking a quick shower, I dressed in a long, flowy, spaghetti strapped dress and put my feet in a pair of open toed sandals. Throwing on my good wig, I grabbed my purse and left the house. The Vista was wheelchair accessible, so I walked my tail to the elevator. The big ass out of order sign stopped me in my tracks and rerouted me to the staircase. The heat was sweltering as beads of sweat formed on my forehead. It was the kind of hot that made you mad enough to fight.

Goddamn black cat ran across my feet as I walked down the stairs. When I tried to kick it, I lost my footing but was quick enough to grab ahold of the banister to keep from falling back on the stairs.

"Oooooh wee! That old lady just fell down the stairs," a little girl outside playing brought attention to my mishap causing her little friends to break out in a fit of laughter as I hoisted myself up.

"Fuck is y'all laughing at? Funky ass wenches,"

"I'm a tell my mama you cussed at us!" one of the little girls yelled out.

"Go get her. I fight kids and mamas!" I was ready for war. Disrespectful ass booger pickers. Rather than wait around for the mammy I kept it pushing. It was too goddamn hot, and I'd fuck around and be in jail for murder like Corrine.

Walking through the courtyard towards the parking lot it looked as though my car had been tampered with. The closer I got I could see that my tires had been slashed. Couldn't be nobody but that little bitch Jamaica. Since my plans were drastically changed, the only option I had was to walk my ass to the corner store for my smokes expeditiously. With the sun beating down on me, I noticed that the girl's car was parked in a visitor's spot on the other side of the lot, diverting directions I walked over to the car. Pulling on the handle, I found the car to be unsecured. With my mind running a mile a minute, I wondered where the fuck could Arei be. Maybe Jamaica had good reason to be alarmed when she was searching for her earlier.

Tucking my tail, I dialed Jamaica's number. She was the only person I could talk to about this situation. I didn't want to get the cops involved for obvious reasons, but I might eventually need to. The phone rang and rang and rang until it went to voicemail. Hanging up, I dialed her number again. This time she answered.

"Jamaica come home. I think somebody snatched Arei for real,"

CHAPTER ELEVEN
AREI

"Get the fuck off of me!" I jerked my body away from my captors. Although my arms were tied behind my back and my eyes were covered, I didn't feel as if I was in any imminent danger. The scent of jasmine and vanilla helped to calm my nerves as I stood with two bodies on either side of me.

"Why is she tied up? Untie her now," a feminine voice spoke in a gentle yet commanding tone.

"How else were we supposed to get her here?" one of the captors spoke up cutting the zip tie from my wrist. Once I was free, I rubbed the indentation that was left behind awaiting whatever was to come.

"If this wasn't a joyous occasion, I'd have your head!" I could tell that the woman was closer to me than she had been previously. It almost felt as if we were eye to eye. As the blindfold was gently pulled off of my face, I looked into those eyes I saw earlier today. It was the woman from Tam's parking lot.

"You were following me earlier," I inched back putting space between us. Had karma paid me a visit and now I was the one being trafficked?

"You're as beautiful as I imagined," the lady smiled and reached out to touch my face. This time when I backed up, I fell into a chair. "You don't have to be afraid of me Arei. I'm not going to hurt you,"

"How do you know my name? What do you want from me?"

"I'm Haleigh. I'm your mother,"

The room spun and it felt like the wind had been knocked out of me. There were similarities in her face and mine. Could she be? Nah she couldn't be…

"You're not my mother. She left me. This has to be some sick joke,"

"You were born November 18, 2005. You have a heart shaped birth mark on the right side of your abdomen, you were also born with a sixth toe that was amputated. Should I continue?" Haleigh inquired playing with a strand of hair that had fallen into my face.

"I was told your family sent you away and that's why I was raised by my grandmother. My dad's mother,"

"That bitch is not your grandmother!" Pain mixed with anger shone in her eyes as she spoke. "Give us a moment," she waited until the two men were out of ear shot before she sat me down and told me her story.

I was floored at everything Haleigh had revealed to me. To find out that she was Corrine's best friend and Grandma Lu traded her off to cover a debt she owed to Fabian. The only thing that was told to me that was true was that my father was murdered when I was a baby. Silent tears flowed from my eyes as we sat in dead silence. Hatred for Grandma Lu bubbled inside of me as I projected my feelings onto Haleigh.

"You're telling me this now for what? You been knowing she had me all this time and you left me in her care! What kind of shit is that?

Why couldn't you have left me with your parents? At least then I would have been in the care of people that had the same blood as me,"

"It's not as simple as you think. My parents are racist pieces of shit. They didn't accept you because your father was black," Haleigh allowed me to digest the reality before continuing. "Yes, I've been able to keep up with you over the years, but I never thought I'd get this close. I'd have this chance… When Lucille called Fabian offering Jamaica to him, I knew I had to get to you,"

"So had she not you were just going to leave me?" Haleigh didn't answer instead she reached for my hands only to have me snatch them away.

"Arei, you have to understand that it wasn't as simple as you think. Yes! Fabian kept me for himself but the only way I could survive day in and out was to know what was going on with you. You've got to believe me. If I could have left and come for you, I would have no questions asked. Shit, I just got my freedom,"

Momentarily I pondered the words she spoke. I wanted to believe her. Deep down inside I did believe her. "If you want to right your wrongs let me go back and get Jamaica,"

"I can't send you back out to the wolves. I wouldn't be able to live with myself if something happened to you," Haleigh threw her hands up in frustration.

"Nothing is going to happen. Grandma Lu thinks I'm naïve anyhow. I'm the one she depends on for this trafficking shit. Jamaica is the only solid person I have, and I don't want to lose her. Plus, I want to serve *grandma* the fate she deserves.

*   *   *

It didn't take much to convince Haleigh to let me go back home to Grandma Lu. It was Fourth of July weekend and there would be so much going on that she would be none the wiser that her old ass was being set up for the okie doke. Grandma Lu had been calling me, but I kept sending her to voicemail. I couldn't find it in myself to speak to her considering I was trying to get my game face on before I saw her face to face. Finally, having spoken to Jamaica I let her know that I'd be home soon, and we had some shit we needed to talk about.

When Haleigh dropped me off at the Vista, she told me that everything would be okay and that she wouldn't be too far if I needed her. Tucking my phone into my back pocket, I didn't push her away when she embraced me. Instead, I wrapped my arms just as tightly around her.

"Alright ma, here is the list of girls and their photos. When I text, you set everything in motion," the night before I had gone onto each of the girl's we'd served social media and gathered as much info about them as I could.

"You called me ma. You just don't know how long I waited to hear those words. I love you baby girl. You be careful,"

Exiting the car, I hustled through the courtyard. My neighbor Shon's daughter was out playing and waved at me. Returning the gesture, I took my time walking up the stairs. That walk was like the green mile. I was truly walking towards my destiny. Sticking my key in the door, I took a deep breath before turning it and letting myself in.

"Jamaica is that you?" Grandma Lu yelled from the back of the apartment.

Rather than reply I just walked towards where I heard her voice coming from and presented myself. I can't believe all these years my life was a lie, and this lady was the source of it all. I could've spit in her face, but I contained myself.

"Arei! Where the hell have you been? You've had me worried sick," Grandma Lu stood up from the kitchen table. "I was this close to filing a missing person's report," she gestured with her fingers.

"Ain't no need to do that. I'm back," turning away I opened up the refrigerator and pulled out a bottle of water. Twisting off the top I drank down the cool liquid to wet my mouth that was now starting to feel like cotton.

"What the hell has gotten into you? You walk up in here all nonchalant and shit. That damn Jamaica done rubbed off on you! Your daddy must be flipping over in his grave,"

"Speaking of my dad. Tell me more about him. I know you got more pictures of him than his obituary," I took a seat at the table and waited for her to put together a lie. Not saying shit about what I knew was going to be harder than I thought.

"He wasn't a picture taker,"

Before I could reply Jamaica was texting my phone to make sure I was home before she returned. Texting her back that I was, she let me know that she was outside. Breathing a sigh of relief, I couldn't wait to lay eyes on Jamaica and fill her in on the bullshit. She wasn't going to believe it.

CHAPTER TWELVE
JAMAICA

My socks were knocked off by the things that Arei laid out to me, although I shouldn't have been surprised at all. I knew at some point that Grandma was going to sell one if not both of us but to know she really set the play in motion to get rid of me was something else. Family wasn't shit. The one I was born into was the bottom of the barrel bogus though. I could only pray to God that being like my mammy and her OG was not in my DNA. I couldn't find it within myself to tell Arei I knew all along that she wasn't any kin. That shit I was going to take to the grave, especially, considering she was taking me out this bitch with her.

"So how soon are we getting up out of here and getting rid of the old bitch?" I questioned plundering through my closet for shit I actually wanted to take with me.

"Within the next twenty-four hours if not sooner. I can't take another moment of looking at her ass,"

"Arei! Jamaica! Come here!" Grandma Lu called out for us.

Rolling our eyes in unison, I snuffed out the blunt we'd smoked and prepared to go see what the old hag wanted. Taking our precious ass time, we finally walked to her bedroom to find her looking out onto the courtyard.

"I hope you two got some rest because it's back to business," she inhaled deeply on the cigarette that she held between her dick beaters. "From here on out, we need to be picking up and shipping girls out like an assembly line,"

"Who is we?" I questioned looking to Jamaica who stood to the right of me wearing the same blank face as I was giving.

"You two bitches that's who '*the we*' is! If you want to have a place to lay ya head and wash ya ass, I think you better get out there and find me some prime young bitches to sell before I sell the both of you like I sold all those other girls!" she screamed damn near choking on cigarette smoke as she dismissed us.

Winking my eye at Arei to let her know that I'd successfully recorded the old hag admitting to selling girls. Getting rid of her ass was easier than we previously thought. Walking out of the room, we decided to set the wheels in motion and get shit over with once and for all.

CHAPTER THIRTEEN
GRANDMA LU

Something was off with Jamaica and Arei. Ever since Arei returned from her little escapade or whatever in the fuck she was on, she's been acting different. Questioning things, she never had an urge to before and behaving as if she had a chip on her goddamn shoulder. Instead of the two little wenches going out to do what I instructed they took their asses downstairs to buy some weed and was currently sitting out in the courtyard with the rest of The Vista's trash ass tenants.

The smell of barbecue wafted from the courtyard below up to my second-floor apartment causing my stomach to growl. I wouldn't be taking my ass out to barbecue in the heat like everybody else, but I did have some wings I could fry up. Suga Free rapped about pimping hoes into the stratosphere while I cleaned, seasoned, and deep-fried chicken wings and peeled potatoes for some homemade fries.

"See I love ya baby. But not like that. Your love ain't never paid no bills or put no clothes on my back…" I rapped along with the song that was now playing as my cell phone rang in the background. A smile formed on my face when I saw Fabian's number. He'd finally called my ass back and I could finally be done with Jamaica's ass.

"Hey my friend. Bout time you called me back I was starting to get worried when I didn't hear from you," the words Fabian spoke to me weren't any that I wanted to hear. The smile quickly vanished from my face as he severed ties with me. Inquiring as to why he would end this good thing we had going on, he offered no explanation just ended the call. It was four fifty-two in the afternoon and I'd just got my heart crushed for the second time in my life. How the fuck will I make money now? Being the hustler I always been, it would take nothing for me to bounce back. I'd just have to work extra hard to keep the girls in line.

With my mind moving a mile a minute the sound of police sirens blared in the background breaking me out of my trance. As I looked out of the window the swat team raced up the courtyard towards the building. Still looking out the window, I was startled when the front door to the apartment came crashing in. My reflexes caused me to grab the frying pan of chicken and fling it at the cops as they ambushed me.

"Arrrgggghhh!" I screamed out as some of the hot grease splashed back onto my arm causing it to burn and blister right away.

"You have the right to remain silent. Anything you say can and will be held against you in a court of law," one of the officers read me my Miranda rights after I was tackled to the ground and roughly handcuffed. They didn't give a fuck that I'd just injured myself.

"It's clear!" another officer yelled as I was ushered out of the house.

"What is this all about? I'm going to sue y'all asses when you find out you illegally broke down my door carting me off to jail,"

"That's what they all say!" the officer who held my arm spoke. All my nosey ass neighbors watched me being escorted down the stairs and through the courtyard towards an awaiting squad car.

Looking through the sea of faces I tried to spot Arei and Jamaica. When I did my knees buckled and if it wasn't for the officers I would have fallen to the ground. It had been seventeen years since I laid eyes on Haleigh, but here she was. Standing next to her daughter. If looks could kill I'd be a goner. If I didn't know before what all of this was about. I surely knew now.

"Ms. Sumpter, what's an old lady like you doing trafficking young girls? That's not Christ like," the detective that sat across the cold steel table questioned.

"I need to see a doctor," was the only response I had for him.

"Com'mon let's make this easy. I have the list of girls. I've talked to at least one of them and your granddaughters are willing to turn states evidence. Just confess to your role and give us your connection. We can cut you a deal of ten to fifteen, so you don't have to live out the rest of your years in prison," the female detective gave her two cents.

"I have the right to see a fucking doctor! Do you see my arm? Matter of fact I need to talk to my lawyer because I don't have shit to say to y'all!"

"Okay. Have it your way. All deals are off the table," with that the detectives left me in the interrogation room with burning arms and alone with my thoughts.

CHAPTER FOURTEEN

GRANDMA LU

The trial came and went quicker than I anticipated. Let the news tell it, I was head of a huge sex trafficking ring, but they could never tell who my cohorts were. Thanks to Haleigh, Arei and Jamaica I was slammed with fifteen counts of human sex trafficking, one count of abduction and two counts of obstructing justice. During the trial Haleigh told how I took her in and sold her off to pay my gambling debt and stole her child. Jamaica testified of finding out I was going to sell her and presented a recording that put the nail in my coffin.

Folsom State Prison is where I am projected to live out the rest of my natural life, all the while paying my debt to society. My daughter Corrine is also serving out her time here, and our initial interaction was horrible. Thinking she was welcoming her mother in with open arms, she and a few of the other women actually jumped me! Yeah, you read that right. Them hoes put hands on me over Jamaica. Corrine said I was dead to her for trying to sell her daughter away. The same daughter that hated her fucking guts. Now I'm here in solitary confinement aka protective custody where I'm only allotted one hour per day to get any kind of air or to do anything constructive.

"Mail call!" one of the C.O.s dropped an envelope into my cell. Thirsty for any form of communication I picked the letter up and saw that there wasn't any name on the envelope.

Sitting down on the steel stool attached to the desk, I opened the letter and read the contents.

Dear Grandma Lu,

It sounds funny now even in written form. Lol. I cannot believe that I actually found it within myself to send you a letter. I want so badly to say that I hate you, but I don't. Whatever the feeling is, it's a deeper emotion than hate. You're such a fucked-up individual and I hope you burn in hell for everything that you ever did. Treating Jamaica like shit. Selling off my mother and all those other girls. I bet you thought you were righting your wrongs by raising me up as if I was actually your grandchild. You're the worst kind of person. You did things to break and defile not only me but Jamaica as well. You treated her like you hated her guts! And why? Maybe because you knew your baby daddy had raped his own daughter and left her pregnant. Thought we'd never find that out, huh? Well Corrine told it all. For the life of me, I can't understand how she continued on in a mother/daughter relationship with you after all that! I wouldn't have but she's not me.

As for me, I'm good. I'm a college student studying criminal law. I plan to spend my life locking up sick bitches like you. Jamaica's doing good too. She has plans of going off to college once she graduates to study child psychology. She's going to help kids, especially those who are exploited and manipulated by trash ass adults. Jamaica turned out to be a better human than you could ever be. No matter what you did to break her, she's winning, and your ass is losing. My mom is doing great too. Her shelter for girls is helping runaways get off the street. After all the shit we went through, God has brought us through and now look at your ass. Welp! This is that last time you will hear from me. May the error of your ways take hold of you and destroy you one day at at time.

Arei

The wetness on my face after reading the letter told me that I'd been crying. I haven't done that shit in years! Wiping away the tears I thought about the things that Arei had said, and she wasn't lying about me being destroyed one day at a time. Hell, my last trip to the infirmary brought with it the realization that my days were numbered as I've been diagnosed with stage four lung cancer. All the hate and disdain I'd carried around with me along with the excessive smoking had my ass in a choke hold. I was fine with it. At least I can say nobody killed my ass. Most importantly though fuck them kids and fuck my life. I was destined to go out in a fucked-up way. It was written and I accept it all.

FOLLOW THE AUTHORS

NICOLE WATTS - KREATIONSK.COM
IG: NICOLEWATTSWRITES

LE'VONE - LEVONNETHEWRITER
IG & TWITTER: @LEVONNEWRITES

ROBIN - HTTPS://LINKTR.EE/FACESOFROBIN

LEONDRA LERAE - FACEBOOK.COM/AUTHORLEONDRAL-
ERAE
IG & TWITTER: @LEONDRALERAE

DRUSILLA MARS - HTTPS://INSTABIO.CC/KUEENDRU

SEVYN McCRAY - WWW.FACEBOOK.COM/NOVELISTASEVYN
TWITTER & IG SEVYN_MCCRAY

Made in the USA
Columbia, SC
08 March 2023

13495785R00161